# Hide and Seek

## RICHARD PARKER

Published by Bookouture
An imprint of StoryFire Ltd.
23 Sussex Road, Ickenham, UB10 8PN
United Kingdom
www.bookouture.com

ISBN: 978-1-78681-240-7
eBook ISBN: 978-1-78681-239-1

This book is a work of fiction. Names, characters, businesses,
organizations, places and events other than those clearly in the
public domain, are either the product of the author's imagination
or are used fictitiously. Any resemblance to actual persons, living or
dead, events or locales is entirely coincidental.

*To Gareth – 'The Beast' Morgan – old friend and
one of the world's good guys.*

# PROLOGUE

In the split second Lana shifted her attention to the drying rack to slot in a washed plate, the stranger dropped over the yard fence. His weight thudded onto the grass and she felt the impact in her chest. Her gaze whipped back to the window and alarm burst from her. 'Cooper!' she cried through the glass, but her blonde, four-year-old son was crouching and filling the scoop of his yellow mini digger with sand at the far end of the long lawn.

She banged the pane but only the stranger turned. He was wearing a child's mask that sat in the middle of his face. It was Snip the Squirrel, Cooper's favourite cartoon character; trademark cheek-bulging smile, and goggles barely containing bulbous eyes. But there was nothing comical about the man's scrawny physique, faded pink tee shirt riding up from his pot belly and close-fitting red shorts. The toothy rodent grin swivelled away before he slid a dirty polythene sack over Cooper.

Lana heard her boy scream and shot to the back door. The new washing machine that had been delivered that morning was still blocking the way. She frantically squeezed past it. 'Cooper!'

She'd taken her eyes off him for only a few moments but when she entered the sunny yard there was no sign of her child.

*No, no, no. This can't be happening.*

She bolted to where he'd been sitting and found the stranger's bare legs scrambling at the rotten, shoulder height fence hidden by the tall border plants, the transparent sack containing Cooper dangling from his fist.

She could see Cooper twisting inside. He was hoisted up and out of reach and her panicked wail energised his.

Her husband, Todd, was at work.

'Help!' She hoped one of her neighbours would be in their yard. If she didn't act fast, the stranger would drop down to the private lane the other side. A guttural exclamation escaped her, and she restrained his ankle firmly with both hands and started trying to lug him back.

He kicked at her, and the rubber sole of his dirty-white deck shoe glanced Lana under her chin and then struck her full in the face.

She didn't register the blows but they forced her to release him. Lana grabbed his clammy calf and then slammed her body against his shoe to trap him there. Digging her nails in, she bit the skin above his heel. She heard him cry out, a high-pitched, feminine screech, and clamped her teeth down as hard as she could.

'Get the fuck off me!' There was surprise and outrage in his hissing voice.

Lana could taste the sweat of his skin and the saltiness of his blood. She heaved hard at his ankle, and he howled and attempted to waggle his foot free. Clutching it, she hinged back on her heels, using all her weight to draw him back or dislocate his leg.

She wanted to shout that she'd murder him before she'd let him take Cooper. But Lana wasn't about to loosen her teeth from the wound and chewed fiercely at it through his fine hairs. The aroma of his foot odour was in her nostrils but she held him fast.

Then the wooden fence shook, and she landed hard on her buttocks. He'd slid back into the yard. She was already on her feet as he rounded on her, his smiling squirrel mask askew on his red features, the sweat glistening in the sparse grey hair prickles on his scalp.

Cooper was squealing inside the sack but the stranger was holding the bunched top tightly shut.

Instinct overrode everything else and Lana flew at him, smacking her shoulder into his chest and locking her fingers onto the slippery polythene. She tried to wrench it from his palm, but even as she leaned away from him and his arm went straight, he wouldn't let go.

Lana jerked it again, and this time the sack was prised from the stranger and thumped onto the lawn. But before she could open it, the stranger had reached inside and tugged Cooper out by his shirt collar. She caught hold of her son's ankles.

Cooper bawled and wriggled as his shirt rode up his body and they wrestled him in opposite directions.

'Let him go!' she heard herself shriek over and over as she watched her son stretching away from her.

Still clinging to Cooper, the stranger turned and stamped at the rotten wooden fence panel. It bounced back into position. He booted it again.

'Help!' she yelled.

The panel cracked with the third impact, and he rammed himself against it. It bowed, splintered, and gave and Cooper was hauled away from Lana.

She maintained her grip and staggered forward so she hit the fence.

The stranger yanked at Cooper from the other side but Lana got her palms around his waist and hugged him to her. She turned herself sideways so he couldn't drag them both through the gap.

The stranger suddenly let go, and Lana collapsed backwards onto the lawn, the wind knocked from her but Cooper squeezed to her chest. She could feel his tiny body pumping as he wept.

'Oh Jesus. Oh Jesus.' *That can't have just happened.*

Wood squeaked as the stranger slid his bulk back through the busted panel, the squirrel face descending as he lunged for Cooper again.

Lana balled herself around her son and rolled onto her front. She felt the stranger's foot stomping her back and clenched her jaw against the further impacts to her head.

Lana hung onto handfuls of grass as he tried to turn her over, and then his foot was violently battering her ribs, before she felt Cooper ripped from beneath her.

When she stood, the stranger had already disappeared back through the broken fence panel. She pushed through it into the lane and saw him fleeing with Cooper under his arm.

'Help!' The plea tore her throat, and she raced after him as he disappeared around the curve of the walled path. She wouldn't lose sight of him. Every cell of her was prepared to kill or be killed to get Cooper back.

But when she rounded the corner he'd frozen. A black SUV was parked up in the narrow space and was blocking his path.

With scarcely a second's thought, the stranger turned on his heel and tossed Cooper at Lana.

Nothing else existed except for the space between her child and the ground.

'Cooper!'

Lana watched her son ascend, striking the sidewall before landing hard on the path. It was like a fist to her stomach.

She didn't register the stranger shove by her as she ran to Cooper's motionless form. But she did hear the sibilant promise.

'Tomorrow.'

# CHAPTER 1

The stranger was called Mr Whisper.

In the weeks that followed the attempted abduction the only name the police had to go on had come from Cooper. Lana and Todd had the same conversation they'd had with their son so many times but today Detective Riggs was present. The officer had suggested they conduct the interview in Cooper's bedroom, where he felt secure.

'Mrs Cross, maybe you could ask Cooper about what happened.' Detective Riggs appeared distinctly uncomfortable sitting on the end of a child's little bunk.

'Cooper, tell Detective Riggs about the man in the yard.' Lana seated herself cross-legged with her son on the snakes and ladders carpet and tried not to flinch. The bruises to her body and face were still a constant reminder of the awful event. She could see from his rigid back that Cooper was wary of the officer's presence and squeezed his leg reassuringly.

'He whispered to me through the fence.'

Todd knelt with them and handed Cooper Frogbert, his favourite toy. 'Just on the afternoon he climbed over it?'

Cooper rolled up his clear blue eyes to think like he always did. 'What did he whisper?'

Cooper briefly regarded Riggs but didn't answer him.

Lana wasn't surprised he was nervous of the officer's bushy beard and booming voice. 'But before that? Did he speak to you then?' She didn't want to push too hard but Cooper had initially said that Mr Whisper had been his friend a long time and she dreaded the

idea he might have been communicating with her son right under
their nose prior to that day.

'I don't remember.'

'Think hard. Is there anything else you can tell us about him?'
She patted his knee through his little jeans.

He shook his head.

'What did he say to you?' Todd put his hand lightly on Cooper's back. 'It's really important you remember, Squidge. Do you
understand that?'

He nodded.

'Think harder,' Lana encouraged him.

''K.' He narrowed his eyes, as if it hurt.

Lana could see he didn't want to and hated making him relive
the experience. She wished she could let him forget, and every
time he was asked the same questions, hoped the trauma wouldn't
affect him on a deeper level. But perhaps there was some detail he
wouldn't find important but that Detective Riggs would.

Todd ran his palm over his son's head. 'Squidge, I promise we
won't ask you many more questions…'

'Mr Whisper was just being nice.'

And that's what broke Lana every time. She could tell Cooper
was afraid of being told off because he'd spoken to the stranger.
Something they'd always warned him about.

'I understand that,' Todd said softly. 'He was a bad man trying
to fool you. Just tell me what he said.'

Cooper seemed desperate to give an answer. 'He told me he wanted
to play. Wanted to come into the yard. I don't remember any more.'

Todd stroked Cooper's toy. 'Promise there's nothing you've told
Frogbert that you haven't told us?'

Cooper looked at the stuffed green animal and then back to
Todd. 'Promise. Is Mr Whisper coming back?'

Lana took his hand. 'No. Forget about him now.' But that was
something she'd never be able to do. And she could see in her son's

anxious expression that he couldn't either. How could he when she kept asking the same questions over and over? And how was it possible to expect Cooper to feel safe living in the same house when she didn't?

Despite Detective Riggs trying to reassure her about the likelihood of Mr Whisper returning, she was determined to get her son away from the place that had become a permanent echo of that sickening afternoon.

It was the house she and Todd had juggled multiple jobs to get the first down payment on; the two bedroom fixer-upper they'd gradually furnished from second-hand stores; the address they thought they might lose from month to month. But somehow, they'd held onto it and built it up. Todd had inherited his father's DIY genes and worked his way through its never-ending patch jobs and plumbing issues.

It had become the home they'd cherished and where Lana had fallen pregnant with Cooper. She'd been toiling in the yard on her beloved borders when Todd had got in from work and she'd told him. He'd hugged her so tight.

It had been a tough birth and, after having to go against all she planned and have a caesarean, the doctors had told her that, because of the resulting uterine adhesions, it was very unlikely she would conceive again. That made every milestone of Cooper's life extra special.

But now every day they remained under this roof was like a stay of execution. All those memories had been sullied, and although Todd tried to convince Lana the episode would eventually melt into the background, she knew he felt the same way as she did.

*Tomorrow.*

# CHAPTER 2

Lana emptied the last dregs of red wine from her bowl glass. It was cold and bitter. She looked over from her seat at the table in the lounge window to where Todd was sleeping, exhausted, in the leather armchair.

She'd repeatedly told him to go to bed, but he'd waited up because he knew if he hit the sack before Lana, she was unlikely to switch off the laptop until the early hours. She squinted at the time at the bottom of her screen. It was after midnight. It had been just before ten the last time she'd looked. It was a familiar feeling of guilt. Todd had to be up at five. He was project managing the installation of power lines in Princess County over the weekend.

She'd told him she was working on the seating plan for the Society of Toxicology's annual convention but he'd guessed she was using it as an excuse to research another sociopath who might have worn the Snip the Squirrel mask.

Lana rose, lifted the blanket from the back of the couch and draped it over him. She leaned down and tenderly kissed his temple. Should she leave him there? He would only wake shivering later. 'Todd,' she said softly. He didn't stir. Lana decided to blow out the candles before she disturbed him. But first she crossed the rug and nudged the door in front of her.

In the compact bedroom beyond, the rainbow air balloon night light was still on. Cooper was lying motionless in his racing car shaped bunk, his long fair hair splayed out over the pillow. She needed to hear the sound of his breathing and lingered in the doorway. His just-bathed aroma briefly overcame the darker thoughts crowding her head.

'You can turn it off, if you like,' his muffled voice said brightly.

'What are you doing still awake?' She moved into the room and leaned over him.

He opened his eyes but kept the left side of his face against the pillow. 'I'll be OK in the dark. Promise.'

'Sure?'

He nodded emphatically and the pillow squeaked. 'No problemo.' That was definitely a phrase he'd picked up from Todd.

It should have been her reassuring Cooper about the dark. But even though the 'tomorrow' his would-be abductor had alluded to had come and gone nine months ago, Lana still anticipated his return every day. Mr Whisper had never been caught.

Lana touched his cheek and it was cool. 'Shut 'em tight. Night, Squidge.'

He opened his eyelids again and frowned his faint eyebrows. That was his dad's nickname for him and she knew better than to plagiarise it. Lana wondered if she'd be allowed to join their club if she weren't such a source of concern for them both.

After the attempted kidnap she'd immediately moved them from their house in the suburbs of Jaxton to a cramped, rented fourth floor apartment in the city. She'd then fitted myriad forms of security and done everything in her power to lock her family inside. Lana knew her fixation with protecting them from the man who tried to snatch Cooper was frustrating their chances of ever getting back to a regular life again. But how could she let it go when every new day held the same dreadful potential?

After three months waiting in terror while the police failed to apprehend Mr Whisper, she'd been encouraged by her therapist to confront the fear that had been implanted in her. To do this Lana decided the best way was to search for Mr Whisper herself.

Lana's hunt had begun online, researching local abductions and monitoring ongoing investigations. To begin with she'd found the details too harrowing, but then they made her consider how lucky she'd been to have wrestled Cooper back from Mr Whisper. As she'd delved further into the specifics, the things that upset her the most were the tales of children who'd vanished without trace. She couldn't conceive of the torment those parents experienced the moment they opened their eyes every morning. There were a shocking number of offenders in the state, and she resolutely sought to find features amongst the images of wanted and convicted predators that slotted behind the Snip the Squirrel mask.

She'd been convinced on two occasions that she'd found him. Firstly, Peter Firth, a social worker with a similar build, who had been standing trial for child molestation. The police had entertained her the first time but quickly assured her that Firth had already been in custody when Cooper was grabbed. They were less sympathetic when she pointed the finger again. The other man, Brandon Fines, was checked out but definitively dismissed. Detective Riggs said their investigation was still ongoing but his updates had gradually become less frequent.

Then she'd heard about the *Right Where You're Standing* app and downloaded it to her phone. It used GPS to direct her to local murder scenes, and she began a physical search, seeking those that had taken children, and hoping the tendency of perpetrators to return to the site of their crimes might afford her a slim chance of glimpsing Mr Whisper.

Lana kissed Cooper's warm scalp and inhaled. It smelt of watermelon shampoo. She turned off the balloon light. 'Don't let the bugs bite.'

'Only three sleeps left,' Cooper reminded her.

She knew he and Todd had been counting down the days to their vacation at Blue Crest Adventure Park. It was what they all badly needed and it bothered Lana she wasn't looking forward to it as much as they were. She'd been so busy but it hadn't been anything to do with event coordination.

Lana had to get away from the apartment and the black hole of her online and physical research into child murderers and paedophiles. And she was finding it increasingly difficult to offload the heavy sense of revulsion the accumulated details of their vile crimes draped over her. But if she stopped being proactive she was certain the panic attacks would return.

When they escaped the apartment for two weeks, Lana sincerely hoped they'd begin to remember what it was like to be a normal family again. Their house still hadn't been sold, so the mortgage and rent combined were steadily draining their savings. She'd agreed with Todd not to discuss their finances until they returned. Lana closed the door quietly behind her.

'You can leave it open.'

She looked back through the crack. The offer wasn't for his benefit. 'OK. Night.'

Cooper's age meant he might eventually forget the episode in the yard. Lana was thankful for that. But he'd definitely picked up on how that afternoon had affected his parents. Cooper never spoke of Mr Whisper now. But he didn't watch Snip the Squirrel either. She still shuddered to think of the man with the pot belly crouching there, talking to her son.

Lana padded back into the tiny lounge. Time to double- then triple-check the locks on the doors and windows before setting the alarm. At least Todd was asleep, and she could take her time.

His head suddenly jerked, and he took a panicked intake of breath.

Lana reached him as he sat upright and darted his eyes about the room. They halted on her but, briefly, he didn't seem to recognise her.

'You OK?' She placed her palm on the fair prickles of his head.

He briefly nodded. 'Yeah…' But the remnants of whatever nightmare he'd had was still ingrained in his expression.

'Come on, babe, bed.' She hugged Todd until she felt the tension drain out of him.

He stood, the blanket falling at his feet as he brushed off the episode. 'You all done?'

He often woke like that now but Lana suspected he'd think it was a failing if she knew just how often. 'I was about to do last-minute checks.'

'Let me do it,' he said, groggily.

'Go on, I'll be in now.'

He nodded. Probably knew it was pointless arguing. 'Don't take too long.' He pecked her forehead.

She didn't answer but skimmed her hand across his hot back as he passed her.

''Night, Dad!' Cooper shouted. He sounded wide awake.

Todd put his head through the door and hissed. 'Hey, you should have been asleep hours ago.'

'Three sleeps to go.'

'I know, buddy. And this one's way overdue.'

Todd clicked the door shut, and Lana opened her mouth to object. But it wasn't Cooper that minded it being closed. She watched Todd disappear into the passage that led to their bedroom.

Three sleeps was all that mattered to them both. But, even while they were away, she doubted Todd would dream any easier than she did.

# CHAPTER 3

Lana got out of their silver Subaru and took in the dilapidated colonial structure, with the metal plates secured over its windows, beyond the collapsed wire fence. The place had been a convalescent home but had been derelict since the early noughties, and an ideal location for Pieter Jink to take his victims. Lana felt goosebumps tighten the tops of her arms.

Situated on the outskirts of town, nine people had been butchered in different rooms of the house; the Fonnet twins had been the last. Pieter Jink had taken them from a school in a neighbouring county and brought them back to Newfield. He'd kept them locked inside an airing cupboard before caving in their skulls with a spade when he was done with them.

On 28 December 2016, while the authorities were still searching for the missing girls, Pieter Jink suffered a single, massive heart attack. He'd been given a family funeral before the trophies that he took from his victims were discovered at his city apartment. He'd bought the out-of-town property as an investment, and the corpses of the twins had been discovered soon after his death, as well as the decayed remains of seven other people buried in the orchard. To date, only three of them had been identified.

Lana's stomach had curdled when she'd seen the image of Jink on the *Right Where You're Standing* app. He was the correct height, and his hair was shorn tight to his head. His build and face were a little slim but the photo had been taken in 2012. He could have put the weight on since. After exhaustive research into his background Lana had discovered that, despite the fact he lived three hundred miles away, Pieter Jink's niece, Robin Dreese, lived in Cedar Grove, a small community just outside Jaxton. And, even though there was no record of Jink's last visit there, Lana couldn't dismiss the reality he would only have been nineteen miles from their home if he'd decided to stop by to see his niece.

She'd attempted to speak with Dreese on the phone, but the number she'd found for her had been disconnected. When she'd called at Dreese's bungalow it was empty. A neighbour told her she'd moved away soon after the revelations about the Jink house. She'd just upped sticks and Lana couldn't find a forwarding address. None of Jink's other family would speak to Lana. She'd passed the information to Detective Riggs, and he'd assured her he would liaise with Newfield PD, but that had been over three weeks ago.

Lana turned to Cooper who was sitting in the back seat connected to his laptop by a pair of headphones. He looked up at her through the window and, briefly, his thin smile of resignation made him look years older. Or was she projecting that because she was delaying the vacation? She held up five fingers to him and Todd and then turned and walked towards the house.

They both knew she'd be longer than five minutes but she moved swiftly to show them she was mindful of the schedule. The vacation they'd won to Blue Crest Adventure Park lay another eighty miles down the interstate. The Jink house was an hour's detour on the way, which meant they had to find a motel and travel on in the morning. But of the many murder sites in the area this was the one that had a connection to Jaxton. Having made Todd and Cooper stop off, however, Lana knew she'd have some serious making up to do afterwards.

It was ten past eight in the evening and the blue sky was just starting to pink above the roof. If she knew nothing of the house's history Lana wondered if she'd have experienced the same sensation she got in her stomach at all the scenes she'd visited: like fat solidifying into a heavy block in her stomach.

Did bad vibrations really remain in the walls after screams had ceased ringing around them? She didn't believe in ghosts but was convinced that terrible events left a permanent mark, even if it was a product of the people who lived nearby. While there were folks to remember and speak of them, a neighbourhood could never properly heal.

Lana took the six steps up to the front door and pushed on the panel.

PROPERTY OF HILLBROOK HOLDINGS

Lana was familiar with the name on the metal plate screwed to the paintwork. It was a subsidiary company of Highseason, a major tourism agent that had started snapping up real estate with dark histories with a view to turning them into 'experiences'. Maybe in a few months' time there would be no way onto the land without paying an admission fee and leaving via a souvenir stand selling Pieter Jink merchandise.

No way in here. Lana descended the steps and felt Todd and Cooper's eyes on her. She headed around to the rear.

# CHAPTER 4

Todd watched Lana tying her long hazel hair into a ponytail as she made her way up the dirt track past the house. It was another way of rolling up her sleeves. What went through her mind when she walked into places like this? In her coral sweat top, cut-off denim shorts, and flip flops she looked so vulnerable in such an evil setting. Until Mr Whisper entered their lives, Lana wouldn't even watch a horror movie with him. Now she wore her fear like armour.

Todd was concerned about her obsession but understood how her new focus kept her anxieties in check. Neither of them wanted the Lana who had become paranoid, fanatical about home security, and paralysed by anticipation. To her, hunting for Mr Whisper felt like she was never dropping her guard and asserting control over the panic attacks that had come afterwards. Lately her sleep patterns had begun to settle down again, and she was almost ready to dispense with her meds.

'Are you worried about Mom?' Cooper asked too loudly.

Todd turned and gestured for him to take off the headphones. 'No, she's fine, Squidge.'

'No problemo?'

'No problemo.' Todd smiled at him and switched on the air con.

'What's she doing?'

'Just visiting.'

'Who?'

Todd considered how to answer. 'She just wants to see where somebody lived.'

'Who?'

'Somebody… from history.'

''K.' Cooper put his headphones back on. History was a school word.

Was Pieter Jink really Mr Whisper? Lana seemed to think there was a possibility. She'd shown him the photos. But Todd hadn't been there in the yard to protect them, so it was impossible for him to have an opinion. And because of that he still felt like he'd let them both down. But since then he'd had to conceal his feelings of inadequacy while they'd dealt with Lana's issues.

He hoped to God Pieter Jink was him. He was in the ground. That meant he was no longer a threat. Then they could go back to being a regular family. He wanted those normal days again; the three of them in Saltshaw Park, feet in the fountain and Cooper chuckling uncontrollably every time Todd took his fingers from the nozzle in the dolphin's mouth and they all got soaked. And Lana actually present with them, instead of casting her eyes about or ruminating over whichever new sordid detail she'd found online.

But after Lana's other accusations had proved to be invalid, he knew stopping here was unlikely to give them the release they desperately needed. And Newfield was three hundred and thirty miles from home. Jink's other victims had been taken from just over the county border. Even if he'd visited his niece in Cedar Grove, why risk driving so far after a kidnap? But there had been no suspects in their immediate neighbourhood. He had to have come from somewhere.

Todd took in the structure skulking amongst the parched landscape. He was going to use the horn if she wasn't out in five. That was always the drill. Even though most of the locations were unspectacular, neither of them wanted Cooper exposed to them.

Todd refused to accompany her, even when looking after Cooper wasn't an issue. But Lana was always quick. And when she returned to the car she would never share her experience with him. She was a wife and mother again, and it was almost as if whatever Lana made herself face in those dark corners reminded her of the wholesome family life she led. She was always so animated when she came back.

Todd told himself it wasn't too much time out of their vacation and that Lana would be more relaxed once she'd done what she had to do. Then they could drive on to Blue Crest so their break could begin properly. Two weeks to forget about debts and the snowballing problems that would be waiting for him when they got back.

He glanced in the mirror at Cooper, and his son was holding Frogbert and making him wave one of his green hands at Todd.

Todd waved back.

# CHAPTER 5

Even though it was nearly sundown the heat still rose up against Lana's bare legs from the cracked mud under her flip flops. At the end of the track she found the orchard, and the fermented odour of fallen, rotting apples caught in her throat.

Lana took in the deep, dead grass the trees stooped in, their laden branches sagging and forlorn. She guessed nobody wanted to pick the fruit that had grown from this soil. Had the police recovered every body that Jink had buried here? Some corpses had been intact while others had been dismembered and hidden under different trees. Slitting their throats had been Jink's favourite method of dispatch, before he pulverised their skulls and cut off the tops of their fingers to make identification impossible.

Lana slid her fingers into the back pocket of her cut-off jeans and pulled out her iPhone.

*Right Where You're Standing* – *RWYS* – was her indispensable app. It was dubbed the 'Wikipedia of Death'. Like a lot of universal software, it had begun life as the work of a student with too much time on his hands. Ted Lepine opened up his serial killer database to allow anyone to share information, and it had soon become the definitive manual for sociopath tourism.

Despite its notoriety for often presenting uncorroborated facts, *RWYS* was swiftly embraced worldwide. Not only did it connect to GPS and inform the user where the nearest murder site was, it also provided the most direct route. It then offered exhaustive bio details of the perpetrator, images of them and their victims and a wealth of associated news clips and footage. It was possible to cross-reference the killer with similar profiles and gain access to a forum to discuss them, as well as put forward your own information and pictures and any theories about unsolved cases.

Accused of indulging the ghoulish side of human nature, Lepine countered that he hadn't inputted anything to *RWYS* since its initial inception and that a very active demographic of contributors had caused it to become the worldwide phenomenon it was.

In 2015, Lepine sold *RWYS* to a major software conglomerate. But their only alteration was to add the voice-over of a well-known actor and open up space for advertisers.

Lana tapped the *RWYS* app icon on the screen. It opened and quickly found her location.

*'Finding nearest murder site…'*

The map zoomed in and a yellow outline flashed around the house and its grounds.

'Murder site of infamous sexual predator, Pieter Jink,' said the velvety voice of veteran Hollywood actor Stanley de Souza. 'Current status: deceased. Jink was never interrogated by police about the nine victims that were found on his property. Jink sexually abused his male and female victims before and after death and retained simple trophies at his rented apartment. These included jewellery that he displayed on a china tree in his bedroom, as well as their clothing, which he vacuum bagged with their ID inside.'

Lana muted the commentary. She'd already exhaustively read up on Jink. She allowed the silence to wash in again and flicked down the page to the photo of Pieter Jink's avuncular features. Again, she tried to imagine the Snip the Squirrel mask in the middle of his face. Below that was an image of the orchard, minus tall grass, police officers and a forensics team dotted around, and mounds of earth in front of freshly dug holes. Beside the one in the foreground were three knotted black refuse sacks, none of them large enough to hold an entire body.

Lana took three paces forward and stepped left. She was now standing on exactly the same spot the photographer had stood. Continuing slowly, the dry grass brushed and tickled her legs, and she stopped at the open grave in the image.

She looked down at the now overgrown turf, imagining how far below it the police had had to dig before they reached the pieces of people there. Under the tips of her blue-painted toes Pieter Jink had crouched, covering over the remnants of something only he understood.

Lana turned back to the house when she heard something rustle in the grass. 'Todd?' But she knew it wouldn't be him. He never ventured into the places she did. There was nobody immediately behind her or on the mud track where she'd entered. Probably an animal.

It was easy to spook herself in the eerie and suspended atmospheres of the grisly haunts she visited, though she was steadily becoming immune to it. She waited for further sounds but none came. Lana held her breath, daring the noise to repeat itself. It didn't.

Her gaze shifted to the rear porch. The same grey metal plates sealed the windows on the bottom and top floor, and she could see the Hillbrook logo on the panel of the back door through the screen.

Lana finished her exploration of the yard, halting at each grave in the picture before making her way to the porch. She climbed the three rotten steps and hinged open the screen. Putting her palm against the grubby white panel she wondered how many times Jink's hand had been on the same paintwork, the pressure of it swinging the door inwards, after he'd been out in the orchard.

The door didn't give and she pushed harder. Lana wanted to make herself peer through every doorway of each room he'd used. But she assumed if Hillbrook had bought the property, the whole place was probably locked down and in the process of being sanitised for paying visitors.

What had she hoped to achieve by coming here? But this was different to the other scenes she'd investigated. Jink was dead and that removed a layer of its menace. It was what she needed to feel – a detachment of the threat, even though she'd doubted there would be any discovery or moment of revelation at the site. Maybe she just wanted her instincts to tell her it was as close as she'd get.

There was a physical similarity between Jink and the man she'd struggled with in the yard, but was the fact his niece had moved away from a neighbouring town grounds to suspect a man who had targeted all his other victims in Newfield? There were no recorded instances of Jink wearing a mask, and the thirteen-year-old Fonnet twins had been his youngest victims.

Mr Whisper had vanished. Sooner or later, Lana figured, she'd have to come to terms with never finding him.

# CHAPTER 6

Todd observed Lana trot back down the path wearing the stolid expression he'd been anticipating; still, a small part of him deflated. But they'd made a promise to each other the night before: they wouldn't allow the outcome they expected from their stop at the Jink house to sour the rest of the trip.

She met his gaze, and he tightened his lips to tell her he understood. He switched on the radio to disperse the silence in the car. The Charlie Daniels Band was singing 'The Devil Went Down to Georgia'. He glanced at Cooper in the mirror but he was still wearing his headphones and watching *SpongeBob* on the tablet.

Lana turned to take one more look at the property and then circled around the front of the Subaru. She wouldn't talk to him immediately. She'd still be processing whatever she'd experienced. But half an hour or so after, they'd have her back.

She slid into the passenger seat.

'Done?' he asked, as if she'd just returned from a more mundane errand.

She nodded once and belted herself in without making eye contact.

Todd started the engine and pulled them away from the godawful place. Sure enough, a few miles from their motel, Lana put her hand on his arm and squeezed.

'Think an early night would be good for all of us.' She tickled Cooper's bare ankle. He chuckled and whipped his leg away and she did it again. 'Want to have all our energy for the park tomorrow.'

*

After they'd booked into the Babbling Brook Motel they carefully carried Cooper in asleep and put him straight to bed with Frogbert.

'Why don't you jump in the shower?' She handed Todd a grey robe that had been washed so many times it felt like cardboard.

He took it, and she switched on the TV, turning the volume low. Through the half-closed bathroom door he watched her triple-check the chain on the door and that their single window was firmly locked. She didn't like him to see her performing her incessant security regimen.

Leaving the house used to take over half an hour. Her compulsive patrols had lessened now but he knew she probably reverted whenever he wasn't around.

Todd took off his clothes, got into the shower and twisted the dial. It was freezing cold but he didn't mind and let the jets cool his scalp and run down to his feet. He knew he'd still have a few more minutes to wait, increased the temperature and soaped himself with some of the watered-down shower cream that was balanced on the rusty tray above the dial.

Then he heard Lana enter the bathroom, and disrobe. She didn't close the door, and he knew better than to argue with her about it. At least they were behind a plastic yellow curtain if Cooper woke and walked in. He felt her hands and then her warm lips and breasts against his back and turned to her, looking into her eyes. They asked him for forgiveness.

Lana slid her palms over the shaved blonde stubble of his head. She kissed his mouth firmly, and he felt the weight of her arms on his shoulder blades. She was always so ardent after. Always needed to wash it off with him and remind herself what she had. Her hot sunbaked skin clamped tight to his, and he inhaled her dewberry scent.

As they both tried to restrain their murmurs Todd wondered how long Lana would need to keep looking for someone she probably wouldn't find. Was he wrong to have indulged it at all, let alone for the months since Cooper's attempted abduction?

But as her mouth slid down his neck and bit his shoulder he was just glad to have his old Lana with him again. Todd pecked her forehead and wished it could soothe her troubled thoughts.

# CHAPTER 7

The following day Todd was blinded by the sunshine when he opened the hot drapes in the motel room, and quickly woke the other two. He bear-hugged Cooper, and his son giggled uncontrollably. 'Whose turn is it next?'

Cooper's eyes rolled to Lana, and Todd grabbed her as she tried to head to the TV and dragged her onto the bed with them. He tickled and raspberry kissed them both and didn't want their laughter to subside. 'Marching orders: I'll pack, both of you in and out of the shower in ten minutes. I'm timing you and there'll be more of the same if you're one second late.'

'Let's go!' Cooper sounded like he needed the bathroom right away.

Lana quickly led him there by the hand.

'Hurry, hurry, hurry!'

Cooper yanked Lana now and the door slammed after them.

They were ravenous and quickly ate pastrami bagels at the little deli opposite the motel. Todd didn't want to linger for a coffee refill, and Lana was stunned.

'I think Daddy got out the right side of bed.' She left the cash and tip on the saucer and quickly rose from the table. 'Wait for us.'

Todd wanted to sweep her along today. The weather had put them both in a good mood and he didn't want to lose the momentum. Pressing problems could be temporarily put on hold. He hustled them into the Subaru and started the engine. 'Soon we'll be riding those rapids in Blue Moon Lagoon. You ready to get drenched?' He looked in the mirror at Cooper.

Lana turned to see him nod uncertainly. 'I think Daddy sounds afraid. You know he hates the water.'

Cooper half smirked.

'You gonna look after him and hold his hand?'

''K.' He nodded enthusiastically; pleased to have been given the responsibility.

'Wagons roll then.' Todd put the car into gear and accelerated to the exit.

# CHAPTER 8

As they reached Sequonda and the warm breeze blew over her through the open window, Lana tried to forget the Jink house and concentrate on her family. In half an hour, they'd all be immersing themselves in one of the cool Blue Crest splash pools and hanging out in a cabana, and she'd promised Todd she'd be present.

They'd won the vacation through their online shopping account, and it couldn't have come at a better time – just the three of them for two weeks. When had they last been able to kick back for so long? Way before Cooper was born – Todd's hours for the power company and Lana's in event managing were often out of sync.

As Todd accelerated to one of the reception booths of the adventure park, Cooper was standing up in the back to see between the seats.

He bounced at his knees. 'Woah, the tree houses!'

Lana craned to see them for his benefit. She was happy he was so excited. Twisting metallic tubes wound down from the wooden huts in the tall pines. She hated those kinds of slides and had suffered an aversion to going into tunnels since she'd got trapped inside some plastic water pipes on a construction site as a kid. Her brother had enticed her in and then connected them so she couldn't get out and just went round and round in circles.

'Hey.' Todd handed the elderly woman dressed in the mauve sweatshirt and baseball cap their printed out e-tickets.

'Hi there.' Her puckered smoker's lips trembled from a long shift of grinning. 'You guys stayed with us before?' She looked directly at Cooper.

He shyly shook his head.

'In that case, I'll slip in some VIP passes to get you fast tracked in the lagoon.'

'How about that?' Todd turned to Cooper for his reaction.

'Thank you.' Cooper beamed.

Lana felt a pang of guilt. If they hadn't detoured they probably could have made it to the park and not had to spend the night at the motel. But she couldn't yet dismiss Pieter Jink as the police had her first two suspects.

'Take the second exit and park up in zone C. You can check in at the reception there.'

'Thanks.' Todd took the tickets and passes, and rolled them to the rear of the line steadily snaking its way towards the mini citadel of rides and accommodation towers.

'Not more traffic.' Cooper sighed and collapsed back to his seat.

'Won't be long now,' Lana placated.

But judging by the sluggish movement ahead it seemed like they still had some time to wait. 'Main thing is we're here. How many tree houses can you count?' She heard him mouth each number.

'Twelve.'

'Wow.' Lana tried a different, more reliable distraction tactic. 'Hungry?'

'Starving to death.'

'You mustn't say that.' Lana opened the glove compartment and took out his lunchbox of cheese chunks and chopped carrots.

Todd regarded it 'Healthy box? How about a slice of pizza when we get there?'

Cooper stuck his head between the seats. 'Stuffed crust?'

'What d'you think, Mom? Healthy box on standby as long as Squidge is good?'

Cooper looked to Lana for approval.

That was a licence she hadn't really wanted to issue but Lana could see that Todd was trying to keep Cooper buoyant. She smiled and nodded.

'Yay!' Cooper yelled and waited for Lana to return it to the glove compartment.

'Only if you're good. If you're not, it comes right back out again. OK?'

''K,' Cooper reluctantly agreed.

Lana kept the warm plastic in her hand as the car inched forward.

Cooper pressed his face further between the seats so his features were stretched and his eyes were slits.

'Don't, you'll hurt yourself.' She handed him a bottle of water.

Cooper sat contritely back with it but then caught sight of something out of the window and his face dropped.

Lana turned to the frieze of cartoon characters to the right of them. One of them was a twenty-foot Snip the Squirrel, his rodent teeth welcoming them into the park.

# CHAPTER 9

Lana was sitting in the bathroom with her cut-off jeans at her ankles. 'Be right out!' she yelled cheerfully. None of them had acknowledged the image of Snip the Squirrel as they'd slowly crawled past it in the Subaru.

But she'd felt the overture of one of her panic attacks before they'd got out of the car to check in and knew she had to take charge of it in private. She told herself she was being crazy. They couldn't hide themselves from every reminder of the event. But Lana felt a familiar claustrophobia, a prickling across the tops of her shoulders and the sensation of the room's dimensions shifting almost indiscernibly.

She told herself what she always did – that wherever Mr Whisper was now it was unlikely he had even spared them a thought since the incident, so why was she still allowing him to monopolise her family's life?

*Get a grip. Move past this. For Cooper and Todd's sake if not yours.*

But her mind had worn the words so flat they had very little definition.

'How's it going, babe?' Todd's voice gently encouraged from outside the door.

He knew what she was doing in there and had been making excuses for her while she got herself back on track. It was a routine he'd become more than accustomed to. He knew Lana was determined not to hold things up again.

*Go have a vacation with your family. Stop torturing yourself. Stop torturing them.*

She stood, pulled up her shorts, pushed the flush button and unlocked the door. Todd and Cooper were standing right outside. She'd barely had time to take in their home for the next two weeks. It was one elongated, immaculate living space – two spacious bedrooms and an expansive lounge, with two huge couches, armchairs and a 40" TV. The kitchen was probably four times the size of the one in their apartment. How could they not have a good time here?

'You all set?' Todd said breezily for Cooper's benefit. He was holding their swipe key.

'I thought we might settle in first. Maybe watch some TV.'

Cooper's face was agog.

'Just kidding.' She smirked at her son. 'What are we waiting for?' Lana gestured towards the door and followed them both to it.

Todd turned to her as he opened it and Cooper scurried ahead. 'OK?'

She nodded emphatically.

They took the elevator from the eighteenth to ground and suddenly they were in the middle of a throng. Lana told herself this was exactly what she needed – other families barging and pushing to jolt her back to reality. Focussing on the logistics of negotiating the crowds would surely banish her abstraction.


The three of them examined the zone map at reception. Blue Crest was much bigger than she'd envisaged. It was like a sprawling mini city that incorporated a water world, forest kingdom, safari, expansive golf course and cabana club where the adults could unwind. There wasn't going to be much of that for them: the whole idea was to spend time with Cooper.

They could have daily childcare, but Lana was still nervous about putting Cooper into the hands of strangers. Waving her son off on the school bus remained an ordeal for her and she relished the notion of having him to herself for the whole break.

They took a shuttle to the downtown district where the VIP (Very Important Parents) towers were situated in the middle of the action. Lana was relieved their own apartment was removed from the hordes.

Cooper's excitement was infectious, and as they wandered around the covered central concourse it was briefly like she had two young boys to rein in. Todd hid behind the support pillars and jumped out on Cooper, making him giggle uncontrollably. It was impossible to work out who thought it was more hilarious.

Cooper was disappointed that he was too young for some of the rides, but after the three of them had taken a rattling cart through The Tombs of the Pharaohs he held onto Lana's arm so tight that her scream was nothing to do with the sharp twists of the track. The attendant pressed an *'I Survived the Ride'* glitter sticker onto his chest as they left, and Cooper radiated pride.

'You enjoying yourself?' Lana asked him as they emerged.

Cooper considered the question. 'Nearly.'

Lana hid a smile. It was Cooper's old ploy to elongate his playtime. He obviously figured if he didn't declare complete fun he would be allowed to continue until he'd achieved it.

Todd recognised the ruse as well. 'Squidge, we've got two whole weeks. Just tell us where you want to go next. Safari?'

''K.' He nodded. His eyes had already alighted on the Buzzsaw Gulch ride. 'Oh wow.' He ran in its direction.

'Wait up!' Todd called after him. 'He's going to be pooped by this evening.'

'So are you.'

'Not that pooped.' He squeezed her hand and then released it to pursue Cooper.

*

The day shot by in a procession of noisy lines, surges of adrenaline, corn dogs and slushies, and Lana realised nothing was going to spoil their fun.

By five, Cooper was almost asleep standing up so they made their way back to their side of the park and grabbed some take-out calzones. Most of the meal remained uneaten, however, as the three of them fell into exhausted sleep on the couch in front of the TV before seven thirty.

# CHAPTER 10

Todd opened his mouth to speak but his words couldn't escape. He was standing in the middle of the lawn watching Mr Whisper stealing over the rotten fence panel – an evil caricature with an overly distended belly.

Cooper was kneeling in the middle of the grass, grinning humourlessly at Todd.

He tried to dash forward to scoop up his son but he couldn't move.

*Come away from the fence! Run to me!*

But even though his lips formed the exclamation nothing but a dry hiss emerged.

Cooper frowned as Mr Whisper thudded onto the ground behind him. The man remained crouching but his body swivelled to reveal Snip the Squirrel's toothy sneer. The eyes of the mask were slanted and the two rodent teeth sharpened to a point.

Todd's muscles were paralysed and he blinked in slow motion. Every time he saw the yard again, Mr Whisper had crawled closer to Cooper.

*Don't look behind you! Just run to me!*

But Cooper was too busy with Frogbert, and now Mr Whisper was at his shoulder, peering over it.

Todd could see and hear Mr Whisper's lashes brushing noisily against the eyeholes of the mask but when his own blinked again he couldn't open them. Through the orange light of his lids he could hear Cooper chuckling.

He had to use every ounce of energy to lift them and when he did Mr Whisper was holding Frogbert, his arms encompassing Cooper's tiny form. He waved one of the little green hands at Todd.

Todd attempted to wrench himself from where he was frozen but his eyes closed again. And the orange filter in front of them was darkening.

*Cooper!* But still no sound could break through. Now his son's giggling turned into squeals. The sort he made when Todd tickled him, and he was almost sick from laughter.

*Cooper!*

They became shrieks of pain.

Under them Lana's voice yelled at Mr Whisper but Todd still couldn't budge an inch forward. He didn't have a mouth now and the blood rumbled in his head as he fought to breathe.

She screamed Todd's name.

Todd couldn't help them. He was suffocating.

'Todd!'

She was close by now. Todd trembled violently with the exertion of trying to see. He briefly glimpsed the yard. But now there was a new dimension to the nightmare. Mr Whisper was lugging a dirty polythene sack towards Todd with them both struggling inside. It hissed across the turf until his Snip the Squirrel mask was the only thing that filled Todd's slitted vision. He could see through the eyeholes of the mask, meet the darting pupils behind it, hear Mr Whisper's breathing and smell the sour breath inside.

'Todd!'


He woke and saw the ceiling fan whirling overhead. Lana was quite still beside him. Todd sat up quickly and put his bare feet on the carpet, reassuring himself he was back in a world where he hadn't lost his son and wife to Mr Whisper.

But it always took a good few seconds to get traction there and, even though he was getting better at dismissing the same night terrors he'd been having ever since Lana had called him at work to tell him what had happened that afternoon, he could still feel the sweat soaking his chest hair.

As he often did, he stood shakily and went immediately to his son. Cooper's presence expelled the last remnants of the nightmare. Todd stood in the doorway, watching the sky blue duvet bounce with his shallow breaths. The guilt of not being at home to protect Cooper and Lana was like stitched internal wounds. Mr Whisper slid a knife into and cut them open every time he had the dream.

No – Todd wouldn't allow that cycle of thought to begin again. Mr Whisper could have moved away or been locked up for a similar crime by now.

It angered him that he'd lost so much time thinking of that pervert. That he'd pervaded their conversations and that Todd had to spend hours reassuring Lana he wouldn't come back. But how could he, when deep down Todd feared he might as well?

When Todd awoke the second time he waited for the usual apprehensions to rack up but, despite the nightmare, the afterglow of the previous day pushed everything else aside. He turned to Lana and found her fast asleep. He picked up his phone and glanced at the time. It was 9.33! He couldn't believe they'd lain in for so long.

That must have been the longest sack time Lana had had in months. They hadn't even unwound with a bottle of wine and her meds were still packed in the case. He was so glad getting away from the apartment was already relaxing her; that, and Cooper running them ragged.

Lana's eyes were still rolling behind their lids. She was such a light sleeper, so Todd got cautiously out of bed to rally Cooper.

He padded through the lounge and saw most of the calzone left on the plate on the table in front of the TV. Usually the Cross tribe would have had it devoured in minutes. They must have been bushed.

A soft thud from the kitchen.

Todd headed there and when he entered the open-plan area found Cooper trying to climb up one of the tall stools at the breakfast bar. He was attempting to reach a tub of Oreos.

'Busted.'

Cooper grinned but stuck to his task.

Todd touched the warm crown of his head as he passed him and bent to examine the dials of the sleek chrome coffee machine. He'd get that going first then wake Lana. She wouldn't forgive him if he let her sleep too late.

He took the sachet of ground beans out of the refrigerator and opened it, his bad dream already forgotten.

# CHAPTER 11

At lunchtime, Cooper decided he wanted a cheeseburger. Lana guessed this was based on the fact that the Pluto Patties restaurant offered planetscape booths and the serving staff were dressed as astronauts and aliens.

After a five-minute wait they got their table and were given some iced water in pouches that had to be drunk through straws because of zero gravity.

'We'll stabilise that when your appetisers are ready,' their space-man waiter explained.

But Cooper didn't hear. He was too busy pressing the sticker he'd earned at The Tomb of the Pharaohs onto his clean tee shirt. He'd transferred it from yesterday's and it kept unsticking.

Todd ordered a Mountain Dew and two glasses of Merlot.

Lana could see he was doing everything he could to maintain the happiness from the previous day. 'D'you need to go?' She put her hand on Cooper's jiggling bare leg.

'Come on, Squidge.' Todd took Cooper to use the bathroom.

A few moments later Lana's phone buzzed in her purse. It was an alert from *RWYS*. She opened the app and saw a user called Ambuscade1 had flagged her about an upload. She'd never heard of Ambuscade1. Why were they contacting her directly?

When she opened it, Lana felt a cold worm of dread slither into her stomach.

It was a photo. A close-up of her, Todd, and Cooper smiling for the lens. When and where had it been taken? She couldn't make out the background.

But it wasn't just the appearance of the image that alarmed her, and the fact that thousands of international users of the app could now access the private snap, it was where it had been posted.

The picture was in the Fresh Blood section – the area of the app devoted solely to new murder victims.

# CHAPTER 12

'If you chew that any slower, we'll still be here for breakfast.'

Todd's good-natured quip eventually filtered through and Lana shook her head. 'Sorry. Guess I wasn't as hungry as I thought.' She was genuinely worried. How had the photo ended up there?

'I could help you.' Cooper was surprised when she slid her burger towards him.

Lana had decided she wouldn't show Todd the picture in front of Cooper. They needed to maintain a secure atmosphere for him. Was she overreacting? But sitting surrounded by meteors, stars and planets seemed to emphasise the fact she felt like she was suddenly in a vacuum. No, she wouldn't allow whoever was trying to spook her to trigger an attack and ruin the vacation. But how could she focus on her family after what had just been posted?

'Are you OK?' Todd asked as Cooper took the bun lid off and picked away the diced gherkin.

Lana nodded. 'Fine.' She smiled at him. 'My turn for the bathroom.'

She closed the door of the cubicle, sat on top of the lid and checked Amuscade1's profile. No details and they'd only joined today. She located the image that had been posted on the app in her phone's archive. It had been taken at Todd's parents' last Christmas.

Could she really have uploaded it by accident? In the past, Lana had signed up to a number of groups on Facebook she had no recollection of joining. It had become a running joke but now she could see how easily she could have released more information to strangers than she was aware of.

Or had her phone been hacked?

*'Anyone know how I can get a photo taken down?'* She typed quickly, posted it on the *RWYS* forum and waited.

*'Hi Lana. Maybe I can help.'*

She knew Styx36 would reply, though not so swiftly. Did he spend his every waking hour on the forum? She assumed it was a he. Styx36 had been keen to speak with her since she'd joined, and Lana now regretted using her real name.

*'Picture uploaded in error. Will inform RWYS but know they take 24 hours to answer queries. Wonder if there's a shortcut.'*

She knew exactly what the response was going to be.

*'Can't see one in your posts, Lana. Where is it?'*

She was reluctant to point him to the exact location. Didn't want him looking at her family. But if he could help her she supposed he had to know.

*'In Fresh Blood.'*

*'How did it end up there, Lana?'*

She sighed.

*'Ambuscade1 uploaded it. Flagged me. Have checked profile but there's nothing there. Probably a prank but want it off asap.'*

*'What will my reward be, Lana?'*

*'Eternal gratitude.'*

*'Sounds good to me, Lana. I'll see what I can do.'*

*'Have to go now. Can you post any suggestions?'*

*'Sure thing, Lana. Hope to connect with you soon.'*

Styx36 used her name way too often.

*'Thanks.'*

Could it even be Styx36 having a laugh at her expense? But how would he have accessed her archive?

There was no way any of her friends could be pranking her. None of them would be so insensitive. She sent an email to *RWYS* requesting the image be immediately removed and got an auto response telling her they were dealing with the message but to be patient in the meantime.

# CHAPTER 13

Lana had expected to be greeted by silence when she reported the situation to the female police operator.

'We'll pass this to our Cyber Crime division but it might be quicker if you email them the specific details yourself. Shall I give you the address?'

'Sure, fire away.' Lana opened the notebook on her iPhone and rested it on the counter of the café charging point she was seated at. She tapped it in. 'Got it, thanks.' Through the window, she watched Todd buying Cooper a red popsicle from the stand in the quad outside. She knew exactly how he was going to react about some lunatic that had attached himself to her through her morbid chat room. But she had to tell him.

'So, nobody has actually threatened you?' the operator asked.

'No, but it's really spooked me.'

'That's understandable. And you can't think of anyone who would want to do that?'

'Somebody tried to abduct my son last year; they were never caught.'

There was a pause. 'Then I can understand your alarm. You did say it was a photo of all three of you that was posted not just of your son, though…'

'Yes.'

'Then let's not rule out this being a prank. But just for safety can you remember the name of the officer in charge of the investigation?'

'Detective Tom Riggs, Jaxton PD.'

'OK, I'm flagging it to them. Just get as many details to that email address as soon as you can. We'll monitor things from here.'

But Lana didn't feel any sense of relief. 'And what should we do in the meantime?'

'If you have reason to believe you're in danger, call us back immediately.'

Lana knew there was no more reassurance to be had and that the operator had done as much as she could. 'OK, appreciate your help.'

She ended the call and emailed a message, her number, and a link for Fresh Blood to the address she'd been given. Why hadn't Styx36 got back to her? His responses were usually instantaneous.

When Lana left the Internet café she grinned broadly for Todd and Cooper's benefit.

'Who were you calling?' Cooper already had red juice over his chin and down his tan tee shirt.

'Grandma. Just making sure everything's OK at home.'

Cooper nodded, immediately lost interest and homed in on the tree houses. 'Can we go there now?'

'Finish your popsicle first.'

Todd followed him across the quad and turned back to Lana. 'Everything all right with your folks?'

'All fine. Todd, I need to—'

But he'd chased after Cooper.

Was she being paranoid? There were some twisted people on the Internet who just liked to cause maximum chaos.

She surveyed the faces of the people sitting on the benches around her. An overweight middle-aged man in a canary yellow baseball cap sitting on his own on one of the plastic box seats caught her eye. He swiftly looked away, his attention returning to the phone in his hand.

# CHAPTER 14

As she watched Todd and Cooper crossing a rope bridge between two pines about fifty feet above her head, Lana's phone vibrated in her purse. She quickly took it out. It was an unknown caller. 'Hello?'

'Mrs Cross?'

Lana didn't recognise the male voice. 'Yes?'

'This is Jed Nickels, Cyber Crime. You contacted us recently and sent us this number?' He sounded Australian.

'That was quick.'

'Just to let you know we've contacted the website you forwarded to us regarding the image that was posted.'

Lana filled the pause. 'And?'

'So… we're just waiting on a response.'

'*I've* contacted them myself and had an auto reply,' she said in exasperation.

'We do have to wait for their feedback before we can move forward. A lot of cases are resolved at this point. I'm sure the photo will be taken down without any problem.'

'But what about the person who posted it?' She squinted through the thick forest ferns beneath the slides.

'That could be more problematic. And, as yet, nobody has explicitly threatened you.'

'So you wouldn't feel threatened by this?'

'I probably would but I have to follow protocol. As soon as I've heard back from them I'll be in touch and we can decide what to do next.'

'Have you had complaints before about *Right Where You're Standing*?'

'I'm sorry but I can't divulge the details of other cases.'

'So what do you suggest we do in the meantime?' A rowdy group of kids ran by her.

'I can't do that until we've evaluated the situation. Chances are the site will cooperate and remove the picture.'

'That still doesn't answer my question about who posted it.'

'Let's take this one step at a time. I've got your cell so I, or a colleague, will keep you updated.'

'And when's that likely to be?'

'Like I say, we have to wait for their reaction before we go any further.' He fell silent to let her know the conversation was over.

She sighed. 'Please call back as soon as you hear anything.'

'Absolutely. We'll be in touch soon.'

Lana slipped the phone in her purse and looked back up at the bridge. They'd crossed to the last tree of the course so were about to emerge from the slide. Safari next, and then it would be time to head back to the apartment. Lana wasn't looking forward to her chat with Todd.

She crossed the soft wood chips of the clearing and lingered at the bottom of the tube. As she hadn't seen any other kids in front of Todd and Cooper, they shouldn't have had to get in line.

A minute later they still hadn't emerged. Lana took a few paces back and peered up through the foliage at the bridge. There was nobody standing on it.

'Todd!' She waited for his reply but none came.

Returning to the slide she called up the dark interior. 'You guys on the way down?'

Her question resonated metallically, and was greeted with silence. She scanned the tall ferns. They definitely hadn't emerged. She would have seen them, even though she'd been on the phone.

The sound of laughter from above. Lana walked back to gaze up at the bridge. She could see two sets of feet pounding the slats.

But her relief was fleeting. It wasn't Todd and Cooper. An infant in a magenta summer dress and a young teenage girl were just reaching the top of the slide.

Lana heard a scream and squeaking from inside the tube. The gangly teenager, wearing miniscule denim shorts, came to a standstill at the edge. Her smile vanished when she saw Lana's expression, and she stood and waited for the little girl.

'Come on, let's go find the others,' the teenager said as soon as the infant slid into view.

'Excuse me.'

The teenager grabbed the little girl's hand and turned to Lana, her eyebrows raised.

'Did you see a small boy and his father up there?'

She shook her head once, expression wary before she turned and led the infant away.

Lana surveyed the bush-lined path that led back to the main gate. No sign of Todd or Cooper. Surely they wouldn't have left without her. They must have seen her from the bridge.

*Don't panic.*

She tried calling Todd but got his answering service.

'Todd!'

The teenager glanced uncertainly at Lana over her shoulder then led the little girl through the exit gate.

# CHAPTER 15

As she swung the metal exit gate and contemplated the crowd mobbing the ice cream stand at the assembly point, Lana's restrained alarm threatened to burst from her chest. She fixed every face. Todd and Cooper definitely weren't there. They knew she was waiting for them. They wouldn't have left without her.

'Sorry, ma'am, you can't do that.' The septuagenarian security guard held his arm across her as she attempted to go back to the tree houses.

'I can't find my son.'

He caught Lana's expression and showed her his palms as an apology.

'Have you seen a boy and his father come by here in the last couple of minutes?'

'Uh…' Turning slowly he narrowed his sight at the throng around the stand.

Lana knew she was wasting time and attempted to push the shut gate, but it didn't budge.

'Now, don't fret.' He fumbled out a touch key and waved it in front of a sensor. 'They're probably still in there somewhere.'

She momentarily closed her eyes tight as he tried a second time, and the gate unlocked. The guard said something else as she returned to the slides, but Lana couldn't hear because she was running, feet thudding under her short breaths.

An adult emerged from the slide and stood to catch his son as he appeared. He smiled at her as she passed him but she focussed on the rope bridge.

'Todd!' She did nothing to disguise her hysteria. 'Todd, answer me!'

She followed the bridge back to the previous tree. There was no slide there, or from the next. They had to have come down from the last one. Why would they have gone all the way back? How long had she been on the phone? Had she shifted her attention from the bridge long enough for that to happen?

*Don't do this to me.*

She jogged towards the start of the course, her head raised to spot them.

She would scream at Todd when she found him. He knew better than this. Please let them have a scene in front of everybody, because that meant she would have found them.

'Jesus!'

Lana didn't apologise to the man she'd collided with. She was still craning up to the rope bridge as she dashed along the bark chips back to where they'd started.

When she got there the line had doubled and families were quickly being filtered through. She glimpsed at her watch but had no idea what time they'd entered the enclosure. Ten? It was forty minutes past now.

'Todd! Cooper!'

'Can I help you?' A short, Hispanic woman in the standard issue mauve Blue Crest uniform approached her.

'I can't find my son. He's five years old.'

'Wandered off?' She unclipped her walkie-talkie.

'He was with my husband. They were up there.' She looked up to the trees again and felt dizzy.

'OK. Let's calm down. I did see a man rush his boy out the turnstiles a few moments ago. Seemed like he'd been sick.'

'My son was wearing a tan tee shirt.'

'This child had a tan tee shirt.'

'You're sure?'

The woman nodded, eyes hooded, as if mollifying a child. 'Let's go see if we can find them.'

Lana strode with her to the entrance. It didn't make sense. If Cooper had been sick why hadn't Todd taken him out at the exit?

'This way.' The woman used a touch key on a small side gate to bypass the crowd.

Lana stepped through and flitted her eyes about the mass of faces in the plaza.

'See them?'

She shook her head.

'They've probably gone to the rest rooms.'

Lana made for the log cabin block in front of them.

'Wait, let me.' The woman overtook her and walked tentatively inside.

Lana turned and reappraised the people around her. 'Todd! Cooper!' They wouldn't have come all the way back here.

'Only three guys in there, no child,' the woman said from behind her.

Lana swivelled and checked the disgruntled face of the obese goth leaving.

'Nobody in the cubicles?'

'Empty.'

'I think you might have seen somebody else's child. Can you let me back in?'

'Sure.' She trotted to keep up with Lana.

'Can you recall anything else about him?'

'Blonde hair.'

'Did he have jeans on?' Cooper had been wearing shorts.

'Green shorts.'

Lana stopped. 'What about his father? What did he look like?' She remembered to swallow; her throat felt as if it had a rock lodged in it.

'Older guy…' She blinked as she tried to recollect him.

'How old?' Todd was thirty-one, same as her.

'Fifties, maybe.'

Lana felt a cold mist settling on her shoulders. 'Pot belly?'

'I wouldn't say that. He had a few extra pounds. He was carrying the boy and holding a big soda cup to his face. That's why I thought he was being sick. I heard him ask my colleague where the bathrooms were.'

It was as if Lana had been sealed inside a polythene bag, suddenly cut off from the happy family world around her. 'Let me talk to your colleague.'

'He's just finished his shift.' She was regarding Lana with increasing alarm. 'But I might catch him in the locker room.' She barked a name into her walkie-talkie.

People were staring at Lana now, more uneasy frowns turning in her direction as they recognised a situation none of them ever wanted to be part of.

# CHAPTER 16

The Hispanic woman was just readmitting Lana to the enclosure when the whoop of a siren turned both their heads. An on-site paramedic ambulance was weaving its way through the pedestrians towards the exit side.

Without exchanging a word they both made their way across the plaza to where it halted.

'What's going on?' the woman asked the security guard that Lana had already spoken to.

'Somebody's injured. Family just found them and called it in.'

'Who's injured?' Lana demanded.

'One of the parents.' He opened the gate for the two-man ambulance crew. 'Follow the path, guys. They're to your left.'

Lana hurried after them and could hear the woman puffing at her heels. There were three people standing in the foliage underneath the slide. As she pushed aside ferns she saw the person lying motionless on his side there. Recognition strangled her exclamation.

'Todd!'

She ran to him and knelt, everyone else briefly draining out of the moment. His eyes were closed. Was he dead?

'Todd, can you hear me?' She put her hand to his face but he didn't respond. 'Todd, it's me. Wake up.' She held her breath until she saw his chest lift.

'Looks like he might have fallen from the bridge,' a muffled male voice said from behind her.

'Can you step back, ma'am?'

Lana lightly touched Todd's shoulder. His expression was unnervingly peaceful. 'Todd.'

'Please, we have to examine him.'

Lana felt hands on her shoulders ushering her clear and watched the ambulance crew checking him over. How could the happiness the three of them shared yesterday have so quickly become this?

One of them shot her a glance. 'D'you know how this happened?'

'No,' she answered, dazed. 'He was with our son.'

Her attention darted to the surrounding bushes but Lana knew she wouldn't see Cooper and was convinced the other attendant had witnessed him being taken out of the park.

'Seal the main gates – my son's missing.'

'I'll see what I can do.' But the woman sounded dubious.

Lana was on her feet and sprinting back to the exit. She would have to leave Todd in the hands of the crew. They would attend to him. She couldn't afford to think about the injuries he'd sustained, she just had to catch up with the man who had taken their son. It was what Todd would want her to do.

'Ma'am!'

She didn't answer. She'd already lost valuable time and they could be halfway across Blue Crest by now.

Back outside, she couldn't get her bearings. Which way was the main entrance? And would he really go in that direction? Her circulation hammered.

'Wait. I'm coming with you.' The Hispanic woman had caught up with her.

'Are there any other ways out of the park?'

She shook her head. 'I only work the gate. Let me think.'

'No time.' Lana crossed the road.

'Wait, they're still building the eastern quadrant. Kids have been slipping in that way for free.'

Lana stopped. 'Which way?'

The woman trotted quickly ahead of her, and Lana followed. Happy expressions became hardened as they both approached, families parting to let them pass as if they could immediately sense Lana's distress.

They rounded a conglomeration of food outlets, and the woman pointed to some tall hardboard panels.

'That's where they've been getting in.'

They both skirted them until they came to a gap with some striped tape across it. The woman ducked under, and Lana was close behind. They were in a large area of churned-up clay where foundations had been laid. Beyond it was a wire fence plastered with trash. Lana could see and hear the busy highway on the other side.

Without hesitating she scuttled down the clay incline onto the large concrete plateau and hurtled towards the area where the fence had collapsed.

'Be careful!' the woman yelled.

But Lana's focus was on the other side of it. She could just make out an area of tall, dead grass there and a dirty, white cubicle. She climbed the bank of clay and easily lifted her legs over the bowed wire.

Sidewinder Chilli Dogs

The fast-food stand's front hatch was locked up. Vehicles zipped by, and she could feel the heat from the blacktop and smell it melting in the sun. She squinted back and forth along the curve of the road. There was nobody parked up but there could have been. How long had it taken her to get here? Only a few minutes, and the woman had said the man was carrying extra pounds. Could he have exited here and already driven off?

'Thanks, Wendy.' The woman was on her walkie-talkie as she clambered the bank of the fence. 'They've closed the main entrance and my colleague is still on-site. Maybe he can remember something more about the guy.'

Lana surveyed the highway.

'Come on, if they *were* here…' She didn't finish the sentence. 'Everybody will be alerted to keep an eye out for them. Perhaps they're still in the park.'

Lana was rooted to the grass.

*This can't be happening.*

'Let me find out how your husband's doing.'

Traffic pelted by blowing warm fumes over Lana. Hundreds of shimmering cars stretching as far as she could see. Was Cooper getting further away with each passing second?

# CHAPTER 17

By the time Lana got back to the ferns under the tree slides the ambulance had gone.

'They put his neck in a brace and took him to the hospital.' The security guard turned from where he was talking to the family and two uniformed, male police officers.

'None of you saw him fall?'

The family shook their heads at Lana. She inspected the area where Todd had been sprawled only minutes before. A few feet away there was a half-eaten red popsicle. Was it Cooper's? Three wasps were feeding off it as it melted into the earth. Momentarily her thoughts were paralysed. Conversations continued but their words were just an incomprehensible drone. The wasps' buzzing melded with the sound. She had to snap out of it, but she could feel the situation incapacitating her.

*Keep looking for Cooper.*

The reality of events had suddenly landed hard, and the sickening notion that whatever she did now was going to be too late nearly brought Lana to her knees.

'Would you mind, ma'am?'

She registered the raised eyebrow of one of the young officers who knew she hadn't heard.

'We're going to take you to main reception where they're reviewing the security footage. We've arranged a buggy.' He nodded behind her.

Lana swivelled to where a pimply teenager in a mauve uniform was sitting on the vehicle staring at the ground.

There was more discussion, they asked her name, and then a hand guided her elbow and gently propelled her towards the seat. She managed to lift herself into it and vaguely registered the woman squeezing in next to her.

The buggy jerked and leaned her from side to side, and as they accelerated along the track she latched onto every face they passed. Any that met her scrutiny swiftly looked away. The woman was trying to calm her, her voice soothing but empty. Nothing would be all right until she had Cooper back.

The journey seemed to be endless but eventually she recognised the area where they'd checked in the day before. Her hand shot in alarm to her empty shoulder.

'My purse.'

'It's OK, honey, I picked it up for you.' The woman pressed it into her palm.

Lana was led to a security booth that reeked of male body sweat. A guy in a mauve shirt gave her a tight-lipped smile as she entered and was confronted by a bank of black-and-white screens.

'Is this your boy, Mrs Cross?' The first police officer pointed.

She leaned forward to study the frozen grey image. Recognising Cooper was like a physical blow. He was crystal clear, even though the man with him was holding the big soda cup over his mouth.

'It's him,' she confirmed emptily, feeling the acid sting of nausea as she examined his kidnapper. He carried more weight than Mr Whisper. Seemed taller. He was wearing denim dungarees and dirty-white sneakers. A dark baseball cap concealed his eyes and nose, and he was keeping his head dipped, the peak pulled down low.

'We're just interviewing the other attendant now. Do you know this man?' The second police officer was standing behind her.

'Somebody tried to take Cooper last year.' Could it really be him?

'This has happened before?' The second officer was incredulous. 'Play it for us,' he prompted the security guard.

The keyboard was stabbed and the footage came to life.

Lana felt her hand over her lips as she saw the man simultaneously restraining and marching Cooper away, all the time clutching the cup and talking to him. A couple turned to briefly observe them but walked on. The man moved faster, and now she could see that the fingers of his hand gripping the cup were also gagging Cooper. The top of her throat sealed up.

They left shot.

'We pick them up here.' The security guard indicated the screen three to the left. He activated it, and the man and Cooper passed quickly through. Cooper's feet were half dragged along the walkway.

'That's it?' The first officer sounded peeved.

'This is where we should have seen them next…' The security guard gestured to the screen below it. But there was no sign of them there. Only a few people milling about a fountain courtyard.

'What's between these two places?' Lana could feel her right leg quaking.

'The water pumping station,' the security guard replied. 'There's a service tunnel.'

'Where does it lead?' the second officer asked.

'How would I know? I've never been down there.'

'Take us.' The first officer was at the door. 'Can we arrange somebody to look after this lady?'

But Lana was already following him out.

'Forget that. I'm coming with you.'

# CHAPTER 18

While the security guard fumbled with a large ring of keys at the door of a grubby blue concrete cubicle, Lana's eyes roved the area not covered by the security camera. The path they were on ran between two tall hedges and led to the fountain courtyard. There were no gaps in the hedges, so she turned back to the door as it opened and the security guard stood aside.

The first officer regarded the set of steps that disappeared into the darkness below. 'If he went this way, he must have had a key.'

Lana leaned in to the doorway and could hear water gently trickling. 'There's nowhere else they could have gone.'

The first officer blocked her way. 'Just let me take a look.' He accepted a torch from the security guard, switched it on and shone it down.

Lana peered past him to where the spotlight illuminated the bottom step. There was a narrow, rusty, iron walkway beyond.

The officer slowly descended, and Lana slipped after him.

'Ma'am, let him check it out first.'

Lana tugged her shoulder clear of the second officer's warm palm. 'If my son is here, I'm not waiting.' She followed, her tunnel phobia entirely forgotten.

'Ma'am!'

'It's OK. But stay behind me.' The officer in front of Lana pointed the torch back up at her.

She squinted against it and nodded. The light above was blocked as the second officer joined them.

Lana felt the temperature immediately drop as they made their way to the bottom. When they reached it the officer in front arced the torch around. The walkway was just about wide enough for one person, and to its left was a drop to a wide channel where the water flowed. There was no handrail to hold onto. Graffiti was daubed on the tiled walls and an aroma of chlorine barely held the smell of mildew in check.

The officer ahead was the first to cough, and she fought one back as her throat tightened.

'Cooper!' Her constricted cry echoed away from them as they listened. The idea that he'd been dragged into this horrible place prompted her to yell louder.

His name bounced down the tunnel again and was swallowed by the gurgle of the water.

'How far does this thing go?' the officer behind her asked dolefully.

His partner didn't answer and swung the beam around.

Lana wondered if they were in the wrong place. Had Cooper been taken out of the park another way? Maybe they'd missed something obvious.

'I'll see if I can get hold of a plan and find out where it leads!' the Hispanic woman shouted after them.

'If you do, go meet us at the other end!' the officer in front of Lana responded. 'Wait…'

The torch dipped.

'What is it?' Lana put her palm against the damp wall and made her way to where he was crouching.

The officer played the light over what was on the walkway.

It was an *'I Survived the Ride'* glitter sticker, partially hidden by a crack that ran along the bottom of the wall.

'Cooper had one.' Was it his? There must be plenty of them that had been discarded. It looked dog-eared but so did her son's.

'Let's not touch it then. Could be evidence.' The first officer stepped over it and gestured for them to do the same.

Lana remembered how she'd almost told Todd about the photo that had been posted just before they headed off to the tree houses. If they'd left then… 'Cooper!' Her ragged exclamation didn't begin to release the turmoil inside.

The officer in front of her started moving faster down the tunnel, and Lana tried to keep up.

'Watch your footing.' The second officer put his palm against her back. 'I gotcha.'

Lana shuffled on, following the beam and sliding her hand along the dank wall to her right.

The sound of a door slamming reverberated.

The officer's torch briefly halted.

Then Lana heard his feet pound, hard, away from her.

# CHAPTER 19

The torch beam furiously bounced as the first officer pumped his arms.

'Careful!' The officer behind Lana attempted to grip the belt of her jeans so she wouldn't fall into the water.

Nobody spoke as they hurriedly progressed along the walkway, the light skimming the tiles beside them for signs of the door.

When it stopped, Lana caught up and saw it was illuminating a rusted grey metal panel with rivets around its edge. She pushed on it.

'Wait.' The first officer put his arm across it until his colleague had joined them. 'Both of you stay here.'

He nudged the door with his shoulder and suddenly the tunnel went pitch-black, the torchlight cut off as it closed behind him.

'I'm not waiting.' Lana shoved through. The panel muffled the second officer's protest. She could see the beam ahead, and suddenly the aroma of urine was overpowering. Rats?

The passageway was plunged into darkness as the officer turned a corner. Lana held her hands out in front of her and tried to keep up.

'Ma'am!'

She ignored the second officer's plea and estimated where to swerve left.

'Halt! Police!' The first officer's torchlight was visible again and bobbed up and down as he picked up speed.

Lana focussed on the beam and saw a shape running away from him.

'I said halt!'

The second officer was now beside Lana but didn't attempt to restrain her. She could see the figure's head crouched low into his shoulders as he put extra distance between them.

Lana's deck shoes harshly slapped concrete but then she ran straight into the stationary first officer. It knocked the wind out of her, and she bounced back from his frame as he directed the torch ahead.

'Where the hell did he go?' he said breathlessly.

They'd come to a dead end of crumbling cinder blocks. The officer skimmed the light along the pipes running the length of the ceiling and then over the walls beside them.

'Wait. Go back.' Lana gulped fetid air and waited for his beam to return to the spot at the bottom of the left wall that looked like a shadow but was, in fact, an irregular opening.

'Just hang back,' the first officer warned.

'You taking a look?' The second officer crouched there.

The first bent to his knees and pointed the light inside. 'Want to wriggle out of there or do I need to come get you?'

Lana could see a figure curled up inside the tight recess. There were soiled blankets and empty plastic bottles around them. They remained motionless.

'OK.' The first officer handed the torch to the second. 'Keep it on him.' He took hold of the figure's boot.

'All right. Jesus. Don't touch me,' a surprisingly cultured voice snapped.

They stepped back as he slid through the aperture. The tattered figure stood, and the beam bleached his unshaven and sooty features. His eyes were bloodshot and his features cadaverous.

'So what's the routine now? You drag me out and I come back in a couple of hours' time?'

'Have you seen anybody come by here?' Lana asked him before the officers could.

He winked against the light. 'It's not just me down here. There's a whole bunch of crackheads further up the tunnel. They're the ones pissing in the water.'

'In the last hour,' the second officer wheezed. 'A man in dungarees and a baseball cap with a child.'

He thought about it. 'Yeah.' He nodded. 'Went straight along the waterway.'

But Lana suspected he was just looking for a way to get rid of them. 'This is really important. My son's been taken.'

His expression didn't flicker. 'Like I said, they were headed towards station C.'

'Look, we're not taking you in,' the second officer assured him. 'Just tell us the truth.'

His pupils darted. 'I didn't see who it was. But someone was heading in that direction. Couldn't tell if it was one person or two. The echoes in here play tricks. Thought it was maintenance, so I split.'

'How far is it to station C?' The first officer took the torch back from his colleague and pointed it directly in the vagrant's face.

'Half a mile or so. Get that thing out of my eyes.'

'There're others along the tunnel that would have seen them?' Lana still didn't believe him.

'You could rob them and they wouldn't notice.'

Sounded to Lana like he might have.

'Let's head back to the waterway.'

The first officer started following the beam the way they'd come, but then he turned. 'And if you're wasting police time I'll be back to drag your ass out of here.'

Lana jogged to keep up.

# CHAPTER 20

Lana and the officers returned to the iron walkway but after they'd made their way along it for some time there was still no sign of the crackheads the vagrant had mentioned.

'Cooper!' the second officer yelled.

'Cooper!' Lana called again. It felt like they'd been shouting themselves hoarse for half an hour. Had Todd woken? Was he wondering why she wasn't beside him? She badly needed him next to her now, had to keep telling herself it was only a matter of time before her family would be reunited. *I Survived the Ride.* She wanted to believe that was a sign Cooper was OK. But had he even dropped the glitter sticker in the tunnel? It seemed as if it were shrinking in on her now. But she couldn't afford to flip out.

'Daylight up ahead.' The first officer switched off his torch so they could see another door outlined by a yellow glow.

They reached it and he yanked it open.

Lana shielded her eyes against the glare and followed him through into the warm air. They were standing at the top of a flight of metal steps leading down to a steep-sided, dry ditch bordered by dead bushes.

'Looks like the original waterway.' The second officer joined them.

Lana scanned the dirt for signs of any footprints but it was strewn with junk.

'Cooper!'

Her desperation echoed back but all they could hear was faraway traffic.

'I'll carry on along the tunnel.' The first officer turned and held up the torch to confirm he was the obvious candidate.

'I'll come with you.'

'No, it's too tight, Mrs Cross. You two follow the ditch.'

'Which way?' the second officer asked sceptically.

'If they did come out at this point, I figure they won't be heading back to the park.' The first officer squeezed by them. 'I'll try and meet you at the next exit point.'

Lana started quickly descending the steps, her feet clunking on steel before she was standing amongst the waste at the bottom. Several rats scurried into a hole on the far side as she crushed a beer can. But she didn't hesitate.

'Tread carefully.' The second officer was beside her and pointed at a discarded syringe.

He led the way, his boots making a trench for her through the debris.

'Cooper!' She was beginning to lose her voice.

The second officer nodded to a precipitous slope the other side that led up to a hole in one of the bushes. 'Looks like a way out.'

Lana halted and peered upwards but suddenly felt she was about to burn out. Her legs wobbled and suddenly the officer was supporting her.

'OK. Hold on. Why don't you hang fire while I check?'

Lana shook her head; she knew she would never make it up there.

'I'll just have a scout around. Wait right here, OK?'

The officer delicately released her and clambered the dirt incline, his rubber soles slipping a few times before he disappeared through the bush.

A noise behind Lana spun her head back to the steps. The first officer was standing at the top of them.

'Can't go any further. The service tunnel ends. Where's Officer Beaton?'

Lana dizzily pointed.

'They must have taken this exit.'

Lana wondered if the vagrant had been telling the truth. Maybe he'd only said he'd heard somebody passing along the main tunnel to keep them away from his territory.

The bush rustled and the second officer appeared. 'There's an old quarry the other side. No sign of anybody though.'

The first officer filled his chest and seemed at a loss.

Lana continued picking her way along the trench.

'Ma'am, I don't think you should go any further,' the first officer cautioned from behind her. 'We can send a patrol car.'

But Lana couldn't allow herself to stop. What was happening to Cooper at that exact moment? Her legs gave again and this time there was nobody to catch her.

# CHAPTER 21

Lana's attention shifted from the polished grey tiles to the closed doors as a crash team shot by in the corridor outside. She'd been seated at Todd's bedside in the ICU for nearly three hours, watching his shallow breathing. A transparent mask covered the bottom half of his face and the respiratory apparatus hissed and whistled over his heart monitor.

The doctors had X-rayed him and told her he'd only fractured one of his ribs. But they couldn't tell her how long he'd be in his coma.

She only had a vague recollection of her journey from the park to the hospital. The officer who'd escorted her to the ward had taken her iPhone number, inputted one for her to call, got her to send him photos of Cooper and said they would contact her as soon as there was any news.

Lana had never felt so helpless. Had she already lost them both? She knew she was still in shock; her tears remained fastened tight as she attempted to process the unreality of the situation.

Todd's eyelids were motionless. She needed him to embrace her, to share the pain that was too much to bear on her own. Lana's whole body was rigid, her fists clenched in her lap, and her top half leaning against them. She wanted to be out there, looking for Cooper, but the police had told her she was in the best place while they did their job.

Waiting with Todd as he lay oblivious compounded her sense of isolation. Where was Cooper right now? Her mind couldn't repel the dark images that presented themselves to her in dizzying succession.

She rose and moved to the bathroom door, because she felt like she'd throw up. The phone in her hot palm buzzed and rang.

*'Unknown caller.'*

'Hello?'

'Mrs Cross?'

'Yes.' She felt her temple buffeting the phone.

'A colleague has asked me to call you right away. There's been a development…'

Lana braced herself for words she knew might be the end of her.

'We've had a response from the website.'

Momentarily, she was bewildered. Then she opened her eyes.

'Ma'am?'

She realised she was talking to Cyber Crime. 'I'm here.'

'The images *were* posted by one of the site's users but they're happy to remove them.'

Lana tried to focus on his words. 'No, I don't want them to do that now. I need to know who was responsible.'

'This isn't the first time this has happened; they're not obliged to give up their details. They also said they're not liable for any disputes between the users of the forum—'

'This isn't a dispute! My child has been taken!'

There was a brief silence before he reacted. 'You've notified Sequonda PD?'

'Of course I have! I have to know who they are!'

'My apologies. Who's the investigating officer?'

Had she been given a name? Probably, but she hadn't taken it in. 'I don't know. I've just been brought to a hospital.' Lana felt even more stranded.

'Don't worry. I'll speak to the department right now. My apologies.' He hung up.

Lana clasped the hot plastic to her chin, the casing creaking as she tightened her grip on it. A noise behind her made her turn.

A tiny grunt had escaped Todd, and she moved quickly to the bedside.

'Todd.' She took his hand. It was only slightly warm. 'Todd?' She studied his eyelids for any sign of movement. 'Come back to me.'

His expression remained indifferent to her plea.

'You have to help me find Cooper.' Lana clenched his hand and dug her nails into his knuckle. Her lip trembled but the tears still didn't come.

His breathing apparatus hissed and whistled. She was alone.

Wait.

The officer had just said 'images'.

# CHAPTER 22

Lana immediately checked the *Right Where You're Standing* app. Her body locked tight: Ambuscade1 had added a new picture below their family photo. The flash illuminated a dark area of dirt. Three holes had been dug, three graves with blue polythene sheeting in the bottom of each.

Lana's insides shrivelled. There was a sack lying in one of the graves, the top tied by thick yellow rope and the canvas bulging with whatever or whoever was sealed within it. She couldn't even begin to contemplate the idea that Cooper was inside. The walls leaned in on her and the room continued to lurch even when she remembered to take a breath.

Lana's fingers trembled as she called the number the officer who had dropped her at the hospital had put in her iPhone.

'Detective Huxtable.' His name echoed.

'Detective.' She could barely form the word. 'This… is Lana Cross.'

'Mrs Cross. I was about to call you. I'll be handling the situation now. We're widening our search at the park.' His voice briefly broke up.

'Another image has been… uploaded to the app.' This was worse than any attack she'd had before. Lana felt as if her heart was about to rupture. 'There're graves. And there's… something in one of them.'

'We've just seen it.' Huxtable sounded unsettled.

'Are you in touch with Cyber Crime? They don't seem to know what's going on.'

'Just spoken to them. This is now their priority; count on it. We'll both be closely monitoring the site, and they're attempting to trace the location of the person who posted the images.' His last words momentarily dropped out again. 'I'm waiting to speak to Detective Riggs. Have you any reason to believe this could be the same man that tried to abduct Cooper last year?'

'The man on the security camera...'

'Yes?'

'I can't be sure. But it could be him.'

'I'll be up to speed on those details soon as I speak to Riggs. Anything else you can add?'

Where could she start? 'Did you find the sticker in the tunnel? I'm sure it was Cooper's.'

'Yeah – we've bagged it and it's on its way to be tested. We're in the process of combing the tunnel but I'm losing signal here. How is Mr Cross?'

Lana's eyes darted to Todd's emotionless features. 'No change.' She could hear an incoherent voice reporting to Huxtable.

'OK, I have to go but I'll be back in touch soon. Just sit tight there. Anything occurs to you, call me right away. Even if it seems trivial. Leave a message. In the meantime...'

What was he about to say, try to stay calm?

'Do you need somebody to sit with you?'

'No. Please, please, just find Cooper.'

'We're doing all we can, Mrs Cross.'

Lana listened to the dead line for a few seconds and then did something she hadn't done since she was a teenager. She prayed to God. Prayed to a God she didn't believe in that her boy was still alive.

# CHAPTER 23

Lana paced in front of the blinds in Todd's room. Outside it was half three in the afternoon. Cooper had been missing for nearly five hours.

Frogbert innocuously looked up from her open purse on the windowsill. Cooper had left him with Lana to take care of before he'd climbed the ladder to the tree houses with Todd.

She picked him up and held the back of his head to her nose. It smelt of Cooper so she inhaled it again. Lana tried to misdirect herself by trying to recollect where she'd bought Frogbert for him but realised it had been a gift.

Who gave him to Cooper? He had so many toys she'd never been able to keep track. They'd donated half of them to the children's home but he'd become very attached to Frogbert. She'd never understood why but when she'd been his age she'd had a threadbare corn dolly she hadn't wanted to give up until it fell apart.

When had his infatuation with Frogbert begun? It was before Mr Whisper had tried to abduct him. But how long before? She met the toy's innocent black glass eyes.

Whose present had it been? Lana couldn't remember. But now she was examining the line of stitching between Frogbert's legs.

If her phone hadn't been hacked how did the kidnapper know where they were?

She opened her purse and extracted her manicure case. Taking the nail scissors she cut along the stitching until the legs parted and white beads poured out of the slit. Lana put two fingers inside and dug about. She didn't know what she was looking for. When she couldn't immediately locate anything suspicious she shook the stuffing onto the floor.

She emptied the last of it and turned Frogbert inside out but there was nothing attached to the interior. Lana examined the remains of her son's toy, gutted and flat in her hands. That was when the tears came. Her chest heaved and she covered her mouth to muffle sobs that were more like exclamations of pain.

'Can I get you anything?' a voice asked, sotto voce.

Lana glanced up at the male nurse in green scrubs leaning in through the door. He regarded the beads about her feet.

She blinked away warm droplets so she could see him properly and eventually nodded to the offer of a drink of water so she could calm herself. Lana knew crying would achieve nothing but her breaths were still coming in sharp tugs when he returned.

'Take a sip.' He waited while she did.

Lana finished the tepid water in the paper cone and handed it back to him. 'Thanks.' Even though he couldn't have been much older than thirty she registered the nurse had a bad comb-over of red hair.

His attention shifted to where Todd was lying and then back to her. There was sympathy in his faint blue eyes. 'Let me know if there's anything else you need.'

Lana wondered how many other people he'd seen in similar predicaments. He was probably cautious about offering any false hope.

'Want me to close the door?'

She nodded and he turned and quietly sealed it behind him.

Lana sat on the edge of the bed and inwardly pleaded for Todd's shuttered eyes to open. She recalled the times he and Cooper pretended to be asleep. It was their double act. Cooper thought it was the funniest game imaginable.

It had started on her last birthday. She'd been working at a function but her boss had let her leave early. After calling Todd she came home to their little apartment at lunchtime to find them both asleep on the couch, facing each other and Cooper curled up against his dad. She'd stood in the doorway listening to them snoring.

She'd spotted a gift-wrapped orchid on the table and picked it up. That was when they both yelled 'surprise!' She'd jumped so much she'd dropped the pot and it smashed the glass top of the coffee table. But Todd and Cooper found that even more hilarious. After attempting to berate them and slow her pounding heart their contagious laughter eventually got the better of her.

The three of them had gone to Saltshaw Park for the afternoon. Cooper had helped her make the sandwiches and pack the hamper. They'd had fun around the fountains and eaten under the pagoda in the Japanese water garden, and when they'd driven home it had struck Lana she hadn't thought about Mr Whisper for one second of the time they'd been there.

Lana put her hand on Todd's and would have given anything to be back in that moment.

# CHAPTER 24

Lana remained on the edge of Todd's bed and checked the photos on the app. They hadn't been taken down but at least no new ones had been added. Then she noticed she had a message on the forum. It was from Styx36.

*'Still want that image removed, Lana?'*

The last thing she needed was him tampering. She responded *'No'* and wasn't surprised when his reply immediately appeared.

*'Why not? Eternal gratitude no longer on offer, Lana?'*

Again she wondered if Styx36 could have posted them. She typed:

*'How could you do that anyway?'*

*'If I told you that I'd have to kill you.'*

Unease scuttled over her.

*'Just kidding!'* He added.

If he really could remove them he must have access to the app.

*'My hacking skills are a little rusty but the RWYS security is very lax.'* He seemed to have read her mind.

The respirator hissed as Lana considered how to proceed.

*'I sense you don't believe me. So I've done it anyway, Lana.'*

She apprehensively refreshed the page. The snap of her, Todd, and Cooper was gone. The grave picture remained. Lana hadn't mentioned it to him so surely he should have commented on it.

*'Now, how about this eternal gratitude, Lana?'*

Lana looked nervously over to the window to check the blind was closed. Why wasn't he quizzing her about the other photo that had been uploaded? Perhaps he hadn't noticed it had been posted by the same person. Or maybe he was Ambuscade1.

*'You have a cute family. I suppose the handsome guy is still on the scene?'*

Lana tensed. Was this a deliberate reference to what had happened to Todd?

*'Yes. He says hi.'*

*'He's a lucky man, Lana. Good to put a face to your name. Adorable kid too. How old?'*

She imagined him looking at the image he'd probably saved onto his own hard drive – if it hadn't been there already.

*'Five. He's very precious to us.'*

*'Been to any dark places recently?'*

Did his sudden change of tack refer to the service tunnel or was she simply talking to someone who didn't care about her child?

*'Namely the Pieter Jink place.'*

Lana stood from Todd's bed. How the hell did he know she'd been there? She recalled feeling a presence when she'd been in the orchard.

*'Bet you're stoked to have that stamp in your passport.'*

But that explained it. Any location a *RWYS* user visited was tracked by GPS and automatically recorded in their Crime Scene Passport. They were accessible to all users. She was sure, though, he was being deliberately allusive.

*'There's another location near you. Hasbland High. You really should check it out.'*

# CHAPTER 25

Despite her attempts to maintain their dialogue, Styx36's status told her he was offline. Lana sent him a message and said she needed to speak to him urgently but he didn't respond. She opened the *RWYS* site locator and the GPS found her.

'*Finding nearest murder site…*'

A pin was stuck on the map northeast of the hospital. It zoomed into the area. Stanley de Souza's voice oozed out of the tiny speaker of her phone. 'Murder site of serial killer Theodore Lane Hewett. Current status: incarcerated. A janitor at the school for nineteen years, he was convicted in 2013, after confessing to the murder of three children he kidnapped and murdered before burning their remains. Lane Hewett retained only one bone from each victim. The pelvic girdles of three girls were found in a hidden compartment in his flatbed truck. His initials were scored into them. A number of other children had disappeared in the area across a period of four decades but no evidence was found to connect him.'

Lana scrolled down the page to a highlighted image of Lane Hewett standing with a group of grinning teachers. His ash brown hair was neatly combed and in a straight fringe across his forehead; it looked like an old photograph. She tried to imagine how he would look with his hair receded and a mask covering his features. It was possibly Mr Whisper, but then she'd thought that of Peter Firth and Brandon Fines.

'His wife, Jeanette, was implicated in the investigation but she escaped a prison sentence due to lack of evidence. Theodore always insisted she knew nothing of his crimes, but DNA found at their bungalow in the school grounds suggested otherwise. Despite petitions from the families of other children who disappeared in the same neighbourhood, Jeanette has remained silent.'

She found a picture of Lane Hewett's wife below his. Looked like it had been taken during the trial, as a guy looking every inch a lawyer stood close beside her. Jeanette was cowering under his umbrella in a plastic rain hood, her eyes narrowed at the camera. Below that was a shot of the police removing bagged evidence from the bungalow.

'Police were unnerved by the casual nature of Lane Hewett's testimony and how he recounted pushing the tip of his blade into the ear canals of victims as the hardest thing he'd ever had to do.'

Was Styx36's suggestion to visit the school more significant than it appeared? She'd been conversing with him online for some months but still had no idea who he was. He *had* taken the snap off the site. Which meant he could have just as easily put it there. She closed the app and dialled the detective.

'Huxtable.' It didn't sound like he was in the tunnel any more.

'It's Lana Cross.'

'Mrs Cross, nothing to report yet, I'm afraid.'

'I've just been speaking to someone on the forum of the app. He's suggesting I go to Hasbland High School.'

'Wait, who?'

'A guy called Styx36. I'm going to send his details to Cyber Crime.'

'Just slow down. You shouldn't be communicating with anyone unsupervised. How do you know this guy?'

'From the forum. Says he's in Syracuse. I still have no idea who he is. He was asking about me visiting Pieter Jink's house.'

'Jink, the deceased serial killer?'

She closed her eyes. 'Yes.'

'You've been to that crime scene?'

'Yes – two days ago. You know the case?'

'Of course. But what were *you* doing there?'

Lana could sense how the conversation was about to go. 'I visit crime scenes as part of my research.'

'For what?'

'I've been trying to find the man who tried to snatch Cooper… conducting my own investigation.' She heard him exhale slightly.

'Bearing in mind that the first incident happened in a completely different state, have you any real reason to believe this could be the same man?'

'The guy in the security footage. He looked a little like the man who tried to take Cooper last year.'

'I've viewed it, and his face is concealed throughout. And in all the other glimpses we have of him in the park. The other attendant couldn't give us a solid description either. Anything else that would convince you? And what's Jink got to do with this?'

'I thought he was a possibility. Jink had a relative who lived in Jaxton.'

'OK. That's significant. But Jink is dead.'

'Maybe it's somebody who knew him – an accomplice.'

'When was the attempted abduction?'

Lana wished that was all she had to deal with now. 'The 6th of August.'

'I'll pull the file on Jink. So this guy online who's been helping you?'

'He just removed one of the images from the app.'

'What?'

'He hacked in and took out our family photo.'

'Mrs Cross, don't let your friend compromise what's online or it's going to get very complicated.'

'He's not a friend.'

'So why did he suggest you going to Hasbland High School?'

'I've just read up on it, and Theodore Lane Hewett.'

'So you're throwing him into the mix now as well? I wasn't part of the investigation but I do know that Lane Hewett is behind bars. Did he say the school's related to your son's disappearance? Or Jink?'

'No. I think he's playing a game. He seems to know what's going on. At least, I get the impression he does.'

'How?'

'Look at the dialogue on the forum. You tell me.'

'Have you asked him outright? We're still waiting for demands to be made.'

'He's gone offline.'

'Look, I'm not dismissing anything but I'm on my way to brief a second search party. I'll call you soon as I'm done and we'll take a look at this more closely then. I'll touch base with Cyber Crime. Don't communicate with this guy in the meantime though, OK?'

'OK.'

'We'll speak soon, promise.'

Was she inventing menace where there wasn't any? Styx36 had said nothing definitive to connect him to what was happening. All of his comments could be interpreted innocently. But he hadn't questioned her about the other picture posted by Ambuscade1 and that was plain to see on the Fresh Blood page.

And why was he still off the radar?

# CHAPTER 26

Lana got out of the cab, swiftly paid the driver and trotted across the road. Despite the warm late afternoon air she could see rain clouds dumping on the neighbourhood the other side of the hedged park to her left. The grey wall of water was rapidly working its way towards her, past a copse in the middle of the scantily populated grass expanse, and threatened to beat her to the main building of Hasbland High.

She was torn up by the idea of leaving Todd in his condition. What if something happened while she was gone? But she was positive he'd want her to be out looking for Cooper and not waiting on the ward for him to open his eyes. Huxtable had her number and could contact her if he had any news. If he wasn't going to immediately respond to what she'd told him, she had to, even if there was only the slimmest chance Styx36 was involved. She'd immediately passed the info about him to Cyber Crime. But now she was here, what or who was she looking for?

The gates were open and a gaggle of teenagers rubbernecked her as she hurried onto the grounds and took out her iPhone. The *RWYS* app pinpointed her exact location and displayed the photo of the officers removing evidence. She continued down the path to the gleaming glass façade of the main block and surveyed the grass banks either side of her for the red-brick bungalow.

Examining the contours of the landscape, she estimated where it should have been, but it appeared the structure had been demolished. In fact, the whole school looked as if it had just had a major makeover.

Stanley de Souza repeated the same information, so she muted him.

A girl screaming spun her head back to the gates. The rain had drenched the teenagers and they had dashed to the shelter of a nearby tree. They watched Lana as it reached her. It was warm on her bare shoulders, but as it plastered her hair to her face, she ignored it and turned on her heel, scanning her surroundings in case she'd missed the bungalow.

Maybe she *had* read too much into her exchange with Styx36. But anything was better than pacing Todd's room until the phone rang.

'You lost?'

She swung around to find a lanky teenage boy had scurried over to her from the group at the tree. 'I'm fine.'

'Looking for somebody?' His hairsprayed, matte black locks were stacked in a solid pompadour that seemed impervious to the downpour.

'No.'

From the giggling behind him it looked to Lana like he was performing for the others.

'Thanks,' she said firmly.

'OK.' His eyes dipped briefly to her breasts.

She realised her crop top must be soaked and instinctively crossed her arms across her chest.

'Just let me know if you need anything.' He raised an eyebrow.

'You don't know if the janitor's house is still here?'

He seemed to be fighting the impulse to look down again. 'Janitor?' He frowned before realisation relaxed his expression. 'Oh… that place. No, that's gone.'

She nodded. 'OK.' The rain came down even harder and she registered how crazed she had to appear. 'Can you point me to where it used to be?'

He blinked his long eyelashes against the raindrops and shook his head once. 'I only started here last term. You could ask Miss McColgan. She's the librarian. Been here for ever.'

The boy turned and pelted back towards the group. As he got under cover Lana noticed a figure was standing at the edge of the copse beyond them in the park outside the school. Was that person sheltering there from the storm too?

Lana kept her gaze fixed on the figure. Whoever it was, they ducked into the trees.

Not taking her eyes from the spot, Lana jogged to the gates.

# CHAPTER 27

Lana crossed the road outside the gates and spotted a gap in the hedge that bordered the park. When she reached it she was looking through an opening to a curving gravel track that disappeared around the edge of the copse.

The rain still hadn't let up and the few people she'd seen in the park on her way to the school were sheltering under trees. Lana passed through the hedge and strode over the wet grass, walking beside the path so her footfalls remained muffled. She squinted into the dense conifers.

As she rounded the trees Lana flinched every time her deck shoes squeaked on the sodden turf. She was looking further down more of the track but there was no sign of anyone. They definitely couldn't have got further than she could see, even if they'd sprinted the whole way.

Her eyes shifted to the foliage to her left. They had to be in there. Remaining on the right edge of the path, Lana hesitantly moved along it, peering amongst the branches, though she couldn't see further than the outer boughs of the perimeter.

She opened her mouth to call to them, but thought better of it. If they were hiding from her there was little point. Lana guardedly cut across the track and entered the copse. Her wet clothes seemed suddenly colder.

Shivering, she turned on the torch of her iPhone and shone it around. Ferns twitched as heavy drops penetrated the canopy above. She stood motionless and listened but could only hear the low rumble of traffic and the rainfall pattering on the leaves overhead.

'Walk out of here,' a man hissed.

Lana went rigid. His voice was very near. She tried to locate its owner with the torch.

'Switch that off and walk out of here.'

'Who are you?'

'Switch it off.'

She complied.

'I wanted to take a look at *you*, not the other way around. And now I know you'll do as I say. If you want to see Cooper, you'll continue to.'

Her son's name on his lips was like an electrical jolt. 'Please… tell me where he is.' She took a step in his direction.

'Any closer and you'll never see him alive again.' His words briefly slipped out of a whisper and betrayed the depth of his voice.

Lana could see a vague outline of the tall man in front of her.

'I'll be in touch very soon.'

She considered running at him, putting her nails in his eyes.

'My associate is with Cooper. I can't vouch for your son's well-being if you lay a finger on me.' He'd clearly sensed her intent.

'Give him back to me,' she said through clenched teeth.

'Go back to your husband and wait for me to contact you.'

Lana didn't budge.

He took a pace towards her, and she stiffened when she saw his hand illuminated by faint light. It clutched a revolver. His other held a folded silver umbrella.

'I'm going to count backwards. If you're not back on the path by the time I reach zero, Cooper's going to suffer in ways you can't even imagine.'

'Tell me what you want.'

'Five.'

'I'll do anything you ask.'

'Four.'

'Please.'

'Three.'

Lana took a step forward, her palms raised. 'Anything.'

'Two.'

The gun discharged.

It was deafening, and wet dirt exploded to her right. Lana cowered and quickly reversed from the shrubs, keeping her gaze riveted to where he was as the warm rain slid down her skin.

'Tell me where he is!'

As the shot reverberated around the park, Lana thought she could still see him standing there. She realised she was looking at the trunk of a tree.

# CHAPTER 28

Lana's phone rang. She ignored it and remained anchored to the spot outside the copse, her right ear whistling from the gunfire. She couldn't see a trace of movement within and wondered if he was exiting the other side. Should she try and follow? She'd been told what would happen if she didn't obey. But this could be the closest she would ever get to the people who had taken Cooper.

Her body trembled as she resisted the urge to step back into the trees.

'Please, I'll do anything you want.' She suspected he'd gone but she waited and listened. No sound of footfalls. 'Speak to me!'

Her phone stopped ringing.

Somebody was shouting behind her. She turned and could see a young couple rapidly approaching. Lana didn't want to linger to answer their questions. She couldn't risk Cooper being harmed by drawing attention to the man in the copse.

Lana hurried along the track and back through the opening in the hedge then marched briskly away from Hasbland High.

He had to be Styx36. He'd directed her to the school and come to watch. She didn't want to take her eyes from her view of the copse through the gaps in the hedge, but did so briefly to look at her phone.

*'Unknown caller.'*

Detective Huxtable? She returned the call.

'C6 West?'

The hospital ward. She'd left her number before she'd set off.

'It's Lana Cross. You just rang?—'

'We've been trying to locate you.'

'I… stepped out for some fresh air.'

'Your husband. Good news. He's woken up.'

Lana's eyes bleared and she exhaled a faltering breath. Todd was back with her again. She could at least release one ball of dread she'd been squeezing tight.

'Is he OK?' But she still didn't shift her attention from the copse.

'The doctor's with him now.'

Lana couldn't allow herself any relief. Not until they had Cooper back. 'Has he spoken?'

'A few words. He asked for you.'

That sounded hopeful. 'What else did he say?'

'He's disoriented but we've got him sitting up. Maybe you should come speak to him yourself.' The nurse seemed bemused.

'I'll be there as quickly as I can.' She hung up. Again Lana considered what she would do if she saw the man emerge. If he was telling the truth about an accomplice holding Cooper, however, accosting him would be out of the question. But if she walked away now, would she always regret this moment?

There was still no evidence of anyone and it was likely he'd escaped the other side of the copse and was already leaving the park. The best course of action was to do as she was instructed. And now, at least, there was a channel of communication via the *RWYS* forum.

But Lana hovered at the hedge for another few minutes before eventually leaving. She had to get back to Todd and the police. Explain why she'd had to leave and exactly what had just happened.

# CHAPTER 29

Lana got out of her Uber cab at Sequonda General, headed to the west entrance and, as she hadn't taken note of her route as she'd left, anticipated getting lost trying to find the ward. But she quickly located a map, found her way to the right elevator, and travelled up two floors before entering the familiar reception.

When she reached Todd's room it was empty, the sheets pulled aside. Maybe she'd taken a wrong turn. Lana was about to leave when she saw the emptied out Frogbert toy on the sill and the beads scattered over the floor. She told herself to remain calm. Perhaps he'd been moved.

She walked back into the corridor and stopped a young nurse. 'I'm Mrs Cross.'

The nurse beamed. 'Your husband's just woken up.'

'Where has he been taken?'

The nurse was perplexed. 'Doctor Gayle should be with him now.'

'There's nobody in there.'

The nurse stepped past her and glanced into the room. 'Strange.' She looked over Lana's shoulder. 'Well, there's Doctor Gayle.'

The rotund, Afro-Caribbean man was crouching over the screen at reception.

Lana followed the nurse to him.

'Doctor Gayle, this is Mrs Cross.'

He took off his bifocals and smiled at Lana. 'Your husband has been asking for you.'

'He's not in his bed,' the nurse informed him.

The doctor frowned. 'I only left him a couple of minutes ago.'

'Bathroom?' The nurse took a few paces down the corridor and pushed open a swing door. 'Mr Cross, are you in there?'

Nobody responded.

The doctor rubbed the stubble on his chin. 'He has to be nearby.'

Lana trotted down the corridor, peering into the other private rooms and trying to stem her rising alarm. With Cooper in the hands of strangers, she could barely focus on another situation. She paused at the TV lounge. A single male was seated in front of the screen with his back to her. But Lana didn't need to see his face to know it wasn't him. Her pace accelerated and she reached the recovery bay. Todd was nowhere to be found.

Panic began to gallop through her.

# CHAPTER 30

'Has your husband ever done anything like this before?' Detective Huxtable was much older than his voice had sounded on the phone. His buzz cut of white hair contrasted sharply with his over-tanned, hangdog features, and she could smell sickly sweet vape smoke on him.

Lana shook her head. 'No. There's no reason why he would have walked out of here.' She felt like releasing the scream that had been building inside her since the park.

Huxtable waited for a patient wheeling a drip on wheels to shuffle past the doorway to the private room. 'Maybe he got confused. He was badly concussed.' He put his fist over his mouth to cough chestily.

'We're checking the other floors,' the petite ward clerk from reception reported. 'He's definitely not on C6. He can't get far, though. His clothes are still locked in here.'

Huxtable thanked her, and she left. He closed the door, poured himself a glass of water from the jug beside Todd's bed and took several loud swallows.

'We're doing everything we can to find Cooper and I'm extending the search to the suburbs beyond the water station. We've also issued the image of the man in the park. Even though his face is obscured, we're hoping somebody might have seen a guy in dungarees.'

Lana stared at the empty bed and fought hard to concentrate on his words. This was crazy. How could Todd have disappeared?

'Just wait here until they've found your husband. Now he's awake maybe he can tell us something about the man who pushed him from the bridge. If that *is* what happened.'

Lana looked up sharply from the mattress. 'What else could have happened?'

'Could he maybe have lost his temper with your son?'

'No,' she said categorically. What was he getting at?

Huxtable examined her reaction through his bushy white brows. 'Could Cooper have run off and that's when our stranger stepped in? I'm just trying to establish a sequence of events and understand why your husband was so eager to leave here.'

'So he threw himself off the bridge?' Lana registered it was getting dark behind the blinds. Cooper would be spending his first night without them. She closed her eyes and visualised him in his racing car bunk, reassuring her that he wasn't afraid of the dark. 'You said yourself; Todd was concussed. He woke up and probably didn't know where he was.'

'And you weren't here to tell him…'

Lana opened them again. He was right.

Huxtable finished the water and gasped. 'You shouldn't have gone to the school.'

'I felt helpless waiting.'

'I understand that.' But his expression said otherwise.

'Todd might not even have… how could I have known how long he was going to take to wake up?'

'So you think Styx36 was the man you saw in the park?'

'It had to have been.'

'And he said nothing about a ransom?'

'No.'

'OK, we've got your statement on that, and Cyber Crime are all over his account. You're sure there's nothing else you can tell me about him?'

'He was in the shadows. I just saw the gun and the umbrella.'

'Blue umbrella?'

'Silver,' Lana repeated emphatically. She'd told him three times. He was trying to trip her up.

'We're pulling the file on Theodore Lane Hewett. Any other idea why Styx36 would suggest you visiting Hasbland?'

'I'd never heard of Lane Hewett before today. What about Jink?'

'He could have been the guy who originally tried to abduct your son but, as he's dead, I think we have to seriously concede that the two incidents are unrelated. But we will try to ascertain if Jink kidnapped any of his victims around the 6th of August last year.'

'He didn't. I've already compared the dates his other victims were taken. The nearest was 12th July. He could have tried to snatch Cooper.'

Huxtable tightened his lips. 'Let's see what the official report throws up first. But with him dead, who's responsible now? Lane Hewett is in prison, so this Styx36 individual could just be sending you on a goose chase.'

'Maybe somebody who knew Jink. His niece moved away from Jaxton soon after his death.'

'His niece?'

'Robin Dreese. I tried to contact her but she'd split. The rest of his family wouldn't talk to me.'

'They'll have to talk to us, if that's necessary. But I want to concentrate on finding Cooper first. I've had a conversation with your Detective Riggs. He said you've already made allegations about two other men.'

Lana caught the scepticism in his tone.

'I know it's not what you want to hear but you must trust us to do our job.' Huxtable put down the glass. 'I have to coordinate things from the station but I'll leave an officer here to help locate your husband. He'll let me know as soon as he does. Meantime,' he fixed Lana with his green eyes, 'let these people look after you, and remain here until they've found him.'

The detective opened the door and turned back. 'Sure there's no feasible reason you can think of for Todd wandering off like this?'

'No.' Lana realised he wasn't about to come strolling back onto the ward. There was something badly wrong.

He nodded and breezed out, leaving the door open. The ward clerk smiled sympathetically at Lana from outside. There was a young, pockmarked officer waiting with her whose uniform looked too big for him. They all started having a low conversation with Huxtable.

It was the first time Lana considered she and Todd would be under suspicion.

She followed him. 'I'm not sitting around, though. Give me a floor to search.'

The young officer looked uncertain.

'It'll take him all day otherwise.'

Huxtable blinked his permission.

'OK, ma'am. This way.'

# CHAPTER 31

'Wanna take this level?' the young officer said businesslike and nodded to the elevator doors as they opened on B. 'I'll cover the ground floor. Got a photo of him on that?' He indicated her iPhone.

Lana blocked the doors with her shoulders to stop them closing. Where was her image archive?

'You all right, ma'am?'

Her brain had momentarily frozen. Lana knew she had to deal with one task at a time. Not allow other dark thoughts to overpower her. She swiped the screen, located the gallery and showed the officer a family shot. It was her favourite, the timer snap of the three of them beaming on her birthday picnic in Saltshaw Park. She shakily enlarged Todd's face with her fingers.

'Got him. Make your way back up to the ward when you're done. If I don't find him, I'll meet you there and we'll search the upper floors. Say, ten minutes?'

'Right.'

She headed for the double doors in front of her. It was now black outside the window. Was Todd delirious from the fall? Maybe the kidnappers had contacted him. But how could they when his phone had been locked away with his clothes? Whatever had happened, more minutes were ticking by while Cooper's life was in jeopardy.

It was visiting hours. Lana quickly passed three private rooms and glanced into each one. People seated in chairs talking in low tones attended all the beds. Next, she made her way onto the main ward where four nurses in powder blue uniforms were chatting at reception. They didn't acknowledge her as she hurried by.

Lana turned the corner into a cloying atmosphere and scrutinised the rows of green curtained beds to her left, glimpsing the occupants as she went swiftly past each one: some asleep, others watching TV or talking to relatives. She rounded another corner to be greeted by the same. Should she just yell his name?

She checked the forum on her iPhone. No word from Styx36 and he was still offline.

She could see a man up ahead in a bedgown. He slipped through a door on the right, and she paused there. It was the shower room. Lana nudged the panel.

'Todd?'

No response.

'Hello? Who's in here?'

'Who's asking?' came a gruff reply.

'I'm trying to find my husband.'

'Well, he ain't in here.'

Lana continued down the ward. She found another long row of beds. As she inspected each her pace accelerated but legs felt weaker. She couldn't allow exhaustion to overcome her now. Two women in bright saris looked up and frowned at her through the curtains as she passed by them.

She butted a door to the fire escape and stood at the top of the stairs so she could get some fresh air to repel her sudden dizziness; the atmosphere smelt of cigarette smoke. Lana hastened to the next ward. Hadn't she seen these people already? But she hadn't encountered reception again.

She was back at the elevator. A fruitless circle completed and no further word from Styx36.

'Are you lost?' A porter was leaning on an empty trolley while he waited.

She didn't hear him and tightly clenched her fist as she looked up at the floor numbers slowly counting down. Lana absently examined the picture she'd found for the officer – her husband's smile captured on the day she'd forgotten all about Mr Whisper, when their happiness had been nothing but a brief reprieve.

Where was Todd?

# CHAPTER 32

When Lana called his name, Todd retreated into the corner of the green-tiled shower room and said nothing. The wall was cold against the rear slit of his bedgown, and fighting his reflex to respond made him feel sick to his stomach.

The emaciated elderly man who had just entered looked back over his shoulder at the door and saw him. Todd shook his head. The man smiled; glad to be part of the deception. He nodded that he wouldn't give Todd away, removed his bedgown and squinted at the dial. His skin was yellow.

'Hello? Who's in here?'

'Who's asking?' the old man answered.

'I'm trying to find my husband.'

Todd held his breath.

'Well, he ain't in here.' He watched the door and awaited a reply, grinning at Todd when none came.

Todd wanted to call out after Lana. He knew how frantic she'd be. When he'd regained consciousness he'd heard the ward clerk talking to the doctor about her, saying how she had to be going out of her mind because her son had been taken and her husband had been pushed from a bridge. And the police were currently scouring the park. That's when he remembered why he was in the hospital. But he couldn't recall anything that had occurred immediately before. His last memory was of climbing up to the tree house with Cooper.

Lana had to be going crazy thinking this had something to do with the attack last year, but Todd knew something she and the police didn't. He had to fix it alone. The idea of his precious son in the hands of the people he suspected had grabbed him rolled acid around his stomach. It was his fault. How could he live with himself if something happened to him? And he couldn't face Lana until he made sure it didn't.

Todd still didn't speak until he'd heard Lana's footsteps finish squeaking away down the ward. He flinched as he shifted position and his rib complained.

'Thanks.'

'You're welcome. My wife never understood the concept of privacy.' The old man attempted to rotate the dial but it was too stiff.

'Here, let me.' Todd groaned in pain as he extended his hand.

'Seems like it's you that needs help. You scared of her?'

'No.'

'Sure. That's why you're skulking in here. Those years are the best ones, though. And they're soon past.'

Todd detected sadness in the man's eyes and got the impression he was alone with whatever condition he had.

'Might get one of those young nurses to come in here and scrub my back.' He winked at Todd.

Todd leaned in and turned the shower on for him then slipped back out of the room. No sign of Lana. He made his way along the row of beds until he came to one that was unoccupied. Ducking behind the cover of the curtain he wondered how long the person who had thrown back the sheets and left a magazine on the pillow would take to return.

Todd opened the drawer beside the bed and took out the overnight bag. It contained clothes but they belonged to a woman. He quickly replaced it and sneaked out again. He'd have to keep working his way down the ward.

# CHAPTER 33

Todd got lucky with a deserted bed in the next section of the ward and found a plastic bag under the chair beside it that contained a pair of sweats, a green college shirt, and some khaki All Stars. He grabbed it and made for the exit, keeping an eye out for Lana before sidestepping into a storage room.

The shelves were lined with industrial-size paper towel rolls and bottles of cleaning fluid. Ditching his gown he swiftly pulled on the sweats and top that already stank of body odour and dropped the All Stars onto the floor. They were two sizes too big for him.

Then Todd noticed the wall-mounted phone. Could he remember the number?

He picked up the receiver and stabbed in the first three digits. Come on. He'd rung it enough times recently. Had his fall scrambled his brain? Think.

As he hoped, his fingers instinctively punched in the remainder, and he heard it ring.

'Yeah?' a chewing mouth answered.

'Cyrus?'

They swallowed. 'Wrong number.'

But Todd recognised him. 'Rusty?'

'Todd,' he said warily.

'I have to speak to Cyrus.'

'No way.'

'Is he there?'

'Jesus, Todd, didn't I make myself clear? There's nothing more I can do, and Cyrus won't speak to you again.'

'This is really important. Cooper's been taken. Please put him on.'

There was a brief pause. 'Taken?'

Todd tried to gauge whether there was any surprise in the reaction. 'Rusty, if he's there…'

'Hang up the phone.' Rusty's tone was suddenly flat.

'This line's safe. Look, the police have got involved but only because I've been in the hospital.'

'I'm hanging up.'

'Rusty, please. Help me, as a friend.' He could hear the sound of Cyrus's voice in the background. 'Is that him? Put him on.'

'No can do,' Rusty said impassively.

Now he could discern the noise of a can dropping out of the drink dispenser machine. They were in the upstairs office. He'd been there once. Knew he'd never be invited back.

'Don't call this number again.'

Todd wasn't getting past him. 'Tell him I'll do anything to make this right. Please, Rusty. I'm begging you.'

Rusty cut the call.

Todd slammed the phone onto the wall cradle and it bounced off and dangled down by its wire. If they refused to speak to him, he had to go to them.

Todd quickly slipped on and laced the All Stars. He didn't care what Cyrus did to him. Cooper was all that mattered.

# CHAPTER 34

Trotting down the corridor to C6 West, Lana found the young, pockmarked officer standing outside Todd's room. 'No sign of him?' she asked before reaching him.

He shook his head.

'Shall we try the floors above?' She pocketed her iPhone. Lana had checked the forum as she'd come up in the elevator but there was still nothing.

'There's been a development. Will you come with me?'

She stopped dead a few feet from him.

'I've just been asked to drive you to the station.'

'What's happened?' A hollow opened inside her.

'Detective Huxtable will explain when we get there.'

She girded herself for the news she'd been dreading. 'You'll explain now.'

'Ma'am, I really don't know any more than that. The sooner we go…'

She fumbled out her phone again and dialled Huxtable. He picked up after the first ring.

'It's Lana Cross. What's going on?' She could hear a car engine in the background.

'We've just found out a uniformed officer picked up someone in the park outside Hasbland High.'

Lana felt herself drain through the floor.

'He's already been taken into custody, and I'm on my way to the precinct now.'

'I told you how he threatened me. He's not working alone.' Her voice rose and dried.

'This wasn't on my orders. A young couple called the police after he discharged his weapon. He was detained at the gates, and the officer found an unlicensed firearm on him.'

'You've got to let him go.'

'We'll just have you take a look.'

'No. If he doesn't think I was responsible for his arrest, he will if he sees me.'

'We'll make sure he won't. And he knows he was stopped because of the couple reporting the gunfire.'

'Has he made any phone calls?' She barely let him finish.

'We'll find out. Please, Mrs Cross, take a breath.'

Had he contacted his accomplice? 'Take his phone from him.'

'Accompany the officer and I'll see you at the station in ten.'

'What about my husband?'

'I'm sending another officer over.'

'So you'll leave Todd wandering around the hospital in the meantime?'

'The clerk is alerting all the wards. If he's spotted, we'll know. Just concentrate on getting over here.'

Huxtable hung up, and Lana turned to the young officer. Her ears were burning. 'Let's go then.'

Hurrying with him back to the elevator, a sheen of perspiration chilled on her forehead as she moved closer towards the moment she put a face to the voice in the trees. What could they do if it was him? Could Lana trust the police or had they already ruined her chances of being able to reason with Cooper's abductors?

# CHAPTER 35

When she arrived at the busy police station, Lana was ushered behind the desk by a female in uniform who didn't seem much older than sixteen. She marched ahead of Lana, knocked once at a door to the right of the corridor and pushed her way inside before there was a reply.

Lana found Huxtable and another stocky plain-clothes officer drinking coffee from china mugs in the tiny, dimly lit cubicle the other side. The rattling air con unit struggled to combat duelling aftershave and vape smoke.

'Mrs Cross.' Huxtable blinked once at the girl and she exited, closing the door behind her. 'Can I get you anything?'

She shook her head, and her attention was drawn to the smoked glass panel behind them that allowed observation of a small, unoccupied interview room.

'This is Detective Miles.'

Miles turned and clamped his lips at her. He was in his thirties, wore a red-and-black plaid shirt, and his lank hair was pulled tightly from his oval face and secured in a short, ragged ponytail. The overhead lights made him appear Neanderthal.

'They're just bringing our guy up now. He can't see us in here.' Huxtable indicated the table and two chairs the other side of the pane.

Lana thought the one-way mirror was just a cliché of TV shows.

'There's still no word about your husband, so we've sent an officer to check the security cameras at the hospital.'

Lana nodded at Huxtable but didn't want to venture any further in.

The older detective's mahogany expression sensed her unease. 'Like I said, he got picked up because of the couple calling it in. He won't think you're responsible.'

If it was the guy she'd seen in the copse, she was torn. Was it better he was in custody and could lead them to Cooper, or did holding him endanger her son even more? Part of her hoped it was the wrong man.

'You'd definitely recognise him?' Miles asked, his voice smaller than it should have been.

'I didn't see his face.'

'But you said he was carrying a silver umbrella?' Huxtable confirmed again.

Beyond his shoulder, the door to the interview room opened.

The tall man behind the male uniformed officer had a grey, zip-up sweat top and a navy blue beanie hat on, and had a black waterproof folded over his arm. He was early fifties and his protruding brow and large wrinkle across the bridge of his nose gave the impression that his squat features had been crushed. It looked as if he normally wore glasses. Outwardly he was calm, but through his thick squinting eyelids his inky pupils darted constantly as they scanned the room. Was it the man that Blue Crest's cameras had captured?

Lana's chest tightened as he entered.

'Just have a seat. Somebody will be with you shortly.' The accompanying officer sounded tinny through the speaker below the pane.

'What's the deal here?' he enquired calmly. 'I told the other officer the gun went off by accident.'

His tone was the same as the man that had spoken to her.

'My permit is at home. One of your officers could've taken me there and I would've been happy to show it you.'

Lana felt her circulation skip as his hand emerged from under the coat with a silver umbrella and put it lightly on the table.

'Can I get you anything?'

'Can we just move this along?' he pleaded good-naturedly. 'I've got to get my insulin injection.'

'Did you mention this to the other officers?'

'No, but then I didn't know I was going to be held up all this time.'

'I'll pass that on and somebody should be right in.' The officer left, pulling the door closed.

Huxtable studied Lana's reaction. 'Think it's him?'

It had to be. She took him in as he scraped out a chair and dropped into it. He was still but his eyes continued to swivel. He reminded her of a chameleon. His attention momentarily halted on her.

Lana stiffly folded her arms, and his gaze flitted away.

# CHAPTER 36

'Like I say, he can't see or hear us.' Huxtable reassured her.

The man sniffed, and the mucous rattled in his nose, and then he narrowed his gaze at the pinboard so that he was in profile. He slid off his beanie and revealed a flattened mop of auburn hair.

'Clarence Belle. Ring any?' Huxtable asked.

Lana shook her head.

Miles clicked his wedding ring against the handle of his empty mug. 'They've run his details and he's got a permit for the gun. No priors.'

Lana examined Belle's bitten fingernails as he interlaced them, opened them, interlaced them. She wanted to pull them out until he talked. 'D'you think he knows he's been brought in for a different reason?'

'Maybe.' Huxtable turned to the cubicle door as it opened.

A uniformed officer with a neatly trimmed goatee entered. 'You wanted to see me, sir.'

Huxtable closed the door behind him. 'You brought him in? …'

'Hooper. Yes, sir.'

'Does he have a cell phone?' Miles didn't turn from his observation of Belle.

'Yes, sir.'

'Has he made any calls since he's been in custody?' Huxtable swirled the slops in the bottom of his mug.

'I can't say for sure, sir. I left him cuffed in the car while I dealt with another situation.'

'He's not likely to, if he knows we're onto him,' Miles opined. 'Unless he's very stupid.'

Lana understood. 'Because there'll be a record?'

Miles nodded. 'If he's our guy, he'll probably ditch his phone as soon as he's out of here.'

Belle stood, put his coat on the table and then strolled about the room with his hands behind his back.

'You see that?' Huxtable said.

Lana frowned. 'What?'

'He's avoiding the mirror. Only glanced at it once since he's been here. He's trying to appear oblivious to it.'

Lana followed his circuit. 'But surely anyone taken into an interview room with a mirror would guess it was one-way.'

'Yeah,' Miles replied. 'Which makes them look at it even more. This guy's going out of his way to make us think he doesn't know.'

Belle sat down again, rocked back in his chair, puffed his cheeks, and checked his watch.

'So what are you going to do with him?'

Huxtable stretched. 'Let him go.'

'Let him go?' Lana barely restrained her exclamation.

'He'll be more use to us that way.'

'He's growing impatient.' Miles stroked his chin. 'We'll check out his insulin story but I don't think that's why he's getting jittery.'

Huxtable slurped the slops and grimaced. 'If we sweat him a bit longer he might get frantic enough to make a mistake.'

Belle clenched his jaw and dropped forward in his chair.

'You're going to follow him?'

Huxtable nodded at Lana. 'I'm not expecting him to lead us to your boy. But sooner or later, if he does have an accomplice, he's going to have to make contact.'

'And then you arrest him? He said if anything happens to him they'll harm Cooper.' She felt dizzy again. This was a job to them.

It wasn't their child's life at stake. Lana tried to repel the memory of him screaming inside Mr Whisper's polythene sack.

'He won't make any calls.'

Lana thought Miles sounded too confident. 'And what about my son in the meantime?' Her attention shifted briefly back to Belle as he stared ahead and blinked repeatedly, almost as if he could hear her.

'One step at a time.' Huxtable loosened his collar. 'If Belle does have Cooper, we just have to make sure we keep him in our sights. We'll see what he does next.'

'And if he does nothing?'

Huxtable's shoulders sagged. 'I'm afraid that's highly likely.'

Lana couldn't believe what she was hearing. 'So how long do we wait? Days? And what about Cooper in the meantime? He's locked up God knows where.'

'I can appreciate what you're going through, Mrs Cross.'

'No, I really don't think you have any idea.' Her cheeks flushed hot.

'You just have to trust us. Unlike most kidnaps I've dealt with, we already have a suspect. I promise you, we're not going to let him escape.'

'I want to come with you. I'm not taking my eyes off him.'

Huxtable pursed his lips, as if he'd been expecting it. 'You can't. You have to let us handle this.'

'I'm going.'

'No. You're not.' He was categorical. 'But I promise I'll keep you updated every step of the way.'

# CHAPTER 37

Todd stood up from his seat at the back of the packed night bus. Lurching and squeezing his way to the front doors he just managed to make it out before they juddered shut and it took off.

The journey had taken just over three hours, and his body had remained rigid as he'd willed the vehicle on from every stop and tried to stem the suffocating panic he felt when he considered who Cooper was with.

He took a deep breath of night air and tried to slow his circulation. Todd had Anwar Ibrahim to thank for his bus ticket. His wallet had been in the sweat pants and, although there were only a few dollars inside, he'd managed to buy it at the station with Anwar's contactless credit card. He would pay Anwar back with interest. If he ever got the opportunity.

He jogged through the smart suburban neighbourhood of Oakdean towards the Langham Cosmetic Clinic and prayed he wasn't too late. It was likely Cyrus Crowther was no longer around. He'd invested in a string of surgeries across the state but the number Todd had was for Oakdean; the place Todd had secretly travelled a couple of hundred miles to from Jaxton when he'd met him in 2016. He obviously still used it as a front for his other business dealings.

He found a sign for the clinic and trotted through a few more blocks of three-storey American Georgian houses, all sporting identical mock columns and paired chimneys, until he hit the gravel drive leading to the reception area.

As the doors slid apart and sighed affluence over him, the middle-aged woman chatting to a doctor in a pink tunic halted him with her best withering look.

'Yes?' she asked, as if he were obviously in the wrong place.

'Mr Crowther's expecting me.' He tried to maintain eye contact but her gaze drifted down to his loose-fitting khaki All Stars.

'Excuse me, Doctor Dale.' She smiled briefly at the man who sauntered back to one of the surgeries. She picked up the phone and dialled a number, stony-faced. 'Name?'

'Todd Cross.'

She nodded and waited for someone to pick up. 'I've got a Todd Cross in reception,' she said, as if he were an infestation. 'Says he has an appointment with Mr Crowther.' She replaced the receiver with finality. 'There's nobody here by that name.'

He expected that but, if Cyrus was around, he hoped his coming to the clinic would enrage him enough to send somebody to intercept him.

'OK, must have got my wires crossed.'

Todd would have to take about twenty paces past her desk to access the elevators to the office where he'd had his meeting with Cyrus. He considered asking her if he could use the bathroom but, at that moment, a girl leaned in through the doorway behind the receptionist to speak to her and she turned her back.

Todd strode swiftly past the desk and gritted his teeth.

'Excuse me?'

He kept going.

'Sir? Wait a moment.'

He reached the elevator and stabbed the button. Cyrus was on the fourth. Would he have time to get in before she caught up with him?

'Sir.' She'd left reception and was rapidly strutting towards him in her stacked heels.

Todd ducked through the door to the stairs and took them two at a time. He flinched and held his finger against his ribcage as he climbed and stopped at the top of the first flight. The receptionist hadn't followed. She would be heading back to the desk to call security. But upstairs was his real problem. He ascended the next three floors and pushed through the entrance.

He was on the conference level, and the main office was at the end of a long sage green carpet. As he rushed along it he peered through blinds at the other rooms. All empty. But then the blue door ahead opened and the man who emerged regarded him with disbelief.

'Rusty.'

'Jesus…' Rusty hastily closed it behind him and hurried to obstruct Todd, his suit flapping around his wiry frame.

'You've got to let me see him.' He attempted to weave around Rusty, but he blocked him.

'Todd, what the fuck d'you think you're doing?' His thinning static-charged sandy air emphasised his alarm.

He didn't know if Rusty was scared for Todd or himself. 'Just let me pass.'

'He's not in there.' He put his palms against Todd's chest.

'Then you won't mind me going in.' He bulldozed past.

'Todd!'

The exclamation stopped him and made him turn.

'Don't.'

'He's my son.' Todd marched towards the door.

As his fingers clasped the handle something solid slammed into the back of his head.

# CHAPTER 38

Warm electric light soaked through Todd's eyelids but it was the recollection of Cooper's predicament that snapped them open.

He was sitting on a chair in one of the conference rooms that he'd seen as he'd made his way down the corridor, and somebody was standing behind him.

'This reflects badly on me, Todd.'

He tried to rise, but Rusty forcefully swivelled the chair to face him.

'Don't get up.'

Todd wondered if he even could. He gripped the arms as the room steadied, his panic rebooted. 'How long have I been out?'

'You shouldn't even be alive.' Rusty's lean features were seething, and he inhaled unsteadily.

Todd put his hand to the back of his head and flinched as he touched the large swelling there. It was still night outside the window, and they were alone. He clocked the fire extinguisher lying on the conference table and the blood smeared around its white instruction panel.

'Cyrus told me to cave your skull in with it.'

'You know I have to call the cops.'

Rusty shook his head once. 'Don't even think that.'

'Do what you want with me but leave my son out of this.'

'We don't have Cooper.'

'Bullshit. After what you said to me on the phone last week.'

'Look, you've had an extension on your extension—'

'You threatened my family.'

'Cyrus wanted to send the crew in but I persuaded him you'd listen to me. That was a mistake.'

'Where is Cyrus now?'

'Gone. And good for you he is. If it wasn't for his schedule he would have buried you himself.'

'I'll pay double what I owe, even if it takes me years. I don't care. Just give Cooper back.'

Rusty rubbed his face with his palms and it was crimson when he removed them. 'I really don't know where he is, Todd. Now, you'd better get out of here before I lose my temper. If you weren't a friend I wouldn't be letting you go.'

'I *will* call the cops.'

Rusty pursed his lips, as if holding back a torrent of words.

'If you touch Cooper—'

'What are you saying?' Rusty lunged and grabbed his throat hard, dragging Todd up with him. 'What d'you take me for? You think I'd harm your kid?'

'If you do anything to him, you'll never get your money.'

'Don't you realise what you've done? Cyrus is majorly pissed with me as well. I vouched for you.'

Todd eyed the fire extinguisher.

'Go on, make this easy for me.'

'I'll find Cyrus on my own.'

'He doesn't have Cooper. Take it from me. Stay the fuck away from Cyrus, or you'll have me to answer to. Now promise.' Rusty squeezed his Adam's apple harder. 'Promise or you won't walk out of here.'

'Get the fuck off me, Rusty,' Todd choked.

'Any idea the deep shit you've dropped me in?'

'I said get off me!' Todd shoved Rusty's slight frame harshly away from him.

Rusty stumbled back, lost his footing, fell sideways, and slammed his temple against the conference table edge.

# CHAPTER 39

Rusty didn't get up. Both his arms were draped either side of his head and a bloody bruise was already darkening above his right cheekbone.

'Rusty?'

His eyes were sealed and still.

Had he killed him? It felt like Todd's insides had petrified around his reaction to the fall. He held his breath until he saw Rusty's paisley shirt moving in time with his breathing.

Todd swivelled to the glass panel in the door to see if anyone had heard. Crossing the room he confirmed there was no way of locking it, so pulled the blind down and hurriedly rolled the stick until it was closed.

He turned back to Rusty but he hadn't budged. He guessed any security guards had been told the situation was being handled after Rusty slugged him but was there anyone else on the fourth floor? Rusty said Cyrus had already left. Had he been telling the truth? Maybe he really didn't know where Cooper was. But Todd had mentioned the police on the phone to Rusty. Perhaps they thought he'd led them right to the heart of their organisation.

Todd slipped out into the corridor and clicked the door quietly behind him. He listened but could only hear the air con unit above him. The other rooms had been vacant when he'd arrived. He padded down the sage carpet to the door at the far end that Rusty had emerged from. No sound of voices.

He peered quickly through its window. The seats around the elongated table were empty. It was where he'd had his meeting with

Cyrus. When he'd got Todd a soda out of the machine and talked to him about fatherhood and how he understood the difficulties of keeping things together for your family. It was Rusty that had introduced them.

Todd had met Rusty in 2011 during a power line installation in Wentsville. They'd kept in touch and hooked up again when Rusty relocated to Jaxton. He left the energy business to work for his uncle. His uncle was Cyrus Crowther. And when Todd had needed money to pay for a private investigator to find Mr Whisper he'd gone against all his instincts because he thought he was rescuing Lana's sanity. He'd initially borrowed five grand. With his credit rating, what choice did he have?

He'd drained their savings account but the PI had told him it was only a matter of time. Todd had continued paying him; he believed it would get their lives back on track. He'd kept it from Lana because he didn't want her to know he believed Mr Whisper was still a threat. That would have fed her paranoia even more. She had no idea how much debt they were in. But when the money dried there were still no results. The private investigator had fleeced him.

'*The last thing I want is for this to become an issue for Lana and Cooper.*' Rusty's implicit phone threat the previous week had emphasised how bad the situation had become.

Todd returned to the conference room. Rusty hadn't moved a muscle. He couldn't allow him to leave until he'd told him where Cyrus was.

Rusty would probably go crazy when he woke. And Todd needed to ignore the voice at the back of his mind telling him he'd already stepped way over the line.

He searched the room. There were two cardboard boxes positioned next to the coffee machine, and he checked their contents. A stack of pink documents filled one and the other contained conference lanyards on yellow ribbons. He snatched out a handful and unthreaded the ribbon from the ID badges. Was he really about to do this?

'Rusty?' He was still out cold. Todd's hands trembled as he took hold of his wrists.

# CHAPTER 40

Lana was sitting in Huxtable's poky office. His desk was neat and tidy and a photo frame was positioned dead in the middle with its back to her. He'd told her to wait there until he returned. That had been nearly ten minutes ago. She glanced at her watch again: 11:28 p.m.

Cooper had been missing nearly thirteen hours. Nobody had said it but from her online research Lana had learnt that after twenty-four the probability of locating a child rapidly diminishes to zero. She knew that notion would steadily debilitate her and was desperate to find something to do instead of being trapped waiting at the station.

She used her iPhone to scroll through Google results. There were a few for people named Clarence Belle, but none of the photos depicted the man they'd taken into custody. Lane Hewett was behind bars but maybe one of the kidnappers knew the murderer. Info on Google told her the caretaker and his wife were childless. A brother or sister? Perhaps the librarian at Hasbland would know more.

One of the websites she'd found Lane Hewett's image on had been set up by a woman named Angela Hamlin. But as she absorbed the text it was clear she was no fanatic. Hamlin wanted him brought to justice for crimes against children he hadn't been convicted of that she believed he'd committed across decades.

'This Todd?' Huxtable entered, holding a printout of a blown-up, black-and-white image. He handed it to her.

It was Todd but the clothes weren't his. 'Where was this?'

'Hospital forecourt. My officers have been reviewing the security footage. Cameras picked him up on two floors. He stole some clothes from another patient and left through the front entrance.'

Lana's frazzled mind couldn't begin to construct an explanation for that. 'When?'

'Soon after he vanished from the ward.'

'He can't be thinking straight.' She imagined him wandering around outside the hospital. 'Is that the last time he was seen?'

'We're accessing street cameras so we can work out where he went after. Can you think of anywhere he'd go in such a hurry?'

'I really can't.' She shook her head at the picture, bewildered. Why was he doing this to her?

'Sure he hasn't tried to get in touch with you?' He nodded at her iPhone.

'No.' And that made his behaviour seem even more out of character. He couldn't be in his right mind. If he was then she had every right to be as suspicious as Huxtable. Lana held it up for him. 'You can see for yourself.'

'Does it have enough charge?'

'Over fifty per cent.' She'd been checking it as often as the time.

'I've just got off the phone to your Detective Riggs. He's working a case in Dearmont but we're sharing information. Said you've already submitted the information about Jink's niece and that he's looked into it. Poor lady is wheelchair bound, Parkinson's disease. She moved upstate to be cared for by her family.'

'Are you going to interview them?'

'From his phone records that were accessed during the investigation, it's clear Jink was nowhere near Jaxton during that time.'

Lana was momentarily speechless. That was one rug he'd swiftly tugged from underneath her.

Huxtable held her eye. 'So I guess we can move on and focus on your forum friend and why he sent you to Lane Hewett's old school.'

'He's not a friend. Please, let me come with you.' Lana was terrified that Belle would give them the slip.

'Let's not go back over that. I'll call you if there's any progress but it's likely we're going to be sitting around a good while.'

'And what am I meant to do in the meantime?'

'D'you want to rest in one of the interview rooms? I'll get Hooper to take care of you.'

'No.' She assumed that meant Hooper would be grilling her about Todd's whereabouts.

'Somebody will keep you updated on both situations. This way.' He ushered her out of his office and across the corridor to another door. He peeked in through its window and opened it.

Beyond it was a smaller room, more like a blue-carpeted cell. A table and two chairs filled most of its space, and the scent of lemon air freshener was overwhelming.

'Please try to stay put. We don't want to be hunting for you as well as your husband.'

Lana figured it was pointless pleading with Huxtable to let her accompany him.

'And try to eat something.'

There was no way she could even consider that.

'Get your strength up. It's likely to be a long wait.'

'Just promise me—'

Huxtable's phone rang and he answered. 'OK. One minute.' He hung up. 'My car's here. Anything you need, just ask.' Huxtable turned and closed the door behind him.

His brisk footsteps echoed off down the corridor.

Lana remained standing, alone in the office, the pixelated printout of Todd in her hand. He'd had the presence of mind to steal clothes. Maybe he wasn't confused. If so, where had he gone and why was he doing it alone? Had she been too focussed on Jink and his family when she should have been more aware of what was happening within her own?

# CHAPTER 41

'Rusty,' Todd said for the fourth time.

His captive's eyes rolled behind their lids and his brow twitched.

'Rusty.'

He blinked awake and took a few moments to take in what had happened since he'd lost consciousness. 'Todd…' He sighed when he tried to lift his arms and found they were bound to the leg of the conference table. He sat up from the floor.

Todd crouched beside him. 'Where's Cooper?'

Rusty flinched as his injury stung. 'Cut me loose and I won't breathe a word of this to Cyrus.'

'No. You tell me now.'

'I've told you. Nobody took Cooper.'

'Why the phone call last week then?'

'I was just letting you know how close to the bone things had got. And don't look at me like that. I told you to examine all your options before you asked for a meeting with Cyrus.'

'You knew it was my last option.'

'And you knew who Cyrus was. What did you think? You'd get friends and family rates? Help! Up here!' Rusty's yell was surprisingly full-throated for a man who had just come round.

Todd clapped his hand over Rusty's mouth.

'Last chance, Todd,' Rusty buzzed in his palm. 'Free me and I'll forget this ever happened.'

The words were hot and moist on his fingers. 'I'm a parent, Rusty. Have you any idea what a parent will do for their child?

Scream again and I'll use the extinguisher.' Todd's heart pummelled his chest.

'Look, we really don't have him.' Rusty jerked his face from Todd's grip. 'And I don't know who has.'

'You're going to call Cyrus.' Todd indicated the iPhone that he'd removed from Rusty's pocket and positioned on the carpet beside him.

Rusty nodded. 'Sure. Whatever you want.' His wrists twisted against the yellow ribbons. 'Untie me then.'

'Tell me the number. We'll do it on speaker.'

Rusty exhaled. 'Look, you owe money and Cyrus likes to make an example of people who don't pay up. He's got a couple of guys who work for him.'

'So we'll call them.'

'Let me finish. Cyrus always operates a three strikes policy. You ignore warnings and he sends in the guys to repossess. Once that's been exhausted, they start breaking bones. First yours, then maybe your wife's. If your wife is good-looking they might even have some fun with her. But taking children?'

Was Rusty's mortified expression a performance?

'It's business sense. Adults take the punishment and keep quiet. You start hurting kids and the authorities get involved. Have the crew been to see you yet? I've been fighting your corner. Buying you time. Telling Cyrus you're good for it. You're all out of last chances, though, so somebody's going to be knocking on your door soon. But snatching your kid right off the bat?'

'You'll say anything to get free.' Todd wondered if he didn't want to believe him because it meant Cooper was further from reach than he'd thought.

Rusty hung his head as if he were exhausted and spoke at his lap. 'Sooner or later, I'm getting loose. You can't keep me here indefinitely. I'm just trying to give you a fighting chance.' He looked up and fixed Todd. 'Because if I'm tied up one minute longer, I really *won't* be standing between those guys and whatever they want to do to you and your family. Come on, Todd. Do the smart thing.'

'Those guys didn't push me off the bridge at the park?'

Rusty frowned hard.

Todd could tell his reaction was genuine.

'Ka-ching,' Rusty said as he watched Todd's expression.

Todd was in the wrong place. But because he was he didn't have a moment to consider the gravity of his trespass. 'I'm wasting time.' If he released Rusty, Todd wouldn't walk out of the office. 'I have to leave you here.'

'Don't do that.'

'I'll tell somebody downstairs. They can come let you go after I've left.'

Rusty glowered at him.

Todd stood but before he'd taken a couple of paces heard the table thud behind him. As he turned, a ribbon was pulled tight across his throat.

Rusty had lifted the heavy leg. He was free.

Todd's spine slammed against Rusty's chest and they both staggered backwards into the conference table. Their combined weight slid it across the floor, and Todd attempted to get his fingertips under the ribbon. Rusty had enough to use as a garrotte.

'I can't let this go, Todd.'

The tension increased and, as it bit into his windpipe, Todd knew that Rusty didn't intend to let him leave the room alive. He thrust his elbow hard into his ribs but Rusty didn't relinquish his hold. He reversed and used his bulk to force Rusty onto the table behind him. They both tipped back and, as Todd landed hard on top of him, the ribbon briefly loosened.

But as they both slithered to the other side of the polished surface the conference table capsized. Glasses and a carafe shattered. Todd's scalp struck the tiles hard, and Rusty grunted underneath him.

Todd ignored the pain and used the few seconds following their impact to slip the ribbon off. He hauled himself to his feet but Rusty remained motionless, legs and feet still resting on the incline of the table.

'Jesus.'

Rusty's pupils rolled up into his head.

Todd didn't linger to find out how badly concussed Rusty was. Choking back the pain in his rib, he stepped around the table. Then he spotted the phone on the floor and scraped it up before lurching out of the conference room.

# CHAPTER 42

Detective Rainer, an older female officer with buns of grey hair wound tight to the sides of her head, entered the interview room and gestured Lana to sit with her.

'Has your husband done anything like this in the past?'

'No. I've already told Detective Huxtable that.'

'Was he taking any medication?'

'No.'

Rainer scribbled on her pad with a stubby pencil. 'What sort of relationship does your husband have with Cooper?'

'What d'you mean?'

The Detective studied her emotionlessly. 'Were they close?'

'He's a loving father.' Lana knew what she was insinuating.

'Has he ever struck Cooper?'

'Never.'

'Does your husband have any enemies?'

'This is crazy, no.'

The questions came in quick succession but although Lana defended Todd's character throughout she couldn't help wondering if she knew him as well as her quick responses indicated.

Rainer didn't appear convinced by any of Lana's answers and walked out without saying if she was coming back. Lana felt sick and was just opening the window when her iPhone bleeped. She returned to the table. It was a friend request from Facebook. When was the last time they'd used Facebook? She opened it and recognised her son in the photo before she read what was beside it.

*'Cooper sent you a friend request.'*

A cold current rippled through her.

'Mrs Cross?' Hooper had tugged the door and was leaning in.

She jumped. 'Yes?'

'Sorry.'

'Any news?'

He shook his head apologetically. 'Just wanted to check you have everything you need.'

'I'm fine.'

'Coffee?'

'No. Thanks.'

'I'll let you know soon as there's any developments. Sure you don't want me to find somebody to sit with you?'

'I really don't.'

'Understood. I'll be just across the corridor.'

She nodded quickly.

He pulled the door closed after him.

Lana accepted the friend request. She waited and tapped on the low-resolution image of Cooper. It was a close-up of his face. His eyes were slits and his lips were stretched into a smile. Or a grimace. Had it been taken recently?

The phone bleeped again. It was Messenger. Now they were friends, whoever it was could contact her directly. They obviously thought the police would be monitoring the *RWYS* forum.

*'Are you alone?'*

Lana immediately responded. *'Yes.'*

*'This has to remain our private channel of communication. Clear?'*

*'Yes.'*

*'As you can see from the image, Cooper is very distressed.'*

Lana's panicked thoughts collided and her fingers momentarily froze. How should she reply? They stabbed at the tiny keys. *'Don't harm him.'* She erased it. *'Please don't harm him.'* She erased it. *'Please let me speak to him.'* Lana sent it.

*'Go somewhere nobody else will hear our conversation.'*

She shot a look to the door as someone walked by the window. *'I already am.'*

*'If the next call is traced I'll bury Cooper.'*

*'I PROMISE.'*

*'No police. Wait while I go get him.'*

Lana remained stock still, gripping the phone with her whole body.

Minutes passed. She scarcely let out a breath and glanced at the time above the Messenger chat page: 12:39 a.m. Surely this wasn't Clarence Belle. Or perhaps he really didn't realise Huxtable was watching. His accomplice?

It wasn't until 12:52 that the phone rang. She answered and held it tight to her ear.

'Yes?' she whispered.

'Mrs Cross? Huxtable.'

Lana wanted to hang up. 'What is it?'

'Sorry, I just called to tell you we're outside Belle's home. He's going nowhere.'

'OK. Can I call you back?'

'What's wrong?'

'I'm just… in the bathroom.'

'I beg your pardon. I'll be as brief as I can. Nothing to report so far, I'm afraid, but we do have another confirmed sighting of your husband. Looks like he got on a bus at the station. Any idea why he'd do that?'

She didn't. It made no sense. Events had overloaded her. 'No. Look, I just need a few minutes.'

'Mrs Cross?'

'I'll call you.' Lana hung up.

'Ring,' she heard herself say. 'Please, please ring.'

# CHAPTER 43

Rusty's iPhone had locked Todd out so he tried three bars loitering on the fringes of Oakdean before he found one with a payphone. There was a lone customer slouched on a stool watching golf on the TV in the dingy interior, fruit machines were warbling against one wall, and the whole place smelt like there had just been a flash flood of bleach.

The tattooed barman appeared as soon as he picked up the receiver from the wall-mounted unit and regarded him with heavy-lidded eyes.

'I'll take a beer.'

'Refrigerator's broken down.'

'However it comes.' He pulled out Anwar Ibrahim's wallet and prayed there were enough bills inside to cover the drink.

A bottle hissed and thumped onto the bar and he grabbed it regardless. He took a swig to make his use of the phone official and realised just how thirsty he was. It was no surprise he was dehydrated. He emptied two thirds of the lukewarm liquid and belched. It reverberated painfully in his rib.

The barman had vanished again and his drinking companion didn't shift his eyes from the screen. Todd fed in the small change he'd found in the sweatpants pocket and dialled Lana.

'Hello?' she answered tremulously.

'It's me.'

'Todd?'

'What's happening?'

'Cooper's been taken,' she blurted.

'I know. Sorry I couldn't call sooner.'

'Where the hell have you been?' she hissed. 'The police are looking for you.'

'I'm fine.' He gingerly touched the bump on the back of his head.

'Why did you walk out of the hospital?'

'There was somewhere I had to go.'

'Where?'

'Listen, I'm about to run out of money.'

'Answer me.'

'There's no time to explain now.'

'You stole somebody's clothes. Do you remember doing that?'

'Yes. I've told you I'm fine.'

'Who pushed you from the rope bridge?'

'I don't know. I was shoved from behind.'

'What aren't you telling me?'

'I had to check something out but it was a dead end. It's not important right now. Is there any news on Cooper?'

'Not important? Where are you?'

Todd realised she could hear the fruit machines. 'In a bar and I don't have much money for this payphone.'

'Why didn't you want me to know where you were going?'

'Not you, the police.' Todd knew that sounded worse. 'I promise, we can talk about it later. Please, trust me. Where are you?'

'At the police station.' Lana lowered her voice. 'They're watching a man who said he had Cooper.'

'What?' Todd froze. 'Which man?'

'Styx36 or Clarence Belle. He's a guy from the *Right Where You're Standing* forum. He sent me to a school, and I confronted him there. Said he had Cooper and that an accomplice was holding him. Now someone has been in touch through my Facebook account and told me not to involve the police.'

Todd tried to process what she was telling him. 'The police have a suspect? Where is he?'

'They're not saying. He's under surveillance at a house in Sequonda. But he might not make a move if he knows he's being watched. The Facebook message said they'll let me speak to Cooper. They sent a recent photo and now I'm waiting for them to call back. I need you here.' Anger burnt through again.

'I've got a few hundred miles to cover first.'

'Where the hell are you?'

'I *will* explain and I'll call you as soon as I'm back in Sequonda so we can arrange to meet. If you've been told not to tell the police, don't. I'm not going to walk into the station to field lots of questions when we need to be focussed on Cooper.'

There was a brief pause as both waited for the other to speak.

'I'll be there as soon as I possibly can. I love you and I'll do everything I can to get Cooper back.'

Todd put down the phone and walked out of the bar. One thing at a time; he had to make the return journey first. Whatever he'd instigated with Rusty would have to be dealt with later. Though he figured it might catch up with him a lot sooner.

# CHAPTER 44

Lana checked through the window of the interview room and was relieved when she saw Hooper sitting at the desk on the phone in Huxtable's office. She'd raised her voice and was sure he'd come to investigate. Should she tell him Todd had called? But the police would want to know where he'd been and from the conversation she'd just had it didn't sound like there would be an easy explanation.

What had he got himself mixed up in? If whatever it was had exposed Cooper to threat she would never forgive him. He'd assured her it was unconnected. Still, Todd was right. Whenever he turned up, Huxtable would demand answers about why he'd stolen clothes and walked out of the hospital.

Could she trust him? She just had to wait until he got back and told her why he'd fled. Lana knew she wasn't going to like what she heard. Even if the police were still searching for him though, she would stay silent in the meantime.

Was there a Hasbland High connection? She searched online for school yearbooks but the archives would only allow her to access those for 2016.

The phone rang. It was a call via Messenger.

Lana stiffened. 'Yes?' She could hear birdsong the other end.

'Are you alone?' a female voice asked.

'Yes,' Lana croaked.

A door slammed and the sound cut off.

'Stay on the line.'

Lana could hear echoing shoes on stone steps. 'Listen, I'll pay a ransom and keep the police out of it.'

'You'll keep this between us regardless.' The woman was breathing heavily. 'One minute.'

The phone went dead.

'Hello?'

No response.

They were still connected. Had the woman hit the mute button?

'There.' The echo had changed now. Sounded like the woman was in a smaller room. 'Say hello,' she instructed away from the mouthpiece.

Lana could hear erratic breathing. 'Cooper?'

'Mom?'

Lana felt her insides lock. It was him. 'Cooper? Say something else.'

More snuffling. 'Come get me. I wanna come home,' he implored.

Lana closed her eyes, trying to imagine exactly where her son was. 'Are you OK?'

'No. A man took me.' Sobbing punctuated his words. 'Please come get me.'

'I will.' Lana blinked away a tear. 'But you have to do exactly as you're told in the meantime. Understand?'

''K.'

'Listen to me.' Lana tried to keep the emotion out of her voice. 'That lady is looking after you until I can reach you. OK?'

Cooper sniffed. 'Is she bad?'

Lana shook her head, as if he could see her. 'Of course not. But you have to do as you're told.'

'When are you coming?'

'As soon as I can.'

'OK. You've spoken,' the woman's voice interjected.

'Please. Can I Facetime? I need to see him.'

'No. And if you attempt to have this call traced—'

'I promised I wouldn't. Just let me see him.'

'I've given you my answer. Don't make demands. I've told you what'll happen if you do.'

'Then tell me what you want.'

'We already have what we want.'

Lana wiped a tear from her eyelash. 'What are you saying?'

'We have Cooper. And we have your attention. We don't want anything more at this stage.'

Lana pressed the phone harder to her ear, as if it would help make her understand.

'I'll send a clip soon.' The woman hung up.

# CHAPTER 45

Lana followed Todd into the front café of a galleria. It was a small red-brick room with no tables but plenty of customers waiting for morning coffee.

Todd found them a corner. 'You spoke to him?'

'He sounded terrified.' Her son's voice so lost and out of reach was playing over and over in her mind.

Todd peered nervously through the clear patches in the steamed-up window.

'So when are you going to let the police know you're OK?'

'When we have Cooper back,' he answered firmly. 'I don't want to be getting grilled when I should be concentrating on that.'

Lana examined his borrowed clothes and then his face. His eyelids were hooded by fatigue. She didn't doubt he was in the same torment as her but she had to know.

'Where did you go, Todd?'

'To see some people. I panicked. Thought they might have taken Cooper. They hadn't.'

'Some people you know?' she said incredulously. 'Who?'

Todd explained how and why he'd borrowed money from Cyrus Crowther and what had happened in Oakdean. 'I can't risk leading the police to Crowther's operation. Rusty's already out for my blood.'

Lana tried to restrain her anger. How could he have been so stupid? Todd had embroiled their family with criminals, and for what? 'I can't believe you kept something like that from me.'

'I'm sorry but if I'd told you I was hiring a PI it would have been like admitting *I* was afraid. I didn't want you to become any more overwrought than you were. I thought it would be the answer to our problems.'

'So what did he find?'

'He claimed he was chasing down a lot of promising leads but he had nothing.'

She closed her eyes. If she'd been more resilient after the attempted abduction would Todd have become so desperate?

'I've eliminated Cyrus,' he stated with conviction.

'You're positive?'

'A hundred per cent. What about this woman who contacted you?'

Lana knew they'd have to finish the conversation another time. She slid out her iPhone and showed him the photo of Cooper on Facebook.

He took it from her and his hand trembled as he comprehended it.

She told him about the photo of the three graves she'd been sent beforehand. 'After I spoke to Cooper she said they don't want anything from us. Just to wait for a clip to arrive.'

'Of what?'

'I don't know.' Lana didn't want him to speculate either. Suddenly the aroma of coffee was noxious.

'Where do the police think you are?' He tenderly rubbed the back of his head.

'Said I needed to quickly grab some food.'

'So this guy is who?'

'I got a message, via the app forum, from Styx36, suggesting I check out Hasbland High School. A convicted serial killer, Theodore Lane Hewett, was arrested there in 2013. Clarence Belle was watching me, and when I confronted him he said he had Cooper. He pulled a gun.'

'What?'

'Shot at the ground.'

'Jesus. I should have been there.'

His afflicted expression reminded her of the day she'd relayed what had happened to her and Cooper in the yard. 'I watched them interview Belle from behind a mirror at the station before Detective Huxtable released him so they could monitor him.' She described Belle. 'They've got him under surveillance at home. He might know he's been followed, though.'

'They're just going to sit around while Cooper's in danger?'

'They're gonna see if he makes a move. Chances are he won't.'

'So we wait for the clip.'

'And try to find a connection between the kidnappers and Lane Hewett. There's little online about Clarence Belle, and Lane Hewett is already in jail.'

Todd blinked as he turned it over. 'Maybe that was misdirection to throw the police off.'

'Huxtable says he's pursuing every lead but his focus is on Belle now.'

'If the kidnappers said no police we have to make sure we keep it that way. Though you should be there if Belle leads them to Cooper. You'd better get back.'

'What are you going to do?'

'Buy a new phone. Have you got the credit cards?'

Lana took one out of her purse and handed it to him.

He slid it into his pocket. 'What about the forum?'

'I don't think they'll contact me there again. Cyber Crime is keeping tabs on it.'

'Probably better we don't call each other. I'll contact you via Messenger. They've got an Internet lounge here. I'll see if I can find out anything more about Belle, and Lane Hewett.' He touched his rib and gritted his teeth.

'Why don't you just give yourself up? You need to have a doctor look at you.'

'No. The kidnappers don't know I'm out of hospital. I can respond to anything they demand of you that you can't tell the police. And I'll be free to move around if they want to keep you at the station.'

'I have to go then.' Lana took her phone from him and headed for the door.

'Let me know as soon as you hear anything from this woman.'

She nodded over her shoulder, exited the café and hurried back across the road.

# CHAPTER 46

When Lana returned to the interview room, Huxtable was seated, waiting for her.

'Mrs Cross?' He glanced at his watch.

'What are you doing back?' she deflected.

'Needed to check in.' He stood and regarded her uncertainly. 'But I've just heard that Belle has taken a walk to Five Rivers.'

'What's that?' Lana forgot her awkwardness.

'Local leisure complex. Don't worry; we've got an officer posted there.'

'Why not just arrest him now?'

'On what grounds? My officer is staying close. If he splits, he might take him to Cooper.'

'You've only got one man down there?'

'Detective Miles. He's not going anywhere without us knowing about it,' Huxtable assured. 'I'm afraid there's still no word on your husband.'

Lana nodded absently then realised the reaction hadn't been sufficient.

'Nothing?'

Huxtable's pupils examined hers. 'No. If we could locate him at least that would be one less worry for you.' He raised his silver eyebrows, prompting a response from her.

'If he was himself, he would have been in touch by now.'

'We *will* find him, Mrs Cross. Then he can put all our minds at rest. You really can't think of any place he'd go?'

'I've told you, there's nowhere.'

'You've tried calling home again?'

'Yes. The in-laws are cat sitting. If he turned up, they'd let me know right away,' she lied. She hadn't spoken to anyone in the family about what was going on. It felt as if sharing the news would make Cooper's disappearance absolute. Momentarily, Lana was tempted not only to tell Huxtable about Todd but about the phone call she'd received. But she wasn't about to disobey the instructions of the people who had proved, beyond doubt, they were holding Cooper.

'No other communications from your friend on the forum either?'

Lana fumbled the phone in her hands. 'No.'

'Maybe it's time you tried to contact him again.'

'But if he's at Five Rivers—'

'I don't think he'll be foolish enough to log on from there. He said he had an accomplice, though. If we get a response, we'll know he does.'

How could Lana dissuade him from the idea? Now she had her own channel to the kidnapper they probably wouldn't use the forum. 'Yes. If you think it's worth a try.'

'Tell him you need to speak urgently. Cyber Crime says it could take days to track a user's location if they don't want to be found. But it'll confirm if we're dealing with more than one kidnapper.'

Lana put her phone firmly on the table, as if she was willing to try anything. But before she had to convince Huxtable further, it rang.

# CHAPTER 47

Lana glimpsed the display in panic.

It was a Messenger call.

'Who is it?' Huxtable squinted.

Lana shook her head, answered and put the phone to her ear.

'Mrs Cross.' It was the woman's voice.

'Yes?' She tried to keep her tone balanced. She couldn't appear alarmed in front of the detective.

'I understand you've met my associate.'

'Sorry?'

'You met my associate in the park.'

Lana tried not to react. 'I really don't have time for this now.' She sighed and rolled her eyes for Huxtable's benefit.

'And he tells me an unmarked car followed him home. He's very angry the cops are involved.'

How could she reply? Lana focussed on what she had to say that wouldn't make him suspicious. 'No, you're mistaken.'

'No more police.' She articulated each word.

'I really don't want to renew, thank you.' Lana hung up.

'Hard sell?' Huxtable didn't blink.

She nodded and hoped she'd made it obvious enough to the woman with her dismissal that she was with someone. And that she shouldn't try to call back.

Huxtable continued to talk at her but Lana couldn't absorb any of his words. When had Clarence Belle contacted the woman? Maybe he didn't care about there being a record of his calls.

*Please don't ring again.*

'And get an update from Miles.'

Lana unhooked her purse from her shoulder and pretended to be rummaging inside so she could hide from Huxtable's scrutiny.

'Lost something?'

What was she looking for? Make it plausible. Find something. She saw it in the bottom. 'Spare tampon.'

'Oh.' Huxtable was suddenly uncomfortable.

'At a time like this.' She resisted taking it out to prove its existence.

Huxtable looked awkward.

'I'm sorry, I need to use the bathroom.'

'Sure. Step out a minute.'

She dropped her phone into her purse and left with it.


It bleeped as she rushed along the corridor. Lana waited until she was in the bathroom before checking it. No clip from the woman. It was an alert from Todd via Messenger.

*'Hooked up.'*

She quickly responded:

*'Go to Five Rivers leisure complex. Clarence Belle is there. He knows police are watching and so does other kidnapper. Only one officer following – Detective Miles – ponytail, black-and-red plaid shirt.'*

Lana entered the stall, closed the door, sat on top of the seat and stared at the phone. She recalled how she used to Skype Todd and Cooper from bathrooms when she was working late so she could be part of the bedtime story ritual. She insisted they always had to have happy endings.

Todd replied:

*'On my way.'*

Just as Lana stood, her phone bleeped again. A clip had arrived via Messenger.

# CHAPTER 48

Lana breathed out hard then opened the attachment. The frozen still displayed something obscured by shadows; she made herself hit 'play' immediately.

The image activated and she could see the lens was being unsteadily panned from a swing door to a daylit window. The picture went even darker as it compensated for the glare. She could make out rows of chairs. Looked like whoever was recording was standing in an old-fashioned hall.

The camera took in a corkboard of children's paintings on the wall and a small stage with a lectern at the far end of the room. A school? Was this where they were holding Cooper? Lana was still anticipating the appearance of her son. The clip ended. Lana sagged but was relieved it hadn't contained what she'd dreaded it would. Was it Hasbland?

When nothing else arrived she opened the *Right Where You're Standing* app and zoomed into it on the map. There was an elongated part of the complex that was obviously the hall. Looked to be of similar dimensions but she figured a lot of school buildings were the same.

'*Do not understand. Please explain.*' She said via Messenger.

She played the clip again and paused it on the children's paintings, examining the messy abstract splodges. What was she supposed to be looking for?

'*I still don't understand. Let me speak to Cooper.*'

No reply came. Huxtable would be wondering where she'd gone.

'*Please tell me what you want me to do. Is this Hasbland School?*'

When no response arrived Lana knew they weren't going to help her any further. She obviously had to work it out for herself. She waited as long as she dared then headed back.

Todd would be on his way to Five Rivers by now. But having been told to visit the high school previously, Lana knew she had to find a way to quickly get over there. She held her breath as she reached the interview room. She could hear Huxtable on his phone.

Lana kept walking and made swiftly for the exit.

# CHAPTER 49

Todd strolled as casually as he could into the reception of Five Rivers and past a long line of morning swimmers clutching towels and floats. He'd been at the local pool with Cooper only the previous week. His son loved to play in the Little Squirts Zone and wouldn't get out until his fingertips were pale and shrivelled.

He knew the payback for his intrusion at Oakdean was rapidly approaching but finding the man who could lead him to Cooper was his only priority. He peered through the window of the pool; it was full of children and their parents. Nobody answered the descriptions of Belle or Detective Miles that Lana had given him.

He made his way into the spa area where there were a number of sealed doors to massage rooms.

Then he spotted a man with a ponytail wearing a red-and-black plaid shirt – Detective Miles. He was seated alone in the corridor on one of a row of orange plastic chairs, talking in a low voice on his phone.

Todd kept walking to the next private room he came to. A masseuse, carrying a stack of towels, was coming down the corridor the opposite way, so Todd decided to try something. He halted and gripped the handle of the room and, from the corner of his eye, saw Miles get to his feet. This had to be the door the officer was watching. Was Clarence Belle inside?

He didn't open the door but intercepted the masseuse. 'Is this the sauna?'

'No, back the way you came and hang a right.' The olive-skinned girl smiled.

'Thanks.' He turned and followed her instructions, passing Miles again.

'False alarm.' Todd heard Miles murmur into his phone.

Todd slipped into the nearby bathroom and found it empty. Opening the door a crack, he could see Miles still relaying the situation via his phone. He could easily observe him from here and wouldn't allow Clarence Belle out of his sight. He just had to stay off the officer's radar, otherwise he might end up at the station. Todd's phone beeped and Miles looked up from his. Todd let the door close and dashed to one of the stalls. He locked it shut, sat down on the lid and waited.

Todd heard the noise of the corridor get louder as the bathroom door opened. Looked like Miles had come to investigate.

'No, not if you're busy,' Todd said loud enough for the police officer to hear. He yanked down his sweatpants to his ankles just in case he took a peek under the door. 'We can do it again another time.' He left a gap for a response to his fake phone conversation.

Footsteps squeaked slowly across the tiles.

'Sure. Just let me know when you're in town again.'

The footfalls stopped just outside the cubicle.

'Let's not get into that again.' He left another interval and could just see the toes of Miles's black leather shoes in the gap under his door. 'We've been over and over that.' He glanced up. The top of the door wasn't high. How tall did he think Miles was? Could he stand on tiptoes and peep over? If he could, he'd find Todd having a conversation without a phone in his hand. He quickly slid the new handset he'd hastily bought out of his pocket and held it to his ear. 'I know but that doesn't change anything.' He carried on improvising and hoped he was convincing him.

The feet shifted from in front of the gap.

But Todd didn't hear the door open again. 'Look, I can't do this with you now. I'll call you later.' He bided his time. Still no sound of exit. 'OK. Tuesday. But I've really got to go.'

The shoes squeaked back to the door.

Todd heard the activity of the corridor again but not the door closing. 'We'll talk properly then.'

The door bumped and the buzz was muffled. Todd didn't immediately move, though. Perhaps he'd closed the door and was still inside the bathroom. 'Yeah, take care,' he added for good measure.

Todd counted to ten then flushed and came out. Miles had gone.

He returned to the door and cracked it. But Miles wasn't in his seat. Todd delicately emerged but darted back when he saw him talking to the masseuse just beyond the private room.

She was shaking her head. 'Not this way.'

Miles spun in Todd's direction, so he tucked himself back in the bathroom. He listened to him stride past and then slunk out and trotted down to the private room.

The door was ajar and the massage bed was empty.

Shit. Looked like Belle had cut and run but he couldn't have got far in the time his police tail had been in the bathroom.

Todd hurriedly followed Detective Miles. When he reached reception the police officer was surveying the faces of the people there. Nobody fleeing via the forecourt. Miles shook his head in exasperation and regarded the elevators.

Todd examined them as he did. By the digital numbers it didn't look like any had recently gone up.

The police officer set off towards the entrance to the squash courts but hesitated at the fire stairs. He opened the door and leaned back to stare up the flight. It closed behind him and Todd stayed put. Miles didn't reappear.

Todd crossed the reception and shoved on the steel push plate. He could hear two sets of shoes speedily ascending the steps.

# CHAPTER 50

There was a loud exclamation before a body came hurtling past Todd down the stairwell. He'd only climbed eleven steps when the detective landed in a heap at the bottom. The sound of his impact on the concrete floor was sickening, and Todd quickly dashed back to help him.

He touched the detective's shoulder. Blood was pooling around his still expression. Todd had seen a colleague die after they'd fallen from a pylon and this man's vacant face left him in no doubt. Horrified, Todd gazed upwards. Nobody was looking down at him.

Hinges squealed overhead. He couldn't lose Belle. Todd started to ascend again and was just about to pull out his phone when the door opened below and there was an exchange of voices. The detective's scream had attracted attention and somebody would summon a paramedic now, although he suspected it was already too late.

As another set of feet came up after him, Todd kept against the wall. His prints would be on the push plate but he'd worry about that later.

He reached the first floor, where a door was still slowly closing, and shouldered through.

Todd scanned the length of the long yellow-carpeted walkway he'd emerged onto. It was busy with people passing along it to connect to the spa café in the adjacent building, and he caught sight of a head moving faster than anyone else at the other end. He kept focussed on it as it trotted towards the doors, and Todd weaved around the people between them. He craned his neck. Like some of the others around him, the man was wearing a white towelling robe. He had auburn hair, which fitted Lana's description. It had to be Clarence Belle.

Picking up speed, Todd shortened the distance but Belle hit the doors and was through them before he could catch up. They slid open as he arrived.

No trace.

There was another door to his right that led to a dance studio. Through its glass panel he just glimpsed Belle disappearing into another swing door.

He followed and read the sign on the panel.

MALE STAFF

Todd cautiously pushed it. In front of him was a wall of bottle green metal lockers. The smell of armpits was potent.

He crept along the front of the lockers to the end. Six more rows extended to the rear of the changing room, and he glanced down the space between his and the next.

A man in staff uniform was seated on a wooden bench slowly undoing the laces of his shoes. Todd moved silently to the second row and found it empty.

A rattle came from the third. Todd stole to it and peered around the corner. He darted back when he saw Belle kneeling there, attempting to get inside one of the lockers.

What could he do, though? Take him by surprise, wrestle him to the ground and force him to talk? Even if security arrived in time and subdued him, handing him to the police wouldn't necessarily make him give up Cooper's location.

Todd hung back. If he'd bolted from Detective Miles he wouldn't go home. But if he believed he'd got out unnoticed, he could lead Todd straight to where Cooper was being held. And as soon as he got an opportunity, he'd contact Lana and decide whether to call the police in.

Todd heard footsteps walking out the other side of the changing room and crossed the ends of the rows until he found Belle standing by a row of pegs beside the exit. A couple of laundry bags were piled by the doors, and he hastily opened the first and rummaged inside. Todd took in his mashed features.

Belle slipped out of his towelling robe and was still fully clothed underneath. Seemed he'd been prepared to run. He found a baggy navy-blue cleaner's uniform and speedily slipped it over his clothes.

Todd stayed out of sight until the doors creaked. Scurrying over to them, he cracked one and could see Belle had grabbed a mop to sell his disguise as well. He watched him get in the elevator before making for the fire exit.

Belle had to be heading for the ground, so Todd tore down the stairs, jumping the last four of each flight and grunting against his sore rib. Entering a smaller, sparsely populated reception, he casually sat on one of the orange plastic seats, slowed his breathing and waited for Belle to appear.

The doors of one of the three elevators parted but as it ejected its occupants, there was no sign of him. Maybe he'd got out on an earlier floor and taken a more circuitous route to get out of the complex. How would Todd tell Lana he'd lost him?

But another elevator opened, and he was relieved to see Belle was the first out. He ambled casually to the revolving doors.

Todd rose as soon as he had his back turned and pursued him outside.

# CHAPTER 51

Lana was in a taxi and on her way back to Hasbland High. If they were to negotiate without the knowledge of the police then leaving the precinct was her best option. Would Huxtable send somebody to the school to pick her up, though? He knew she'd been there before. However long she had, it was better than trying to communicate with the kidnappers while he was sitting on top of her.

She checked Messenger. Nothing.

The driver spoke to her in his mirror. 'Philomena Street is going to be crazy. I'll take you behind the park, if that's OK.'

She didn't know if it was a ploy to inflate the fare but nodded anyway, and opened *RWYS*. The GPS found her position.

*'Finding nearest murder site...'*

Lana studied the image of the police removing bagged evidence from the bungalow. It no longer existed. But maybe there was something in the hall.

The cab driver dropped her in front of the school, and she cast her eyes around for signs of somebody watching. Todd was hopefully monitoring Clarence Belle but there was at least another woman involved. There didn't seem to be anyone in the park acting out of the ordinary, nevertheless, Lana kept glancing back at the copse as she entered the grounds.

At the reception desk she approached a young girl wearing spectacles and earphones.

She smiled and pulled out an earbud to hear Lana.

'I'm here to see Miss McColgan.' Lana was sure that was the name the teenager had given her when she'd first visited.

'She's in the library. I'll call her down.' She picked up a phone.

'That's OK. Just point me and I'll find her.'

'End of the corridor, first staircase, second floor.'

'Thanks.' She hurried along the corridor, and slowed when she reached the double doors to the hall. She pushed through them.

It was modern. The windows were a different size. There was no corkboard of paintings. No stage. And it looked half the size. Had she wasted valuable time coming back here?

She returned to the corridor and was suddenly overtaken by panic. She was no nearer to finding Cooper and had just exhausted the last slim option she thought she had.

*Am alone at Hasbland. Please tell me what to do next.'*

She sent it to the kidnappers and waited. When no reply came she used Messenger to try to get a response from Todd again:

*'Call me now.'*

What had happened to him? Had he run into Detective Miles? Or Belle? And where could she go? Not back to the police station. Huxtable would want to know where she'd been, and why, and she couldn't risk involving them. What was the relevance of Theodore Lane Hewett and the school, or was Todd right about it all being misdirection?

Lana went to the first staircase and climbed to the second floor. She found the library door open.

An elderly lady with a bowl cut of henna-dyed hair was kneeling with a teenage boy. Both of them were stuffing paperbacks from a tall stack onto a revolving stand.

'Miss McColgan?'

She looked up, smiled thinly and nodded, irritation just lurking on the fringes of her expression.

'I wonder if I could speak to you.'

'I've told the principal I can't make any exceptions if books are returned late. Even if parents try to soft soap me.'

'That's not why I'm here. Could I have a word in private?'

Miss McColgan blinked, as if getting up was going to be more effort than she wanted to make, but got stiffly to her feet.

Lana offered her hand. It was ignored.

'We can go through here. Keep going, Dwight.'

Lana followed her into a tiny office, mostly occupied by a foldable bike.

Miss McColgan shifted a stack of books off the chair in front of the messy desk.

'That's OK. I just wanted to quickly ask you—'

Miss McColgan sat heavily in it and sighed.

'About Theodore Lane Hewett.'

Miss McColgan smiled and appraised Lana anew. 'You police?'

'No. But I'd really appreciate anything you could tell me about what happened here.'

'Journalist?' The old lady was suddenly animated.

'No.'

'Who are you then?'

Lana considered what else she could tantalise her with. 'TV. Just researching a potential documentary.'

Miss McColgan attempted to restrain her excitement. 'Which channel?'

'I can't say but I was told you were the best person to speak to.'

She seemed satisfied by that. 'I knew Theodore. Will you need to interview me on camera?'

'If you're willing. What are some of the things you can tell me about him?'

Miss McColgan got up from her chair and walked to the door. 'OK, Dwight, you can leave early. Not a word to Mr Lipton.' She watched him go and then pulled it shut. 'So, who's going to be presenting this?' She sat back down again, lacing her fingers as if holding in her eagerness.

'I can't say yet. I'm just conducting preliminary interviews.'

'What d'you want to know?'

'Has anybody come by here asking about him?'

Miss McColgan frowned.

'We know there's at least one other channel thinking about a similar show.'

She shook her head. 'No. Least, they haven't approached me.'

'OK. Good.'

'Nobody really comes here since they demolished his old bungalow. Still see his wife on occasion.' Miss McColgan fingered the large amethyst stud earrings that made her earlobes look red and sore.

Lana recalled what the app had told her. 'She still lives locally?'

'See her shopping for groceries from time to time.' She took a tissue out of the sleeve of her ivory blouse but didn't seem to have a job for it.

'Know where she lives?'

'South side of town somewhere. Never really spoken to her. She deserves her lot.'

'What d'you mean?'

'Heard she got liver cancer. Not long for her now. Maybe they're wrong about the bad ones always surviving.'

'You think she knew about what her husband was doing?'

''Course she did.' She unfolded the wrinkled tissue. 'They found blood in the house. He always said it had come off his clothes but I don't think it was just Theodore torturing those girls. If they looked at what they took out of their home now they'd probably be able to find all sorts of new evidence. But who's got the time? There's people being murdered every day, and she'll never live long enough to go to prison.'

'So you never spoke to her, even during the time she lived on the grounds with her husband?'

'Wouldn't ever meet your eye. Perhaps because she was ashamed about what her old man was doing. If you ask me, she turned a blind one to more than his affairs.'

Lana hadn't seen any details of those.

'Never understood why the young girls went for Theodore. He was old enough to be their grandfather.'

'Are you talking about the pupils?'

'Nothing was ever proved but I dread to think how many girls he molested that we didn't hear about. Then there was Ms Doyle, religious studies teacher. She'd left a year before he was arrested.' She balled the tissue up again and replaced it in her sleeve.

'What happened to her?'

'Gave her notice and left. Everyone knew she had a thing with Theodore. Quiet as a church mouse. They're always the ones to watch. It was her first year of teaching. Odd girl. Nobody warmed to her so that's how she got friendly with him. I often wondered if Jeanette chased her out but neither of them would say boo to a goose.'

Lana realised Miss McColgan would go on all morning if she let her.

'Jeanette Lane Hewett is the luckiest woman alive. If she wasn't part of what happened to those poor girls she at least let it happen. Couldn't believe she walked out of the court. Could have had the decency to move away. But she stayed right here. I could never understand that. Maybe she thought that her sticking around would make people believe she was innocent. A sane person would have left – whether or not they were guilty. I suppose you'll be speaking to her.'

'I haven't approached her yet.'

'Don't hold your breath. She's never spoken to anyone about it. Least not publicly. Could have given those girls' parents peace of mind. Told them what exactly happened. But she won't.'

Lana had to try Todd again. 'Thanks for your time.'

Miss McColgan seemed disappointed their chat was over. 'You'll be in touch then?'

'Absolutely.'

'If you talk to Jeanette, don't say hi for me. I still have nightmares about what she and Mr Whisper did.'

# CHAPTER 52

'Mr Whisper?'

'Mr Whisper. That's what the kids used to call Theodore. Staff as well.'

Lana suddenly tasted the sour, sweaty skin of his ankle.

'Are you all right?' Miss McColgan's features were uneasy. 'Looks like you need this more than me.' She rose from her seat.

'I'm fine. Really. Are you sure about this name?'

'Theo had thyroid surgery when he was a kid. You could barely hear what he said. That's how he got so close to people. Had to whisper in their ears. Think it got him the sympathy vote. Not from me, though. Always thought there was something unnerving about him.'

Lana had assumed Mr Whisper was a moniker Cooper had given him. Had Lane Hewett used his own nickname? She'd tried to establish the details of her son's conversation through the fence, but Cooper had been too young to give her any clear answers. He'd just shrugged his shoulders and told her he didn't really remember.

'Mr Whisper?'

Miss McColgan nodded irritably.

How far was Hasbland High from Jaxton, and had he really travelled that far to target Cooper? And why Cooper?

'Are you really from a TV show?' Miss McColgan asked dubiously.

Lana absently shook her head. 'Thanks for your time.'

She turned and left the office. Theodore Lane Hewett. A name to the face that had haunted her since he'd escaped from the back lane. It had to be him, and he was still alive, rotting in a prison cell for the murder of three girls.

'You're welcome,' Miss McColgan called acerbically after her.

But if he was convicted in 2013, he couldn't have tried to snatch Cooper. She was back in the corridor and descending the steps.

She had to find out if he was still locked up.

Todd still hadn't responded to her message. She had to speak to him.

Downstairs, Lana supported herself against the wall at the bottom of the steps and tried to slow the surge of blood thrumming in her head.

# CHAPTER 53

Lana walked out of the main block into the busy school grounds. She hardly heard the kids' break time chatter around her.

There was no doubt she'd found a link between the attempted abduction of Cooper last year and his kidnap from Blue Crest. Whoever had taken him had been pointing her at Theodore Lane Hewett, propelling her towards Mr Whisper.

It made a nonsense of her own investigations – Firth, Fines, Jink – and she was being manipulated into uncovering the man Cooper had said had stolen over the fence.

*Tomorrow.*

It was the realisation of her and Todd's worst fear. Her apprehension hadn't been misguided. All those months they'd tried to convince themselves the danger had passed it had been lurking and biding its time. Somebody had been meticulously planning to make good on the promise, and they were clearly enjoying tormenting her.

Was it because Lana assaulted the intruder that day and robbed him of what he believed he was entitled to?

But if Lane Hewett was incarcerated, Clarence Belle and the unknown woman had to be helping him. So what was their connection to him?

Lana recalled how excited they'd all been when they'd won the vacation. Had that simply been bait to lure her family to exactly where they wanted them?

# CHAPTER 54

'Hubbard?' a nasally female voice answered.

Lana approached the main gates of the school. 'I'm just calling to find out if you still have a Theodore Lane Hewett as an inmate.'

'Are you a family member?'

'No.'

'Can I ask what it's concerning then?'

'I just need to confirm he's at Hubbard.'

'Just a moment.'

An acoustic guitar strummed in Lana's ear as she was put on hold. The *RWYS* app said he was there. She peered through the hedge at the copse. Nobody in evidence.

'Hello?'

'Yes?'

'He transferred out of here in 2014.'

Lana halted. 'Where did he go?' She heard nails rattle over a keyboard.

'Coitsville Psychiatric.'

He wasn't where he was supposed to be. 'Is that a prison?'

'I don't know, darling. That's all I got written here.'

'Why was he transferred?'

'Even if I had that information, I wouldn't be able to give it you.'

'Is there somebody there who can?'

The woman sniffed. 'Not right now. Everyone's on a recalibration course.'

'It's really important I find out.'

'I understand, sweetheart. If you want, you can give me your number and I'll get someone from admin to call you first thing tomorrow morning.'

Lana sighed. 'OK.' She reeled off her number but the woman didn't repeat it.

'Uh-huh. Someone will call you then. Anything else I can help you with?'

'No, thanks.' Lana cut the call and immediately opened the results of her Google search for Lane Hewett again. She quickly located the website about him that had been set up by Angela Hamlin, the woman who wanted him convicted for a catalogue of other local unsolved crimes. Maybe she could shed some light on his current whereabouts.

There was a photo of Angela's austere, spectacled features, and her phone number underneath.

'Hello?' a man answered.

'Can I speak to Angela?'

'No,' he barked abruptly. 'Who is this?'

'I've just found this number on her website.'

'Angie's not here. In fact, I don't know where she is.'

'Sorry, who am I speaking to?'

'Her father. I usually look after Stacey for her today but neither of them is here. Looks like I've had a wasted bus journey. If you do get hold of her, tell her I'm not hanging around here past lunchtime.'

'Sorry, I don't know Angela.'

He hung up on her.

Lana hit the contact email address for Angela and sent a message asking if she could call her number urgently.

# CHAPTER 55

Todd accessed Messenger with his new iPhone. Lana had sent the same plea three times.

*'Call me now.'*

He dialled, and she picked up.

'Can you talk?' Lana sounded more out of breath than he was.

'For the moment.' He shrank further into the doorway of a nail salon as Belle appeared in the window of the burger place opposite.

'Did you find him?'

'Yeah.' He watched Belle hoist his frame onto a tall stool and dump a carton on the shelf in front of him. 'He pushed Detective Miles over a stairwell.'

'What? Is he OK?'

'I don't think he survived it. I left people attending him and managed to follow Belle out.'

'Oh my god. Are you all right?'

'I'm downtown. He's just stopped off for lunch. Burger-zilla. Sitting there in the overalls he stole from a changing room. Just looks like a cleaner on his break.'

'Huxtable has been trying to call me. Now I know why,' she said, grimly.

'Looks like Belle can't go home now.'

'He hasn't seen you?'

'Don't know. He might be using his stop off as an excuse to spot me. I'm not going to take my eyes off him but seems like I've got time to catch my breath.' He could hear traffic the other end. 'Where are you?'

'I've been to Hasbland. They sent me a clip of a school hallway but it wasn't there.'

'You're positive?'

'Positive.'

'And nobody followed you this time?'

'Not that I saw but doesn't mean they didn't.'

Belle unwrapped a chicken sandwich.

'I know who Mr Whisper is.'

Belle took a big bite.

'What?'

'Mr Whisper.'

Todd no longer saw Belle's jaw working the meat and felt the familiar prickle of dread he'd been experiencing ever since he'd come home from work and found the police on his doorstep.

'It was the nickname of the guy they arrested at Hasbland for murdering three children.'

'How d'you know?'

'Librarian at the school. It's Theodore Lane Hewett. He's still in prison. At least, I think he is.'

It was a question Todd never expected to have answered. 'You're sure?'

'Yes. He's been transferred to a psychiatric hospital in Sequonda. I've just googled it. Appears to be one of those progressive, low security places. I've called but I'm just getting an answering service.'

There was a brief silence between them.

'So who am I chasing?' Todd tried to focus on Belle dabbing at his mouth with a paper napkin. 'His accomplice? I don't like this. You've been lured there. What are they trying to tell you?'

'I've tried to get them to communicate but they won't respond.'

'Somebody is seriously messing with us.'

'Someone who knows us and what Mr Whisper did. I even think our whole vacation was a set-up to bring us here.'

Todd felt anger spike as he observed Belle poking a straw into the lid of his Pepsi. 'Shall we call the cops in on this now?'

'No,' Lana said adamantly. 'We're doing exactly as we're told. But now we've got an edge. Hopefully Belle will think he's free to go where he needs to.'

Belle chewed and stared out of the window.

'Maybe he's in there biding his time until he feels confident about not being followed.'

'Just keep out of his sight.' Lana's voice dried.

'I'll wait as long as it takes.'

'This could be our only chance of finding Cooper.'

He knew she was right. Whoever else was involved could be monitoring Lana. They didn't even know he'd woken up. 'So, we're waiting to hear from this woman.'

'Yes. As far as I know, she's the nearest to Cooper.'

'So that's at least three of them involved, if you include Lane Hewett.'

'But if one of them was Mr Whisper why point me to the place that would reveal who he is?'

Todd shook his head as Belle sprinkled a sachet of salt over his fries. 'So you can't say for sure if this Lane Hewett is definitely locked up?'

'I'll keep trying to call the office. I also found a website set up by a woman named Angela Hamlin. She's dedicated to having Lane Hewett convicted for a file of unsolved cases. I've tried contacting her, but no luck, so I sent an email and left my number. I'm hoping she might know exactly where he is.'

A bus halted in front of the burger place, and Todd craned to see through the windows to where Belle was sitting. But as people got on and sat down his view was obscured.

'Todd?'

The bus pulled away. Belle was still there.

'It's OK. See what you can find.'

'Call me as soon as he's on the move again.'

Belle crammed some curly fries into his mouth and his whole face seemed to fold as he ground them up.

'I will. Where are you going now?'

'I can't go back to the police station.'

'Get into a cab. Go somewhere public.'

'I'll keep trying to contact the kidnappers, but I get the feeling they're not going to respond until I've worked out the significance of the clip they sent me.'

'I'm going to be putting my phone on silent. If I don't answer it's because I can't. I'll let you know where he's going as soon as I can.'

'OK. Just be careful. Love you.'

'Love you, speak soon.' Todd put his phone in his pocket and leaned back. He couldn't afford to blow this. He was the nearest to the people who had Cooper and he wouldn't stop pursuing Belle until his family were safe. Todd contemplated him as he alternated between fries and sips of drink. The police would be searching for him, so where was he going next?

Todd didn't have to wait long to find out.

Belle finished his chicken sandwich, stood from his stool, yanked the door of the burger place and stepped back out onto the street.

# CHAPTER 56

Lana got into another Uber cab and tried to prepare herself for the next destination. Having been in the observation cubicle with Detective Miles just hours earlier, she was disturbed by what Todd had told her about Belle pushing him over the stairwell. Belle didn't seem to care about consequences so what did that mean for Cooper? She had to keep it together. Todd was behind Belle. There was still hope of them finding him.

The Coitsville Forensic Psychiatric Institute was thirty miles out of town but there was another, nearer, stop off to make first. Online, Lana had found only sketchy details of Jeanette Lane Hewett's life following her husband's arrest and imprisonment. However, it was apparent she'd reverted to her maiden name – Gunson. If Miss McColgan was right about Jeanette never having moved out of the south side, she wouldn't have many Gunsons to eliminate before she found her.

Ten minutes after she'd scoured the local directory, the cab dropped her outside a second-hand bookstore. The place looked closed. But it was the only window in the row that wasn't shuttered.

SPEEDY BOOK EXCHANGE the smog-obscured sign struggled to say.

'Sure you want to get out here?' The young Chinese driver nervously regarded the demolished buildings on the other side of the road. They were fenced off by barbed wire that had snagged every piece of airborne debris. It fluttered frantically as a breeze whistled through the empty street.

Lana climbed out. 'Mind waiting?'

'Sure. But be quick.'

Lana crossed to the bookstore. Number 447. There was a light on in the window above. Did Jeanette live over the shop? There was no other door. She pushed on the panel and it swung inwards. She turned back to the driver and held up five fingers before making her way inside.

The store was large but the walkway of carpet tight. Yellowing paperbacks were stacked up from the floor in front of the shelves either side. The precarious columns of romance titles were considerably taller than Lana and gave off a musty aroma that tingled her nose as she approached the counter. There was a humming heater in front but as she got nearer she saw it was a dehumidifier working overtime. Judging by the patches of damp on the peeling jade walls, it was fighting a losing battle.

Lana remembered her mother swapping books at a stall in the flea market when she was a kid. She didn't realise places like this existed any more.

'Just leave them on the counter and help yourself, Molly,' a disembodied female voice called out.

Lana glanced around but couldn't work out where it had come from. 'Hello?'

Her greeting activated a rustling nearby, and Jeanette Gunson emerged from between two of the bookshelves to Lana's right. She was wearing an indigo headscarf that drained the scant blood in her complexion, and was much thinner than in the photos on the app. Lana knew Jeanette was in her sixties but she appeared to be nearer eighty. Seemed like Miss McColgan had heard right about her health issues.

She stepped out from the gap between the shelves to reveal a tiny kitchen behind her. The overhead lights bleached her yellow skin. She was painfully lean, her bare arms poking from a claret apron that clung tight to her bony chest. Spectacles hung on a chain.

'Sorry, I thought you were somebody else.' Her expression wrinkled in apology.

Could this frail woman have been party to perpetrating horrific crimes against children? 'I need to speak with you urgently.'

Jeanette's face immediately darkened. 'About what?'

'I wonder if you'd mind me asking you some questions. About your husband.'

Jeanette closed her eyes, as if wishing Lana away.

'I know it was a long time ago and that it must still be very painful for you—'

'No. You don't know.' She still didn't open them and squealed in air through her nose.

'I wouldn't be here if it wasn't really important.'

'Who are you? Police?'

'No.'

'Then I'm calling them.' Jeanette reached into the pocket of her apron and produced a phone handset.

'Please. There's no need.'

'I have nothing to say to you.' Jeanette scowled at Lana, her finger poised over the keypad.

'Just give me two minutes.'

Jeanette punched the keys three times and held it to her ear. 'Police. I have an intruder.'

'I think he may have attempted to abduct my boy.'

'Join the line. It's no concern of mine.' Jeanette presented her back to Lana and continued her phone conversation. '447 Randolph.'

'He tried once, and failed, and now my son has been kidnapped. If you're calling the police, ask for Detective Huxtable. He's going to want to speak to you next anyway. Look, I know they transferred your husband to Coitsville. I just need to know if he's still there.'

Jeanette walked out of sight into the kitchen. Lana didn't hear any further exchange on the phone.

A moment later, Jeanette reappeared, clutching the handset. 'I haven't seen my husband since the day he was convicted,' she said, as if she were making a statement to the police. 'But there's always somebody coming through that door who's got other ideas.'

'I need to find Cooper, he's only five. And the people who took him are pointing me in your husband's direction.'

'There's a lot of crazies in the world. I've learnt that the hard way. They're still coming at me. All these years later. But he can't harm anyone now. No matter who tells him otherwise. I wish everyone would let us be. I'm sorry, there's nothing I can do to help you.'

'Do you recognise this place?' Lana fumbled out her iPhone and located the clip she'd been sent. She hit 'play'.

Jeanette huffed and lifted the spectacles to her eyes. 'What is that?'

'The kidnappers sent it to me. Is it a familiar place to you?'

Jeanette frowned at the screen and shook her head.

But Lana could tell she hadn't examined it properly. 'Please, look again.'

Jeanette squinted. 'Don't recognise it.'

'Maybe somewhere else your husband worked?'

'I really don't,' Jeanette said flatly. 'I'm sorry you've wasted your time.'

'You mentioned something about people talking to your husband.'

Jeanette pursed her lips in denial. 'When?'

'You said people had tried to convince him otherwise. Who were you talking about?'

'I told you, all sorts of kooks got interested in Theodore. That's all.'

'Maybe you can convince Detective Huxtable of that.'

Jeanette's eyes hardened. 'There's nothing to tell. I tried to contact Theodore once during the first year of his sentence. Just by phone. I was trying to salvage our finances and needed some account passwords. Theodore took great delight in telling me he had a regular visitor. Some guy who had started corresponding with him and asking him about what he did. Said he was going to write a book about him. Never happened, of course, but Theodore was made up at the time.'

'What was his name?'

'Search me. Don't know how long the visits continued after that because that was my last phone call with him.'

'What about the people coming here?'

Jeanette sighed. 'There was probably one a week in the early days. Plus the kids who liked to squirt gasoline under the door. Not as often now but I'm always waiting for somebody to take me by surprise. Like you.' She put the handset on the counter.

Lana noticed the display was dead. Was there even a battery in it? 'Could he have been one of those?'

'Who?'

'The guy who was writing the book.'

'Maybe. Nobody said they were visiting Theodore but I always threw them out of here soon as I saw that look in their eye. I got to know it before they even opened their mouths. Like they wanted to touch me because it was the nearest thing to touching Theo. I suppose they got less interested when they moved him to Coitsville. His grandfather and father had dementia. It's always been in his family.'

'Dementia?'

Jeanette nodded. 'In 2014, I get a call from Hubbard. Tells me I'm still the only person listed as his next of kin, and they're transferring him to Coitsville, and why. I told them I didn't care and not to call me again. They didn't.'

'You haven't spoken to your husband since?'

'That man ceased to be the moment they took him away to his cell. I'm still his wife, though. I made the vows. Sickness and health.'

'You OK, Jean?' A squat, bespectacled black woman with white curls was standing in the shop doorway. She was holding a thin yellow plastic bag of paperbacks.

'Hey, Molly. Yeah. You done with the last lot then?'

The visitor eyed Lana obliquely. 'The doctor's keeping Harden in another two weeks so I got nothing else to do.' She breathlessly sidled up to the counter, and Jeanette took the bag of books from her.

'Should've closed early. Don't take too long picking.' Jeanette spun pointedly back to Lana. 'This lady will make some room for you now.'

Was being hounded by weirdos what had made her so devoid of sympathy, or was that an indicator of what she could have been capable of in the past? It was clear their conversation was over, and Lana didn't have time to press her further.

Jeanette started sorting through Molly's books as if Lana didn't exist, and a few seconds later she was outside and crossing the street back to the driver.

# CHAPTER 57

Todd still hadn't worked out if Belle knew he was being followed or was just doing everything in his power to ensure he wasn't. After leaving the restaurant, Todd had tailed him into a dimly lit residential neighbourhood then back onto the main drag only a block away from Burger-zilla.

He'd allowed Belle to stay a street ahead and never turned a corner to the next until he had. Belle didn't check if anyone was behind him. Only his desultory route indicated he might be nervous about being watched.

But having pushed the officer down the stairwell, Belle had every right to be skittish. Hadn't stopped him chowing down on burger and fries, though. How could he have done that? Perhaps he'd reconsidered taking the backstreets because that's where the cops would hunt for him first. Maybe he thought staying in plain sight on a busy sidewalk was what wouldn't be expected.

Police sirens prompted Belle to turn left into a plush shopping complex, and Todd loitered and counted ten before doing the same. Belle had got on the escalator and was halfway up. Todd took the one beside it and fixed him as he ascended.

Belle disappeared over the top, and Todd hastily climbed the steps. Reaching level one he casually searched for Belle. He was standing by a silk tie stall, his flattened expression aimed back at the escalator he'd ridden up.

Todd kept his eyes ahead and didn't move them back to him. He could just see Belle at the periphery of his vision, motionless. Todd allowed three or four retail windows to pass before he dawdled at a bench and sat down. He slowly turned in the direction he'd just come.

Belle was gone. Todd resisted the temptation to stand and immediately retrace his steps. Perhaps *he* was being monitored now.

But then he caught sight of blue overalls on the escalator. Belle was heading up to the next level. Todd rose and squinted at the opposite end of the concourse. There were escalators there as well. Should he take one of those and cross level two to intercept him? Perhaps Belle might stop at the top of his to see who came up after him.

But he might lose him. There were so many outlets on each floor. Todd knew he didn't have time to deliberate. He trotted to the second set of escalators, which were clogged with people. Todd tried to weave around them but there were several couples blocking his way. Maybe Belle would go straight up to the next level from two. If he did, it was game over.

He squeezed through the couples as they neared the top and surveyed the busy tiled floor. He could barely see the escalators at the far end. If Belle was walking in his direction Todd knew he had some ground to cover before he came upon him. He dodged through the shoppers until the escalators were in sight. No trace of him on the one going up but he could already have reached level three.

Slowing, he walked and pretended to be taking in the window displays and anticipated Belle materialising from the crowd. But he didn't. Todd inspected the doorways of the last two stores. If he'd gone inside, the other customers had swallowed him. Shit.

Todd reached the first escalators and looked back. No glimpse of him. Had he gone back down the escalator? Todd moved to the railing and peered at level one's fast moving current of heads. No Belle.

As he'd pursued him up two escalators Todd elected to ascend the last one. It led to the food court. He'd have a quick scout for him there. Before he did, however, he ducked in the last store and bought a brown leather effect baseball cap with his credit card.

He put it on and pulled the peak down over his face. From what Lana had told him, Belle knew all about them. Maybe he'd even pushed Todd off the rope bridge. He took the moving steps two at a time and then slowed as he reached the top and was in view of anybody in the court. Food counters were on platforms at both sides. Todd didn't gaze around but made straight for the longest line at Pizza The Action.

Standing at the back he slipped out his phone, pretended to have a conversation and then took in the rest of the space.

Even though it was lunchtime the tables were only half full and he rapidly scanned them. He spotted Belle sitting alone at one beside Barista Veloce on the other side of the platform. He was nursing a tiny espresso cup and was riveted to the escalators. Todd returned his attention to the line.

It moved slowly. How long would Belle take to drink his espresso? He'd only been on the food court a matter of minutes, so he could only have just sat down.

Todd didn't turn until he had his slice and was walking to a table. He didn't focus on Belle but could see him seated the other side of the escalators. Todd found a table of four red metal chairs behind a group of kids on their iPhones and concealed himself there. He took a bite of his pizza and pulled out his phone again. He chewed, even though he knew he couldn't swallow the dry dough. He randomly touched the screen before glancing up.

Beyond the kids, Todd could see Belle still staring at the escalators. He slowly raised the small cup to his lips but seemed in no hurry to leave.

It didn't appear Belle had become suspicious of Todd. Even though his mouth was still full, he tore off another piece of pizza with his teeth and dipped the peak of his cap so it covered his face and he could keep tabs on the bottom half of Belle from under it.

A couple of minutes later Belle slowly rose and gently pushed his chair back under the table. Todd didn't budge. Perhaps he was now satisfied that nobody was shadowing him. Todd told himself to stay calm as Belle stepped onto the moving step and dropped out of sight.

As soon as he had, Todd rose and swiftly slalomed his way between the tables. He pretended to be having an animated conversation on his phone. Better still; make it an argument, he thought. If Belle was lurking down below then it was unlikely he'd suspect someone shouting on his cell.

But as he descended there was no sign of Belle on the second level. Todd took the next escalator down. He spied Belle just hitting the bottom of it. Todd hastened down half the steps and then concealed himself behind a guy hugging his girlfriend from behind. Maybe Belle now felt confident enough to continue his journey to wherever Cooper had been imprisoned.

# CHAPTER 58

Coitsville Forensic Psychiatric Institute was originally a purpose-built military convalescence hospital for shell-shocked veterans of the Second World War. It was constructed on a patch of fallow land in 1942 with a man-made boating lake created to aid patient therapy.

That was all the info Wikipedia had to offer Lana, and as her young Uber driver pulled up out front of the decrepit red-bricked building, it didn't give the impression that it had been renovated since. Above the forecourt was one single lamp on a thick overhead wire, and a dull glow emanated from the glass-panelled doors at the entrance.

'I didn't even know this place was here.' The driver had got them directly there with his satnav. 'Want me to wait again?'

Lana knew she was turning into a decent gig for him. 'If you don't mind.' She got swiftly out of his silver Hyundai and hurried to the reception and could hear the squawks of birds on the lake behind the decaying four-storey structure.

The door was a dead weight as she tugged it back by its tarnished brass handle and walked straight into the smell of antiseptic and stale cooking. There was nobody at the grand marble reception in the centre of the cracked, red-and-white chequered tiles, but she could hear voices echoing down and gazed up at the three balcony levels above. She found a buzzer on the desk and pressed it, but it didn't make any noise.

'One moment.' A strident female voice bounced off the walls.

A door slammed and feet squeaked down stone steps. A squat woman descended from the stairs between two shuttered service elevators, wearing a mint green uniform and an elongated paper nurse's hat that gave her extra height. Lana wondered if it signified her authority or if she was running the whole place alone.

The middle-aged woman didn't greet her but simply raised her eyebrows as she reached the reception desk.

'I hope I haven't missed visiting hours.'

That irked the nurse, and she suddenly gained a few feet in height as she stepped up behind reception. 'I don't have any appointments for today.' She checked the computer screen before her and was satisfied she hadn't made a mistake. 'No.'

'I'm sorry, I didn't realise I had to make one.'

'Everyone makes an appointment. We don't have anyone to monitor visits this afternoon.'

'I've come a very long way, and the lady I spoke to yesterday said it wouldn't be a problem.' It was a gamble.

The woman rolled her eyes. 'Well, Josefina only works part-time, so she doesn't have the authority to make those sorts of decisions.'

'I'm at your mercy here.' Lana suspected it was the right thing to say. 'Maybe you have the authority?'

The nurse seemed affronted Lana would think otherwise. 'Who was it you came to see? I may be able to find a tech but we are short-staffed.'

'Theodore Lane Hewett.'

The nurse blinked and tapped the keyboard. 'And are you family?'

But Lana had registered the glimmer of panic in her eyes before she'd turned back to the screen. 'Yes.'

'ID?' the nurse demanded.

'I'm his granddaughter.' Lana could tell from her reaction that the nurse knew she was lying.

'ID,' she repeated with a smile as starchy as her uniform.

Lana took out her driving licence and held it out.

The nurse looked at it but didn't and then rattled a few more keys. 'Lane Hewett. Don't recognise… no, nobody here of that name.' She fixed Lana, her expression blank and final.

'Can you check again?'

'I can but it'll be the same result.'

'I know he was transferred here from Hubbard.'

'Recently?'

Lana thought her enquiry sounded too innocent. 'No.'

'Then when, exactly?'

'In 2014.'

'And you're family?' The nurse raised her eyebrows again.

Lana put away her licence. 'You're telling me you've never had a Theodore Lane Hewett here?'

'I didn't say that. But there's no record of him on my screen.'

'Is there not a database you can check?'

'Effie!' A male voice yelled down from above.

Lana glanced up to see a man with a stubbly chin leaning over the lowest balcony.

'I'll be right there.' The nurse appeared glad of the interruption. 'Sorry if you've had a wasted journey.'

'You didn't answer my question.'

'I only have access to the details of patients in our care.'

'Who else can I speak to then?'

'Dr Blascoe.'

'Could I speak to him?' Lana asked in exasperation when the nurse didn't elaborate.

'He's not here.'

'When will he be back?'

The nurse considered it. 'Hard to say. He's had a death in the family. Bereavement leave.'

'Can I leave a message for him?'

'Sure.' The nurse tightened her jaw.

But Lana had second thoughts. 'Perhaps it's better I call him.'

'Like I say, he's on bereavement leave.'

'Effie!'

'Right there, Josh!' But the nurse stayed put.

'Do you have a number for him?'

The nurse exhaled. 'Sure.' She rapidly scribbled it down on a pad, forcefully tore off the page and handed it to her. 'But like I say—'

'Bereavement leave.' Lana snatched the paper and turned on her heel.

# CHAPTER 59

Belle had once more led Todd into a residential neighbourhood but this one was distinctly less salubrious. They passed rows of identical, brown brick bungalows, the majority of which were boarded up. There were groups of tattooed kids on every corner, and dogs barked constantly from the confines of the homes that were occupied.

He didn't imagine there was much family life going on behind their front doors and wondered how many of them were drug dens or storage facilities for contraband.

It didn't seem to bother Belle, and his pace remained steady as they cut through a burnt-out square of grass where a group of children were assembled around the tyre swings. Nobody was playing. They were all in a leery huddle, as if killing time until they were old enough to join the gangs, and eyeballed both of them with hostility.

Belle took a left down a narrow alleyway of high, slatted wooden fences that bordered the houses either side, and Todd hung back and let him reach the other end and turn right before following. Wherever he was headed, he'd eluded the police and gone around in circles to make sure he wasn't pursued.

Maybe Cooper was only minutes away. He couldn't afford to reveal his presence now.

He gave Belle as many seconds out of sight as he dared and then stole as quietly as he could down the alleyway, paused at the end of the creosoted fence and peered around. No sign of him in the similar passage beyond but he proceeded carefully, listening for Belle's footsteps and any glimpse of him around the curve. It straightened out. There was none, even though it stretched away for at least a hundred yards. Todd's attention shifted to the gates in the fences. They obviously led to the backyards of each house. Belle must have ducked through one of them.

He halted and strained his ears for the sounds of any activity behind them. Nothing. Should he risk scaling one and taking a peek? Then he heard a door slam. Where had it come from? Shit. He couldn't even pinpoint which side of the alleyway it had been.

Todd could discern a key turning and a lock snapping into place. That was definitely to his right. He gently tried the circular handle on the slatted gate. It started to give. He hesitated. If Belle was jumpy about being followed he might be watching from a window. He glanced to the top of the fence but couldn't even see the roof of the house behind it. He was completely concealed. But Todd decided to wait a good few minutes before attempting to access the yard.

With his adrenaline firing, Todd didn't trust himself to judge how much time elapsed so counted the minutes in his head. After three had passed he figured he should call Lana first and let her know exactly where he was before he made any attempt to enter the property.

He reached into his pocket and was just fishing out his phone when an arm crooked solidly around his throat. Todd struggled to get free but the bicep tightened him against the chest behind him.

Belle must have gone straight through the house and circled around.

Todd tried to yell, but his larynx was crushed. The arm steadily squeezed out the daylight.

# CHAPTER 60

Lana was perched on the edge of her seat in the back of the cab and cut the call she was making. She hadn't been surprised to get Doctor Blascoe's answering service. Now she had nowhere left to go.

She'd repeatedly called Todd's number and was getting the same. Maybe Belle had led him somewhere without coverage. But that only made her fear for her husband's safety even more. There were no further messages from the kidnappers and nothing from Angela Hamlin.

Lana scoured her website again – there were dozens of incidents of missing children and attempted abductions she'd recorded that may or may not have been perpetrated by Lane Hewett. She sent Angela another message and conveyed her desperation.

'You done with me after this?' Her young Chinese driver with the dark, two-block hairstyle was studying her in the mirror.

It was the first time she'd really taken him in. 'I don't know. Can you drive slower?'

He nodded and decelerated.

Lana dialled Detective Huxtable. Maybe he'd made some progress.

'Mrs Cross.' He sounded like he was barely keeping his anger in check.

'I'm just calling to tell you I'm safe. And so is Todd.'

'You *do* know where he is.' There was no surprise in his voice. 'You shouldn't have ignored my calls. Belle has escaped.'

She remained silent.

'And we think he killed my officer.'

The confirmation churned her. Even though she'd been anticipating it, Lana had desperately hoped Todd was wrong. Now Belle was a suspected murderer, the implications for Cooper shifted the reality around her. She had to hold on. Remind herself that Todd would kill Belle before he let him harm their son.

She wondered if Detective Miles had a family. 'I'm so sorry.' But Lana couldn't let on she already knew.

'You'd better both get to the station and explain yourselves.'

'Todd and I have to work this out on our own. We've been told the police can't be involved.'

'What have they demanded? You can't negotiate on your own. You need our support. If anything happens we can respond immediately.'

'Cooper's life is too precious to risk.'

'Two men were seen fleeing Five Rivers. Know anything about that?' He didn't wait for her answer. 'Did you send Todd in there?'

Were they already running a trace on her call? 'I have to hang up.'

'Listen, the situation is escalating. Another child has gone missing.'

Lana's finger paused on the 'end call' button. 'Another child?'

'Cayla Maddock. And her mother, Zoe, too. We're withholding the details from the media but we won't be able to keep a lid on it much longer. Please, don't make this situation any more complicated. We need all of the information at our disposal for the best chance of finding these children.'

'Where were they taken? From the park?'

'I'll tell you. Once you've come in.'

'No. How old is the child?'

'Once you've come in.'

The conversation had gone as far as it could. 'I've got no choice. Don't look for us.'

'Wait! Think about this.'

Lana watched the driver's eyes darting between the road and her. 'I'll call you as soon as I can. I promise.' Lana hung up, and his gaze was still on her.

'Sounds heavy.' He dropped down a gear.

'If you want to let me out here you can but I must ask you not to tell anyone where we've been.'

The driver's attention flitted to the boulevard and back to her again. 'It's OK. I don't have any other jobs after this. Seems like you could use some help. Tell me where you need to go.'

'I really don't know.' She tried Todd again.

*Pick up. Please.*

She got his answering service. Had he got too close to Belle?

'We're just hitting downtown.' The driver stopped at some lights. 'And there's a cop behind us.'

Lana didn't turn. She closed Hamlin's site and opened Google.

'Sure you don't want to speak to them?' He waited, eyebrows raised.

The lights changed.

Lana took a breath before shaking her head. 'No. Drive on.'

'OK.' He obeyed. 'Though we can't just keep cruising around all evening.'

But Lana quickly found what she needed.

# CHAPTER 61

Todd awoke as somebody passed by him. Their movement unblocked a bright light. The first thing he saw was the floor, which was concrete. He could just discern a muted electrical buzz. Was he sitting on a chair in a garage? There were scraping noises behind him. Where the hell was he?

Todd opened his eyes fully and squinted at the grey, shuttered metallic door in front of him.

'Put it back on him,' a clipped male voice said.

His view of the door was obscured as a piece of material was tightened over his face and yanked back. As he struggled he could only breathe in his hot, acrid breath. Todd put his hands to the hood. His feet weren't bound either.

'You've got me at a disadvantage,' the pithy voice admitted. 'I've had to improvise. But resist or try to get up from this chair and I'll slit your throat.'

Todd stopped squirming. When had Belle spotted him? At the food court?

'Make a peep and this will be over very quickly.'

Todd felt something sharp pressed into the hollow of his left cheek and flinched. But he remained silent.

'You're a fast learner.' They didn't decrease the pressure on whatever blade they had at his face. 'One sound, remember, is all it'll take. That includes talking at any level above a whisper.'

They rammed the blade firmly into his cheek, and he felt it pierce the skin. It was excruciating but he suspected the alternative wasn't an idle threat. He clenched his teeth and insides against releasing the pain.

'What were you doing in the alley?'

Todd swallowed a lump of the agony and tried to suck air in through whatever material was over his mouth. 'Take me. Just release Cooper,' he whispered. But he needed to scream.

'Who the fuck is Cooper?'

'His boy,' a different, dry voice explained. 'Remember what Rusty said.'

Todd opened his eyelids against the hood.

'Afraid *he* can't help you now. Cyrus is pretty pissed with him too,' the second voice sighed.

Where the hell was he? He assumed Belle had taken him into the house. 'Cyrus sent you?'

'Little too loud, Todd.' The first voice was right inside his ear now.

Todd couldn't restrain a howl as the point of the knife was screwed harshly into his cheek.

'Ssshhh.' His captor kept twisting the blade.

Todd bit his tongue, his shoulders pumping as he went rigid in the chair.

'Been following you since you left the clinic, Todd,' the first voice continued. 'But now we know you're not working for the cops, Cyrus doesn't give two shits. He just needs me to make an example of you.'

Why the hell had he ignored his instincts about getting mixed up with these monsters? Now he was in the middle of a situation that would have arisen even if he had told the cops about Cyrus when he'd woken in the hospital.

'Please…' he hissed through the hood. 'Take me back to the house. That's where they're holding my son. Just let me get him out of there. You can do whatever you want with me after.'

The tip went in harder. Todd could feel it scrape against his molars. The blade must have gone right through the muscle. Yellow bubbles filled his vision. Was he going to pass out?

'That could work. You game, Zach?'

There was no reply from the second man.

'Where have you brought me?'

'Far enough away to make it inconvenient. Unless Zach is prepared to sacrifice the gas. It's his car. What do you say, Zach?'

Again he didn't respond but Todd knew the fact the man's name had been used meant he wasn't going to walk out of wherever he was alive.

'That's a no go, Todd. Can't say I blame him. Gas has got pretty expensive the past few years, so it's a significant consideration for him now. 'Fraid we can't accommodate you.'

'Let me talk to Cyrus, please!'

The blade squealed against enamel again, and he gritted his jaw as the increasing pressure gradually forced his head sideways.

'I told you to keep it down. And haven't you got it yet? You never get to see Cyrus again. Rusty must have made *that* clear. You don't see Cyrus, and you certainly don't go busting in on him and his closest associates.'

Todd breathed out sharply through his nostrils. 'I've got the rest of the money I owe him,' he lied.

'We're beyond that now. That's past. You've been written off as a loss. But Cyrus has to prove to his partners that this was a one-off.'

'Please…' Todd's head shook with the exertion of holding back the knife.

'Cyrus took a real shine to Rusty. But we're going to be calling on him right after we're done with you. Does that tell you how much leverage you have here?'

The metal slid hard into a gap in his teeth.

'I'll give you the money.'

The blade tension weakened slightly.

'What are you saying, Todd? You want us to rescue your boy?'
Todd nodded.

The knife was pulled out of his cheek and withdrawal was worse. His body convulsed.

'Zach?'

Todd waited, but there was still no reaction from the other man.

'It would certainly cover us for the gas. How much exactly did you owe Cyrus?'

'Fourteen thousand.' Todd swallowed salty blood.

'Is that what your boy's life is worth? And ours as well. You want us to risk ourselves against the nutjob that has your son for a lousy fourteen grand?'

Todd knew he had to get up from the chair and attack them – him, against two paid killers. Cooper needed him. 'It's all I have.'

'But it's not, Todd. It's Cyrus's money. If you haven't learnt anything about business etiquette I was hoping you'd at least got your head around the concept of paying your debts.'

'You can take everything in our account.'

'We're going to, Todd. Because, even after you've disappeared, your lovely wife, Lana, is going to have to work off what you owe.'

The throbbing in Todd's face ceased.

'Cyrus will put her on the street.'

Todd's whole frame trembled, but as his calf muscles contracted and he began to rise from the chair, the hood was pulled taut across his face and the weight of the man with the knife pinned down his shoulders.

The blade was against Todd's jugular, the point pushing against the delicate barrier of skin between it and his blood's release.

'Help!' The word burst from him.

'Jesus, Todd, be original,' the first voice chuckled.

'Help!'

'Fuck's sake, Dee, just finish him.' Zach's panicked voice was closer.

'I'm going to.'

Dee's hand covered Todd's mouth through the hood. Then fingers pinched his nostrils.

'Hold it,' Zach warned.

The blood surged through Todd's temples as the blade point paused.

Footsteps echoed rapidly towards them, from beyond the shuttered door.

His captors were as frozen as he was.

'Not a sound,' Dee whispered.

Where the hell were they?

# CHAPTER 62

Todd heard the shuttered door rattle as a fist was banged against it. 'Everything OK in there?' a young, male voice enquired.

'All good,' Zach replied, good-naturedly, when Dee didn't.

'Heard shouting.'

'That was me,' Dee explained and tightened his hand over Todd's mouth. 'Fucking crate landed on my toe.'

'Uh, you OK?' The guy outside the door didn't seem convinced. 'Give you a hand?' he offered uncertainly.

'Appreciate that but we're more or less done here,' Zach said, all pally.

There was no sound of the man leaving, only the electric buzz.

'Thanks again!' Zach called through the door.

The man's footsteps hesitantly retreated, but halted after seven paces.

'What happened to the old security guy?' Dee whispered.

'He was talking about retirement. Perhaps he went and did it.'

'We're not paying this guy?' Dee readjusted his footing.

'Search me. I think he's still there, though.'

They listened but there were no indications he was.

Todd gulped.

'Go check it out. If he's gone, we'll finish him.'

Zach exhaled through his nose and then scuffed over to the shuttered door.

Todd could make out his breathing as he loitered there.

'Well?'

'I'll have to open the door.' Zach kept his voice low.

'And show him exactly who we're going to be keeping in storage…' Dee sniped.

'Maybe you should call Cyrus. Find out if this security guy's on the payroll.'

'If he was, he would have known better than to butt in.'

Todd fought to suck in air. What did he have to lose now? If there was even a slight chance someone would hear, shouldn't he try to break free? They were going to kill him as soon as they were sure the security guy had left. He prepared to launch himself from the chair but tried not to telegraph it to Dee by tensing his muscles any more than they were.

'I can hear him talking,' Zach hissed.

Dee was motionless.

A low male mumble, some distance away.

'Could be on his phone to the cops.' Zach sounded worried.

'Quiet,' Dee snapped.

The voice had ceased.

'Go speak to him. Be persuasive.'

The shutter was rolled up, and Todd briefly felt cool air drape over him. It slammed again and Zach's footsteps squeaked and receded.

Dee positioned his mouth so he was talking gently against Todd's eardrum. 'I know what's in your head. Truth is, you shouldn't even be here for this, so just… soak it up.'

The blade prodded his jugular.

'Move half an inch and no more bonus lungfuls of air.'

Todd flinched as Dee's lips clicked. He knew the blade would be jabbed straight into his neck if he even attempted to move. But maybe the guy outside would call the cops. What would happen if he did? Would they kill the security guard? If officers were on their way, they'd have to split. Would they still finish him?

They both waited for Zach to return.

# CHAPTER 63

Lana gripped the shoulder of her driver's cold leather seat as he climbed the steep hill to the exclusive Larchmont Heights neighbourhood on the outskirts of Sequonda. Was the missing mother and child connected to Cooper's disappearance? The only way to find out was to give herself up to Huxtable. But she couldn't risk Cooper's safety doing that.

There was still no response from Todd. What else could she do in the meantime but wait to hear from him and the kidnappers? And the one person they seemed intent on pointing her to was Theodore Lane Hewett.

The car levelled off and they were driving along Galpin Drive, which was bordered by neatly kept privets and taller hedges concealing palatial homes. They caught brief glimpses of the houses through the electric gates of each one.

'These places are like embassies.' The driver slowed.

Lana had found an online lifestyle interview about Doctor Tim Blascoe 'living in the gated confines of Larchmont Heights'. Below the details of his work on the reform therapy lecture circuit, there was a photo of him posing with his sports cars on the circular forecourt of his grandiose property.

He was the complete opposite to what she'd expected. He was young, for a start, early thirties, tops. He had closely cropped but thinning red hair, a beard of a darker shade, and intense grey eyes magnified by horn-rimmed spectacles. He'd been installed at Coitsville since 2011, which meant he was only in his twenties when he'd landed his appointment as head of the institute.

The driver halted the Hyundai as they reached a yellow-and-red striped automated arm at the end of the left turn off. 'Pelham Way. Unless you've got a pass, looks like this is as far as I go.'

He switched off the engine. 'And before you ask, I'm cool to wait.' The driver swivelled to her and smiled reassuringly. He released his belt.

'What's your name?'

'Li Jun.'

'Lana.' How old was he? Twenty-two? 'You're getting a huge tip, you know that?'

His face hardened, and his deep frown told her she'd offended him. Li Jun jerked his head for her to get out of the car.

Lana walked behind the little unmanned sentry box beside the arm and made her way up the broad sidewalk. There was nobody in the sunny street. No cars parked up. The residents obviously had plenty of garage space.

It took her a good couple of minutes to cover the plots of six luxury houses before she located Blascoe's circular forecourt. She crossed the street to the Italianate home and rang the buzzer on the pillar beside the gates. There was a red Buick Regal GS parked up behind them. Eventually the speaker crackled.

'Yes?' a bored woman's voice said.

'Is Tim around?' She tried to sound casual.

'Who is this?'

'A friend.'

'Which friend?' she scoffed.

'I need to speak to him urgently.'

'About what?'

'Is he there?'

'No. And if you don't leave I'll call security. Look up.'

Lana found a camera positioned at the top of the pillar.

'Control are seeing you same time as me. Still a friend of Tim's?'

Lana stared directly into the lens. 'If you're not going to let me in, can I please leave a message?'

'OK,' she agreed, after a few seconds consideration.

'Sure you'll remember this?'

'You're being recorded,' the voice said superciliously.

'Good. Tell him I was at Coitsville today. I'm a relative of Theodore Lane Hewett. I need to know where he is. It's very urgent.'

There was no response.

'He can call me any hour.' Lana reeled off her number. 'Got that?'

'You can leave now.' But her voice had lost its belligerence.

'Make sure he gets it.' Lana kept her eyes locked on the camera. 'OK?'

The woman didn't reply, so Lana trotted back to the car. Who the hell was she? Blascoe's housekeeper? Wife?

'Any luck?' Li Jun asked as she slid into the back seat.

'No.' She closed the door and called Todd again. Answering service. And nothing from the kidnappers. What had Cooper experienced during her fruitless search? She felt sickening panic gaining momentum again.

'Back to town?'

It was a few seconds before Li Jun's question filtered through to her. 'May as well.'

He put on his belt, started the car and swung it around in front of the sentry box. 'You look absolutely exhausted. Maybe you should get some rest.'

'I can't.' She glanced at her phone: eighteen per cent power. 'But I have to charge my cell.'

He accelerated. 'No problem. Power it up here.' He put his palm out over his shoulder.

'Thanks.' She handed it to him.

'Sure you don't want me to take you to the cops?'

'No. I can't.' But where else did she have to go?

'I'm pulling over.'

Li Jun parked them under the purple blossom of a jacaranda tree. 'Why?'

Keeping the engine running, he plugged in her phone to the lead trailing from the dash. 'Maybe you should have a think about where exactly you want me to take you.'

Lana shook her head. 'I don't know. But I can't stop. If I do, I'll think about what's happening to Cooper.'

'Your son?' He turned to her.

She bit her lip.

'And somebody's taken him?'

She tensed her face against the tide of hot emotions breaking behind it.

'I can't even begin to imagine how it would feel if somebody took my daughter.'

Lana met his eye.

'I know. I'm too young, right?'

She nodded.

'Everything I do, I do for her. We nearly lost Mei Lin when she was born. She came too early: twenty-three weeks old. I couldn't believe such a tiny bird could grow. She's two and a half now.'

Lana could see he was far from the college kid she'd believed him to be.

'So why is this Doctor Blascoe so key to finding your son?'

'I don't even know if he is.' Lana explained the situation.

'Well, if you want to keep moving, I've got to get gas.'

'Fine. I'll pay for it.'

Again, Li Jun appeared affronted. 'Just sit tight.' He put his hands back on the wheel but a whirring noise behind him made him peer in his mirror.

Lana rotated in her seat. The arm at the end of Pelham Way had lifted and a vehicle shot out. She couldn't make out the male driver in the red Buick as it zipped past them.

'That's the car that was parked in Blascoe's drive.'

'He's in a hurry.' Li Jun was about to pull out.

'Wait.' She put her hand on his shoulder. 'Just a few more seconds so he doesn't see us.'

They watched the car reach the top of the hill and then drop down out of sight.

'OK, go.'

Li Jun accelerated and took off after the Buick.

# CHAPTER 64

Even though Dee had released his mouth, Todd still struggled to breathe through the wet material over his face. The tip of the blade remained firmly against his jugular. Long minutes had passed, and Zach still hadn't come back from investigating whichever security guard might have called the cops on them. The only sound was the low electric buzz.

'Fuck's sake,' Dee cursed under his breath. He dialled a number with one hand and then sighed when nobody picked up.

A gunshot. The volume of it made both of them jump, and the knife slid and pricked Todd's throat. It echoed off the walls of the confined space outside the shuttered door, fading with each repeat.

Dee swallowed, and they both waited for Zach's returning footsteps.

They didn't come.

Dee tried the number again but quickly hung up.

Had the security guard shot Zach? And if so, were the cops on their way?

Dee's breathing got shallower. 'Get up,' he eventually demanded but kept the blade against Todd's neck. 'And turn around.'

Should he try to overcome Dee while he was distracted by Zach's disappearance? But Dee only had to exert a tiny pressure on his neck to finish him.

'Step around the chair and walk forward.'

Maybe he was just going to kill him before he fled. If he was going to do that though, why didn't he just stick him with the knife?

'Take one step to your right and then walk forward until I say stop.'

Todd complied, and the hood loosened.

'That's far enough.'

Todd heard a handle rattle and the low buzzing getting louder. There was a chill against his waist. The hood slid off, and he was looking down into a chest freezer. Through the mist he could see a dark shape lying in the bottom. The man's suit was as frostbitten as his skin; his lips were parted, and his frozen eyes were yellow and cloudy.

Dee's palms were against Todd's back, and he shoved him forward and then grabbed his ankles and upended him so he slid into the freezer.

Todd's wounded cheek connected harshly with the dead man's icy features, and he immediately turned and stuck his right fingers over the edge of the chest.

'Don't make a sound in there.' Dee slammed the heavy lid down.

Todd yelped as it banged on his knuckles and quickly withdrew his hand and clutched it with his other.

'What did I tell you?' Dee secured the door above him.

Todd was in freezing darkness and could feel the solidity of the body underneath him. He turned on his back and frantically kicked up at the door with both feet.

'You stay quiet until I come back or I'm going to leave you in there with Antonio for good.'

Todd battered the door again but it was locked tight. He had to get back to the house Belle had led him to. 'Let me out!' Stinging cold moisture was already settling on him.

'One more time and I'm not going to make it quick for you.'

Todd sat up and put his mouth against the tiny crack of light along the edge of the lid. 'Please.' His shoulder stuck to the wall, and he quickly pulled it free.

The shutter rattled as it was raised and lowered again.

Todd readjusted himself, felt the sharp features of the corpse against the back of his head. He repeatedly booted the door. If Dee dealt with the security guard and opened it again, Todd knew he wouldn't be alive long after.

# CHAPTER 65

Over the sound of his teeth chattering Todd heard the shutter rise and fall and tried to peer through the crack under the locked lid of the freezer. 'Who's that?'

Nobody responded but there were footfalls on the concrete floor. 'Answer me.' His chilled stomach quivered uncontrollably.

'You're in no position to make demands.' It was Dee's voice.

Todd sagged. 'What happened?'

Dee didn't answer.

'Where's the security guard?'

The lock snapped, and the freezer door opened. When the fog cleared Todd could see Dee was pointing a handgun inside at him.

Dee was thirty-something, with close-cropped silver hair. There was blood spatter over his angular features and the lapels of his slate grey suit. 'I think the best course of action would be to shoot you in the head and let the cops find you here.'

Todd's eyes latched onto the barrel of the gun as he waited for it to discharge.

'But having spoken to Cyrus, he doesn't want you left behind.'

Was Dee toying with him?

'Climb out. And do anything that doesn't look like climbing out and I tell Cyrus why I didn't have a choice.'

Todd obeyed and didn't glance back at the body he'd been lying on top of. He took in his surroundings. They were in a yellow metal room about twelve by twelve feet that was empty except for an open crate – that, he assumed, they'd used to transport him in – the freezer unit, and the chair he'd been seated on.

'It's a stay of execution. Cyrus is willing to hear your side of the story but you have to move fast. Cops will be here soon and, if we're trapped, I won't allow you to answer any questions. Singing from the same page?'

Todd nodded.

'Then go.' He gestured with the gun. 'I'm right behind you.'

The grey shuttered door was still partially closed and Todd had to duck under it to get to the corridor outside. Similar rooms stretched away from him.

They were obviously in a storage facility. So this was where people who disappeared ended up: on ice, until they could be properly disposed of. Maybe that was just Dee's way of processing clients. But whatever he said, Todd didn't believe for one moment that he was about to have an audience with Cyrus. With the police on the way, Todd was just being taken someplace else to be dispatched.

What was Dee doing?

A whoosh and he quickly emerged. Smoke pursued him under the door.

'Follow the signs to A Bay. And don't speak to anyone. Cops have to cross town so we've got a decent window.'

Todd negotiated the maze of corridors to A Bay, wondering when his best opportunity would be to try an escape attempt. But with Dee's gun aimed at his spine, he didn't doubt it would be easier for Dee to leave Todd dead than try to wrangle him as the cops arrived.

He would have to be transported from one location to another, however. Getting the attention of a driver was going to be his best bet, or even making them crash.

He walked into a reception where doors led out to the parking zone but halted abruptly.

Two bodies were lying in front of the desk. The first was a young guy in a security uniform. His throat had been slit and his blood had crossed the floor to the far wall. The second was an obese guy in grey sweats with a gunshot wound to his chest. Todd assumed it was Zach. He choked back a reaction.

A smoke alarm started wailing.

'Don't worry.' Dee jabbed the handgun harshly between his shoulders. 'Keep walking.'

As they stepped over the blood, Todd looked up at the security screens above. He saw them both in multiple images and noticed that Dee had pulled a beanie low over his face.

'Stop.' Dee retrieved a key from Zach's pocket.

'Move.'

Todd pushed the doors wide and smacked into the warm afternoon air. There was a handful of cars and cargo vans in the small lot outside, and he could hear approaching sirens.

'The white Prius,' Dee directed him.

Its lights flashed as it was unlocked with the remote. Todd hovered by the passenger side.

'You're driving.' Dee kept the gun low. He threw the key at him.

Todd didn't catch it and it clattered to the gravel.

'Fuck's sake.'

Todd scrabbled it up and crossed paths with Dee. He opened the door, slid into the seat and fumbled with the key.

'Don't play for time.'

Todd switched on the engine, and Zach's paused music recommenced. Roy Orbison was promising to return to Blue Bayou.

'Take her to the gate.' Dee passed Todd a ticket from the dash.

The sirens bounced off the flyover that loomed over them.

Todd glided up to the machine and slid in the ticket.

They waited for it to be spat out and then again for the arm to rise.

'Go,' Dee said calmly.

They pulled out of the parking zone and dropped down a long ramp that led to a spotless, palm-lined industrial park. Todd turned right as he was instructed, heading in the opposite direction to the sirens.

# CHAPTER 66

As they hit the outskirts, Lana and Li Jun knew exactly where Doctor Blascoe's Buick was leading them.

'Looks like bereavement leave is over,' Lana observed.

Minutes later, Blascoe turned his car off into the red-brick institute, and Li Jun crawled and halted before they reached the gates.

He switched off the engine, and the only sound was the trill of a lone bird out on the lake. 'Seems too much of a coincidence he'd head over here in such a hurry after your home visit.'

Lana nodded. 'Whatever's happening now, I need to know what it is.'

'What are you going to do?'

'I've no idea. I have to get back in there, though.'

'I'll come with you.'

'No. You've already done enough. Can you wait for me?'

'Of course.' He rolled his eyes.

'And keep an eye on my phone.'

'You've got ten minutes. Then I'll come find you.'


Lana got out of the car and stealthily skirted the dry ditch that led to the gates.

Doctor Blascoe's car was parked up near the main building. Lana entered the forecourt and sidled up to the doors. She peered through the thick glass panels but couldn't see anyone at reception.

She heaved the handle for the second time and hesitated inside the tiled foyer to listen to incoherent exchanges echoing down between a familiar female voice and a querulous male. It was difficult to tell if he was a patient or member of staff.

There was another noise under the conversation – feet ascending stone steps. Sounded like Doctor Blascoe was on his way up there.

Glancing up to the balconies, Lana swiftly crossed the floor and paused at the bottom of the stairwell between the service elevators. The footsteps above continued for a few more seconds and then a door squealed and closed. First floor, second? Lana started to climb.

At level one a sign told her the Ambrose Ward lay beyond.

'Doctor Blascoe,' the nurse said from above. She seemed pleased to see him.

Lana could only hear her side of the conversation. She scaled another ten steps so she could eavesdrop through the door to level two. Suddenly it creaked open, and she promptly descended again.

'She was here, trying to tell me she was his granddaughter.'

'You told her nothing?' Blascoe's sonorous voice bounced off the wall.

'No.' She sounded peeved he thought she might have.

Lana ducked through the entrance to Ambrose Ward and found herself in another corridor, looking down rows of closed blue doors either side. As their voices got louder, she prayed they wouldn't follow her. She readied herself to dart into one of the rooms.

'But you didn't deny Lane Hewett was here.'

'I told her he wasn't currently a patient,' the nurse sighed, as if they'd gone over this before. 'I gave her your office number. Said you were the only person to speak to.'

They reached ground. Lana breathed.

'OK. And you noted her name.'

'Lana something. I'll just check.'

'Bring it to my office.'

Their footfalls separated. Did she really need to be skulking up here now she was sure Blascoe was hiding something? She had to know where Lane Hewett was. Every second she wasted was another moment Cooper was in the clutches of the kidnappers. She crept back down the steps to reception.

The nurse was at her station going through some papers. Lana turned left and continued down the corridor. Blascoe's office had to be this way.

But as she rounded the corner, Lana stopped dead. She'd walked into a very familiar place. Paintings were pinned to a corkboard. Paintings she'd assumed to be the work of children. A lectern was still positioned on the stage. It was the hall the kidnappers had sent her the clip of.

'How did you get in here?'

Lana spun around and found Blascoe standing behind her.

# CHAPTER 67

Compared to his website image the doctor's hair was cropped even shorter; he'd shaved off his red beard, and there were extra pounds around his jowls and waistline. His sneer was far from the benevolence he projected online.

'I need to speak to you about Theodore Lane Hewett.'

'You can't just walk in here when you want.'

'I tried contacting your office.'

'I'm on leave.' His grey eyes flickered as his presence there immediately invalidated the excuse.

Lana had busted in before he could have his confab with the nurse, and she was determined to exploit it. 'If he's not here, I just need to know where he was transferred.'

'Theodore Lane Hewett?' He crinkled his features, as if struggling to recall him.

His whole body language told Lana he was being deceitful. 'Yes. He came here from Hubbard in 2014.'

'You'll have to make an appointment. I've one hundred and sixteen other patients under my care. See Nurse Tate. She's at reception.'

He should certainly have been bawling Lana out more about her intrusion. She didn't allow him time to think. 'But this is very urgent.'

'So urgent you trespassed at my private residence.'

It appeared he was quickly finding his feet. 'I didn't trespass. I asked if you were at home. And I was told you weren't.'

'I wasn't.' He took a breath, as if keeping himself in check. 'Now you'll just have to adhere to protocol.'

'Why can't we discuss it now?'

'I told you: I'm busy.'

'Even though you're on leave.'

He opened his mouth and then looked over Lana's shoulder with palpable relief.

'Everything OK here, Doctor Blascoe?'

Lana followed his gaze to find Nurse Tate had entered the hall behind her and was regarding her with the faux innocence of someone who knows exactly what's going on.

'You remember me.'

Tate raised her eyebrows at her. 'You came back,' the diminutive nurse stated sardonically, as if it were a pleasant surprise.

'Could you show this lady to reception? She wants to make an appointment.'

Lana returned her attention to Blascoe and saw how the interruption had allowed him to compose himself. 'Would it make any difference if I told you this was a genuine matter of life and death? The safety of my son depends on this.'

Blascoe's cynical smile evaporated when he saw the conviction on her face. 'It'll take some time to access a patient's file. Isn't that right?' He glanced shiftily at Nurse Tate.

Lana didn't turn to see her reaction. 'So, you've no recollection of Lane Hewett and what happened to him?'

He shook his head once.

'Then, if you're not going to help, maybe I should make some noises about you obstructing me.'

Blascoe didn't blink. 'Nobody's obstructing you. You've barged in here talking about life and death, demanding patient information, and I don't even know who you are.'

'She said she was a relative,' Nurse Tate informed him again sceptically. 'Even though Lane Hewett doesn't have a granddaughter.'

'Recalling more than you did this afternoon, Nurse,' Lana replied without taking her eyes off Blascoe.

Blascoe cleared his throat. 'If you are a relative, you can apply in the appropriate way and we'll be more than happy to accommodate you. Mrs...?'

'Cross,' Nurse Tate answered for her.

'You definitely do remember me then.' Lana was positive they both knew exactly what had happened to Lane Hewett and would put every obstacle in her way to conceal it. 'Why are you doing this?'

'Doing what?' He frowned.

'Lying, colluding. I heard all of your conversation upstairs.'

Blascoe's expression didn't alter.

'You drove over here because I came searching for you at home and now you're playing for time so you can hide whatever it is I shouldn't know about Lane Hewett.'

'This is nonsense,' Blascoe blustered.

'No, it isn't. I have to know where Lane Hewett is, and if you don't pull his file for me tonight I'm involving the cops.' Lana should have been surprised at the words coming out of her mouth but knew it was Cooper driving her on.

If Blascoe was lying to her about Lane Hewett what else was he capable of? Lana considered where they were standing. Had Blascoe recorded the footage? She whipped around to Nurse Tate but she was still standing in her position inside the doorway. She looked askance at Lana, as if her behaviour was unstable. Lana kept her in the corner of her eye.

'Look, I'm not interested in whatever situation you're protecting here. I promise I won't involve the police if you just tell me what I need to know.'

Blascoe snorted. 'Whatever situation *you're* in here, Mrs Cross, I'm afraid I can't help. I tell you what, though, swing by tomorrow and we'll see what we can do. But if we have a repeat of this scenario, I'm afraid it's me that's going to be calling the police.'

Was it a bluff or did Blascoe know for sure she couldn't call them? Lana suddenly felt in danger. 'OK, I'm getting back in my cab…' She added the detail to let them know someone was waiting for her outside. 'But I'll be back tomorrow morning.'

'Make it the late afternoon. It could take some time for us to locate his records.'

Lana nodded at Blascoe. She hastily exited the hall, glimpsing Nurse Tate's quiet amusement on her way out.

# CHAPTER 68

As Lana pushed against the weight of the main entrance door she wondered if she was overreacting. There was no doubt Blascoe had something to cover up. Could he really be involved in snatching Cooper though?

But whoever the kidnappers were, if they knew about her personal investigations they'd rightly assume that, as soon as they'd made her aware of Lane Hewett, she'd be chasing down his last place of incarceration.

'Mrs Cross?'

Her gaze dropped to the entrance and the figure standing to the right of it. She took a pace back. Lana recognised the forty-something tech that had shouted down to Nurse Tate on her first visit. His jet black hair appeared wet and was slicked back from his snub-nosed features.

'Heard your conversation with Doctor Blascoe.' The man stepped forward. 'You got to see his nice side.' He was wearing navy blue overalls, the V-neck of which exposed the explosion of hairs on his chest. His bare arms looked like they had their own dark sleeves. 'They're fucking, know that?'

Lana didn't like the grin he was wearing.

'Him and Nurse TaterTWOT. Total Waste Of Time. Been there myself. Like heaving away at one of the catatonics.' His demeanour was that of a surly teenager.

She wondered how long he'd been stuck in his job. 'Do you remember Lane Hewett?'

'No.' He shook his head quickly and gauged her reaction as if it entertained him. 'Been working here five months; one of the other techs used to wipe his ass for him.'

'Who was that?'

'Roy something. He left and moved down south somewhere.'

'Do you know how I can contact him?'

'No. Ain't heard from him since. Used to come out here for a smoke with him from time to time. He was a dealer on the side so his samples were good.'

Lana could tell he wanted to drag his story out. 'What happened to Lane Hewett?'

'Roy told me. What are you? Reporter?'

'No.'

'Private investigator?'

'Look, I don't have time to waste. Can you tell me or not?' She knew what his next question would be.

'With Roy gone I'm really the only one who can fast track the information you need. How badly d'you want it?'

'How much?'

'Five hundred dollars?' he asked hesitantly.

'OK.'

'A thousand dollars,' he immediately added when he saw how readily she would pay.

'A thousand. But you'll have to tell me now.'

'Fifteen hundred.'

'A thousand. Talk.'

'Could lose my job if they know I'm speaking to you.' He cast a glance back at the entrance.

'I've said I'll pay.'

'You're walking around with that sort of coin on you?'

'No. You'll have to trust me.'

He briefly closed his eyes. 'No dice.'

Lana plucked out her coin purse and examined the interior. She'd put a third of their vacation fund inside and left the rest in the safe at their Blue Crest apartment. 'I've got $470.' She took out the bills. 'You can have this now and I'll pay the rest later.'

'You wearing any jewellery?' But his eyes had already alighted on the single ring on her finger.

'It's my wedding band.' But Lana knew that would mean nothing to him. 'What about my watch?'

'Looks like you got that from a grabber. The ring'll be fine. Just as security. I'll give it back when you come up with the $530.'

There was no time for sentiment. Lana tugged but it was difficult to remove. She grunted and tried to yank it over her knuckle.

He watched impassively.

Lana manage to wrench off the ring, folded the bills over it and held it out.

He came forward to accept them.

She snatched her hand back. 'Tell me now.'

He smiled and nodded, as if reminding himself he could easily take the money from her if she tried to withhold it. 'But you have to promise not to go right back in there hurling accusations. If you do, they'll know how you came by them. Deal?'

'Deal.'

'Lane Hewett ain't here no more.'

'I know that. Where has he gone?'

'Not far. According to Roy anyway.' He seemed as if he were about to relax into the story, but caught her expression. 'Roy came in one morning, in January 2015, to be told Lane Hewett had died in his sleep. TaterTWOT told him to strip his room and put his stuff into storage. But Roy overheard her and Blascoe having a very heated conversation about the old psycho. Somebody had taken their eye off the ball. Lane Hewett had been taken out of his room for some fresh air. He was wheelchair bound by then so nobody paid him any mind when they took him out back. Roy saw Blascoe looking for Lane Hewett around the boating lake. One of the patients had drowned there the previous year and they couldn't afford for there to be another. Place had almost been closed down the first time. So, seeing as nobody visited the senile old cunt, they just took his name off the books.'

January 2015. That was way before Mr Whisper had attempted to snatch Cooper. 'His body's still in the lake?'

'Maybe. It's never been drained. Or perhaps Blascoe and his bitch dragged him out and buried him somewhere.'

'Or maybe he's not dead at all.'

# CHAPTER 69

As Li Jun drove her back to town, Lana considered all the time she'd spent in fear since Mr Whisper had dropped into her yard. How many hours had been drained away searching shadowy sites online and in person in the hope she'd be able to fill in the portion of his face covered by the mask?

Theodore Lane Hewett was Mr Whisper. He couldn't be dead. His attempted abduction of Cooper had been in 2016, over a year and a half after he was believed to have drowned. His nickname, and the connection the kidnappers were flagging with the clip of Coitsville, couldn't be a coincidence.

If the tech was to be believed, the murderer had been lying at the bottom of Coitsville's boating lake, his skeleton rotting, the day she'd fought with the intruder at the fence.

They couldn't have found the body.

She examined the ghost of the ring around the base of her finger. Losing it seemed like a horrible omen. How long had it been since she'd heard from Todd? And it felt forever ago the woman had allowed her to speak to Cooper.

'It's not fully charged.' Li Jun passed the phone back to her.

'Thanks.'

He'd told her there'd been no messages but she checked anyway. Nothing. And no response from Todd or Angela Hamlin.

'You going to tell me what happened back there?'

'Nothing clear-cut.' She had the tech's version of Roy's story. If it were partially true it certainly explained Doctor Blascoe's behaviour.

And, in the absence of any visitors calling there to see Lane Hewett, it was no surprise they'd managed to sustain the deceit.

If he and Nurse Tate thought Lane Hewett had drowned, and covered it up to avoid an investigation into something that had already happened once at Coitsville, she could understand why they'd been so eager to get rid of her. What did they hope to do in the meantime? Lose the file?

She'd promised the tech she wouldn't go back in there to confront Blascoe. It wouldn't have achieved anything anyway. They weren't going to admit to burying a patient in the grounds. Lana didn't believe they had. Maybe Lane Hewett had been faking early dementia symptoms and his need for a wheelchair and had bided his time before escaping. And with Doctor Blascoe doing all he could to keep it quiet, nobody would have gone after him.

'I'm running on fumes. Have to get gas.'

She had no choice but to expose Blascoe's duplicity and would contemplate the consequences of that later. Now, though, she wanted to provoke a dialogue with the kidnappers and ask them to let her speak to Cooper.

She typed: *'Coitsville Institute. The recording is of the last known address of Theodore Lane Hewett. Am I talking to Mr Whisper?'*

Lana sent the message.

# CHAPTER 70

'If you're thinking again about opening that door and jumping out you know I'll turn this car around and come back to pick you off.'

Todd kept focussed on the busy road ahead through all the empty Taco Bell wrappers and cartons on the dash. The pain in his cheek and knuckles had emerged from his adrenaline. He could still taste blood in his mouth, and his shirt collar felt tacky.

There was plenty of night traffic about. Maybe he should drive them straight into another vehicle. But even if he did, Dee could still shoot him. The handgun was sideways on his captor's lap, his finger on the trigger, the muzzle only a foot away and aimed directly at Todd.

The signs told him they were on the east side of town and putting more miles between them and his son. He had to keep himself alive for Cooper. Only Todd knew exactly where Belle was. But maybe he'd fled. Perhaps he'd seen Todd being taken by Dee and Zach and the place was now empty.

Zach's CD still played low, and Roy Orbison sang 'California Blue'. Todd's heart felt like it was bouncing off the walls of his ribcage but he kept scanning the illuminated industrial landscape around him. He'd have to keep looking for an opportunity and take advantage of any moments Dee became distracted. But those were going to be scarce.

'Where are we going?'

'See Cyrus.' Dee's phone rang before he had time to elaborate. 'Yeah, we're clear.' Dee switched it to his right ear so Todd couldn't hear the other end of the conversation. 'Didn't make it,' he answered phlegmatically. 'Had to leave him behind. Zero time for clean-up. Torched storage. Nothing I could do.' Dee grimaced as he waited for a response and gestured for Todd to keep his attention on the road. 'No, he's retired. We didn't know that when we went in there. With me now… Very well.' He hung up and put the phone back in his suit pocket.

Seconds rolled by.

'Was that Cyrus?' Todd didn't need to ask.

'Yep. He's happy to hear you out.'

That was bullshit. Wanted to personally take care of Todd himself more like.

'Where are we meeting him?'

Dee sniffed. 'I'll give you directions when we're closer.'

But Todd understood the nature of the conversation he'd just had. 'OK. I'm sure we can iron this out.' He needed him to think he was anticipating a meeting. If Dee believed that, he was less likely to expect an escape. 'Is he nearby?' He glimpsed Dee's expression.

Dee rolled his eyes suspiciously at him. 'Get off at the next intersection.'

Todd glanced at the sign. They were headed out of the city. 'Cyrus somewhere out of town?'

Dee nodded slightly but said nothing else.

# CHAPTER 71

While Li Jun filled the tank of the Hyundai, Lana remained in the back seat, scrolling through Angela Hamlin's website again. Her eyes alighted on a familiar name.

Zoe Maddock.

Detective Huxtable had just said she'd vanished with her child. She tapped it open but there was scant information about her, only that she lived in Blackfort, which was forty miles north of Sequonda. A neighbour had barely rescued her daughter, Cayla, from being taken from her pushchair by an unidentified man in 2012.

A cold wave crashed through her.

Had Cayla almost been a victim of Mr Whisper, too? And, as with Cooper, had he made good on his promise to return?

Her phone buzzed as she looked at it.

*'Cooper has a clever mother.'*

It was a reaction to her last message but it almost seemed like a response to her new discovery.

*'I'll Whisper your next instructions soon.'*

Lana replied: *'Please let me talk to Cooper.'*

She waited, and jumped as Li Jun replaced the fuel cap. He trotted across the forecourt of the gas station to pay. They were the only car filling up, and there was one guy half asleep behind the kiosk. Night-time traffic slid sporadically by as she counted the seconds.

*'He's too busy having fun with me.'*

The words were like fingers around her throat. She frantically typed:

*'Please.'*

She guessed her begging was exactly what they wanted.

*'Why don't you come join in? We're getting ready for a special pool party. I'll get Cooper to design an invitation.'*

Lana was desperate to keep their dialogue going but how should she answer that?

Li Jun got back in the car and clocked her expression. 'Lana?'

'He's just contacted me.' She took a wavering breath, explained what had happened and didn't lift her eyes from the screen.

Her phone vibrated again.

*'He's working on it.'*

# CHAPTER 72

The streetlights dropped away and the buildings became sparser as the freeway took Todd and Dee away from civilisation and into parched scrubland. If there had been an opportunity to escape, Todd had blinked and missed it.

There was a hotel and casino out on its own up ahead, and its neon looked like the last illumination before the deep darkness beyond.

'When you reach it, pull off into the lot.'

'Why are we stopping here?' Todd had been anticipating the instruction to drive off the road and over the dunes but knew his relief would be short-lived.

'See Cyrus,' Dee said, like he had a thousand times already. 'It's his place. Just park us up by the main entrance.'

Todd attempted to find a bay. It was surprisingly busy.

Dee read the digital display screen above the revolving door. 'Prime Rib Special Night. No wonder. Better still, take us to deliveries.' He pointed at the sign.

Todd knew the first part of their arrival had been a piece of play-acting. They were always headed for deliveries. As soon as they were at the rear of the casino he was positive Cyrus and his associates would be waiting. He tried not to let it show as they left the lights of the front reception.

Without thinking, his foot came off the gas and the Prius slowed.

Dee turned to him as they stopped. 'What are you doing?'

A car honked behind them.

Todd very deliberately opened his door and put his foot onto the concrete. 'You can't shoot me here,' he heard himself say.

'Get back in the car.'

He dipped his eyes to the gun. 'You won't. Not here. There're too many people.'

There were. Cars circling and trying to find a space. All eager for cheap rib.

Dee sighed. 'What you gonna do, Todd?' But there was irritability in his voice. 'I won't let you leave. There's nowhere for you to—'

Todd closed the door on him and strode fast. He crossed behind the car and stepped up onto the sidewalk that led to the entrance.

'Stop.' Dee was out of the vehicle too.

He waited for the bullet in his back. There was a crowd gathered at the entrance. They were blocking his access to the revolving doors. He elbowed in and one woman yelled at him. Todd darted into the door and suddenly had to slow his pace as it sealed him in a segment. He shuffled inside and glanced through the glass. Amongst the irate faces, he couldn't glimpse Dee. Was he summoning his colleagues? Dealing with the driver behind?

Todd was in the scented air con of reception. It was teeming with people playing the slots, and forming a line at the entrance to the restaurant. He was safe here. But how long would it take them to locate him? It was unlikely anyone would question him being strong-armed out of a casino. He had to find a payphone. His cell was probably still back at the storage place.

But before he could head for the escalators, Todd checked the revolving door. The crowd he'd muscled through were just on their way in; there was still no sign of Dee.

He hurried back into it, a thin sheet of glass between him and the glares of the disgruntled party before he was back out at the drop-off point. A cab was just emptying out an elderly couple, and he slid by them and hunkered down in the back seat.

'Hey, drop off only. The taxi stand is at the restaurant exit,' a man berated him from outside.

Todd pulled the door shut then leaned forward to the middle-aged, female driver wearing pink-rimmed spectacles. 'Get me back to town and I'll give you a hundred dollar tip.'

'Get out of my cab.' She eyed the injury to his cheek like it might be contagious.

'Please, two hundred.'

'Wait at the stand like everyone else.'

'Name your price then.'

More heated exclamations outside the cab. Cars beeped behind them.

'I'm not getting out of this cab. Please, I really need you to help me here.'

'Get this asshole out of here, Yash,' the driver shouted through her window.

The door opened and a paunchy man in a tired red coat and gold epaulettes stepped back for Todd. 'Right this way… sir.'

# CHAPTER 73

Todd climbed out of the cab, his eyes scanning the faces behind the doorman. There was no sign of Dee. Had he seen him go inside and followed or was he watching the commotion and biding his time?

'Get in line at the stand like everyone else!' the doorman barked. 'Drive on, Rita.'

The cab departed and another rolled up to drop off. Todd loitered there. The doorman studied his face wound with weary eyes. Skirting the vehicle, he made for the busy lot. He was safe amongst people but wondered if Dee's associates were monitoring him on CCTV. He rapidly weaved around the parked cars towards the exit.

'Watch it, prick!'

He froze in front of the Nissan that had broken for him, held his hand up in apology but didn't linger. How far were they from town? Could he walk back? Todd thought twice about leaving via the main exit and approached the high hedge to the left of it. Maybe he could find a gap there.

The hedge was made of plastic, coated by dust and was full of trash that had blown off the freeway. Todd leaned his shoulder against it and exerted his weight. The branches were made of wire, though, and he couldn't break through. He turned, half expecting to see Dee approaching. There were plenty of bodies bobbing about in the darkness but none that were coming in his direction. He trotted to the far corner of the lot and squeezed past a parked orange Silverado pickup.

There was a step up and a small gap where the plastic hedges met at a right angle. Todd thrust himself through but the aperture wasn't wide enough. Grunting, he bent back the artificial branches sufficiently to get his leg out and put his foot on the sidewalk the other side. As he wriggled further in, the metal painfully compressed his tender rib, but grunting, he managed to get his arms then the rest of his body clear.

Vehicles hurtled past on the freeway. Todd quickly found a gap and dashed to the median strip.

Beyond him were pylons and a sliver of moon being smothered by dark blue clouds. Todd sprinted to the other side and slid down the dust bank there. The casino was no longer visible, and he could scarcely see his hand in front of his face. Blood coursed irregularly through his cheek, bruised knuckles, and the lump at the back of his head.

The terrain was going to make his return journey even longer but he knew he couldn't afford to be anywhere near the traffic. His feet crushed cans and plastic bottles, and the aroma of a carcass rotting nearby was suddenly overpowering. Disturbed flies buzzed around him, and he stepped cautiously and tried to stay in line with the rim of the road.

He'd escaped, and even though it was only a temporary reprieve, it at least meant he was free to return to the place Clarence Belle had led him. But would Cooper still be there – if he had been in the first place?

It was going to take him a good while to get back to the outskirts. He couldn't risk trying to flag down a car when Dee was hunting for him. Todd stumbled over a hubcap. He had to speak to Lana. Find out where she was and if the kidnappers had been in touch.

# CHAPTER 74

An attachment was delivered to Messenger, and Lana immediately opened it.

'What is it?' Li Jun turned from his front seat. They were still parked at the gas station waiting for the invitation to arrive.

Lana examined the image and felt anger billow. It was a photo of a crayon picture that was undoubtedly Cooper's. And he'd obviously been told exactly what to draw.

The face had a turned-down mouth and tears rolling from the eyes. The golden curls were unmistakable, and there was a crude cage around his features.

'What is it?'

Below it was an address: '573 Brennington.'

She read it aloud, and Li Jun immediately consulted his satnav. 'It's eleven minutes away, on the west side of the city. Right where the water park used to be.'

'What's there now?'

'Nothing. They shut the place down for redevelopment but I don't think they've done anything with it since.'

'Can you take me there?'

He shot her a look of incredulity. 'You can't go there on your own. You've got to call in the cops.'

'No.' She let him see the snap of Cooper's drawing.

'Jesus, you can't just play into their hands like that.'

But Lana was already typing her response.

'On my way.'

'Lana, just take a moment to think.'

'No more waiting. Cooper needs me.'

'Even if they lock you up in the same cage?'

'I have to protect him.' The raw urgency of that instinct had become overwhelming. 'If they tell me to go someplace, I'm going.'

'Once they have you, how do you protect him then?'

Lana knew he was right. 'But what choice do I have?'

'If you refuse to call the cops—'

She shook her head. 'No cops.'

'Then we head over there and take a good scout around.'

'I'm not endangering you as well. Just drop me off.'

'I'm not going to leave you there.'

'You're not coming with me.'

'Then you can find another ride. Good luck with that this time of night.' Li Jun looked front and folded his arms.

'You know I don't have time for this!'

He twisted his body to her and his features were strained. 'Lana—'

'What if I turn my Skype on? You can listen in and then if it seems like I'm in danger—'

'You *will* be in danger.'

'If it seems like I'm in danger, you can call for help.'

'They'll probably take your phone right off you anyway.'

'Are you going to drive me or not?'

'It's my call?'

'Yes.' She was aware of the enormity of what she was asking. 'Cooper is everything to me.'

'They know that. And they still haven't told you what they want.'

'This is the only way to find out.'

'But Cooper—'

'Don't say it.' She held up the image to him again. 'This is his. I've heard his voice. Cooper is alive.'

'I pray he is. And you have to demand to see him before you agree to do anything they ask.'

'I will.' Lana didn't blink as she held his eye.

He eventually nodded. 'OK. I'll drive you. But the moment I think you're in danger, I make the call.'

'Agreed.' She understood his predicament. But her only priority was getting to where Cooper was.

Her phone buzzed.

*'Already waiting. Cooper's so excited to see you.'*

She silently showed it to Li Jun.

He regarded her sternly. 'You're positive?'

'Of course not, but we have to get going.'

Li Jun exhaled and started up the car.

As they sped down the darkened road ahead she felt an odd sensation of resignation. Lana knew she couldn't control whatever was waiting for her and, despite what she'd promised Li Jun, that she could only do now, what any mother would.

# CHAPTER 75

Todd halted and turned the second time he heard the noise – a scuffing sound, some distance behind him. He strained to listen as a heavy truck passed by on the freeway above.

As its engine faded, Todd discerned gravel rolling down the embankment. He held his breath and attempted to peer through blackness. It was soon followed by plastic being crushed underfoot. That was no scavenging animal. Todd was in the perfect place to be disposed of. He wondered if his pursuer had brought a spade to bury him.

He started striding even faster, further into the scrubland, while trying to keep the dull glow from the road above in sight. He wondered if the crunch of his stealthy footsteps was echoing back.

Pausing to get his bearings again, he spotted a figure at the top of the bank about fifty yards ahead. How many of them were there? He had no choice but to go deeper into the landscape. He'd have to circle around him to get on the freeway to access the city. Todd could see it beyond like a sprinkle of glitter across the horizon. It hadn't got any nearer, and he wondered if he'd miscalculated how long they'd been in the car before they'd reached the casino.

He crouched, sucking in the pain, as the figure descended the gravel and their shape melded with the shadowy terrain. A harsh gust of wind blasted his back and muffled his ears. Then he picked up footfalls to his left. They were skirting the bottom of the ridge in his direction.

Todd stayed low and crept backwards. He had no cover, only the junk and low gorse bushes around him. Perhaps it was better to remain still and hope they went past.

Movement to his right; the first set of feet was already catching up. Should he stay put? If he kept quiet they could only rely on accidentally bumping into him.

The paths of the two men intersected.

'Anything?' He heard the first unfamiliar male voice whisper.

'He's here.' It was Dee.

Todd saw the light from one of their phones arcing around them. He instinctively ducked, even though it was too weak to reach him.

'I said don't use your torch,' Dee scolded.

'What are you doing?'

'Downloading an app.'

'What the fuck for?'

'Infrared viewer. I'll soon spot him.'

Todd froze. There was no doubt he would from that distance. It was unlikely he'd find anywhere to hide behind him. Todd gritted his teeth and gingerly slunk back towards the bank, anticipating treading on a piece of glass and giving himself away.

'Done?'

'Forty fucking dollars?' Dee was mortified.

'You gonna download it or not?'

'Jesus, got to put in my password now.'

Todd moved briskly, hoping their dialogue would mask him.

'Shit. I updated it recently. What the hell was it?'

Todd was in line with the conversation and stopped at the bottom of the slope.

'That's it. Downloading.'

He waited with them, could make out their faces lit up by the screen.

'OK.' Dee extended the phone.

'Wow, that's cool.'

'Can't see any sign of him.' Dee slowly advanced. 'The range on this is shit.'

The other man accompanied him. 'You think he ran all the way out there?'

'If he was scared enough. If he was thinking straight, though, he would have stuck to the road.'

Todd put one foot on the incline and prepared to launch himself up it.

'I think he'd head back into town but we'd better cover both ways.'

'Which way should *I* take?' The other man sighed stoically.

'Which way d'you think?'

'And when should I stop walking?'

'When you run into him or you hear from me. Or do you want to be the one to explain to Cyrus why we lost him?'

'I didn't let him go,' he said quietly.

'Huh?'

'Nothing.'

'Just get going,' Dee chided him.

'As you've got the city lights to guide you, can I get the infrared?'

'Get your own.'

'Come on, Dee.'

'You got a phone, you pay the forty bucks.'

'I'll need it out there.'

'Look, if he makes it into town I'm going to have a harder job finding him than you.'

'Yeah, right.'

'Then I'll be calling on his wife. That'll bring him out.'

'Can't we just do that anyway?'

'No. And he's going to be in the next state if I stand here talking to you all night. Call me if you get lucky.'

The two figures parted, and Todd remained motionless as Dee scrabbled past, panning his camera across the scrubland.

Todd waited for both sets of shoes to fade completely and then clambered back up the bank and carefully onto the edge of the freeway. They hadn't parked a car up, so had obviously crossed over from the casino.

He hadn't put much distance between it yet but didn't feel brave enough to return there to hop in a cab. He'd be caught on the cameras and someone else could still be looking out for him. Todd didn't fancy his chances of flagging down a ride and was sure remaining on the edge of the road would be dangerous.

Pausing for a gap in the traffic, he crossed back over to the other side. The same vista waited for him there but he dropped down the steep gravel. Todd was probably going to make the same time as Dee; he'd wait for him to emerge the other end before slipping into the city behind him.

# CHAPTER 76

KERSPLASH!

Li Jun's headlights illuminated the wholesome family on the huge sign as they frolicked around the name of the water park. But as they drew closer, Lana could clearly see the rust spots in the image.

The arrow below the eroded hoarding pointed left into a fractured road strewn with trash bags. There were no other cars. Not a soul in sight. At least, not that she could see.

'What a grim place,' Li Jun whispered as he slowed the cab.

'Is this 573?'

'No. It's another couple of blocks away and round to the right but I'm stopping here so I can check this out.'

'No.' Lana put her fingers on the handle. 'I'll go the rest of the way alone.'

'Remember our deal.'

'Li Jun, I'm really grateful but there's no time,' she said finally. 'I'll take it from here.'

'I'm calling the cops now then.' He held up his phone.

'Look, give me your Skype details quickly.'

He did and she connected with him. His face appeared on her phone. 'I'll keep this switched on.'

'Please, don't do this,' his image said to her.

'But only if you stay in the car.' She slid the phone into her jeans pocket. He had to be as terrified as she was. But Lana was impatient to get out of the vehicle. Cooper could be nearby. 'Just give me ten minutes.'

'Five. Then I call them.' Li Jun nervously surveyed the wall of fly-tipped furniture and junk piled up on the kerbside.

Lana reached forward and gently squeezed his tense shoulder. 'Thank you.'

He turned, his expression grave. 'Please, take care, Lana.'

As she climbed out of the Hyundai, Li Jun said something else but she'd already closed the door on it.


Lana didn't glance behind her as she started down the middle of the road. Looking right she saw the precipitous water slides. They were deeper black than the sky and behind barbed wire fences hung with signs repelling trespassers. Was Clarence Belle here? The woman? Were they holding Zoe Maddock in the same place?

Something bad was waiting for her, something that had long planned this moment. It didn't matter that Li Jun was back there. She'd been at their mercy since they'd taken Cooper, and everything would happen as they wanted it.

If Mr Whisper was up ahead she knew what transpired would have nothing to do with the scenario she'd always envisaged when she finally faced him. Lana would offer to take Cooper's place. She would beg and be prepared to withstand any pain to see him released. And even though she doubted she would be walking back in the opposite direction, Lana was positive Todd, if he was still alive, would completely understand.

# CHAPTER 77

Lana had covered about fifty yards when her phone bleeped. She halted and took it out of her pocket.

Li Jun's face frowned back at her. 'What is it?'

'I've got an alert. Hold on.' She pressed the button to access her other apps and confirmed it was *Right Where You're Standing*. Lana opened it.

*'Finding nearest murder site…'*

A map of Sequonda, with a pin stuck in it, opened and zoomed in. A yellow outline flashed around the water park.

'Unsolved murder site,' said Stanley de Souza. 'Eight-year-old Toby Morrow went missing on the 9th July 2001 after visiting this water park with his family. After a two-day hunt for the boy his body was discovered jammed behind some pipes in the water treatment unit. He'd been strangled and sexually assaulted. In the absence of any witnesses to his abduction, police never found the perpetrator.'

Lana's neck bristled. Was Toby Morrow another of Mr Whisper's victims?

'After a five-year investigation, the police still had no leads. No additional information.'

Lana closed the app and hit Skype. 'A child was murdered here.' Lana's voice broke. The implication of that sapped the last drops of hope that she might find Cooper alive.

'Come back to the car. You can't go in there.'

Lana shook her head. 'I can't allow Cooper to be with these people any longer.'

'Let the police handle it.'

But Lana had already made up her mind. 'You have to be quiet now.' She put the phone back in her pocket as she came upon a dark cluster of outbuildings.

Concentrating on putting one foot in front of the other she turned right into a narrower street. Water splashed steadily from an overflow pipe above, and a single orange light barely illuminated it.

Kersplash! proclaimed the sign at the end. Parking said the one below it. Lana made her way along the sidewalk, peering into the shadows to her left. Somebody could easily be watching her from there.

But nobody had approached her by the time she reached the end of the street and found the tall, closed corrugated metal gate to the parking lot. There was a door within it, and she shot the catch. The whole frame clanged and it shuddered open. There was no light the other side, and she couldn't see further than the couple of feet of asphalt that were vaguely lit by the orange glow from behind her. Dense black lay beyond.

Now, pure fear halted Lana in her tracks, and she wondered if Li Jun could hear the thud of her heartbeat. She didn't step over the lip. Once she did, they had her.

The geography of the car park was suddenly revealed as tall lamps with spherical heads flickered on, delineating the empty spaces. They knew she was here. But the bulbs didn't make her feel any safer. Lana was now completely exposed.

The arms of the four ticket machines were raised as if in greeting.

Lana wanted to tell Li Jun what was happening, but it was obvious she was now being monitored. There were cameras positioned on poles around the bays. Was that how they were tracking her or were they hiding somewhere near? Her eyes scoured the area but there was no cover until the darkened reception the far side.

Lana inhaled and stepped through. She left the door in the gate open and walked self-consciously to the ticket machines. Passing through the nearest she noticed her reflection growing in the smoked panes of the one-storey building ahead. Soon she could see her own anxious features as she squinted for movement inside.

The glass gave nothing away but a vague glow from within. She put her hand on the metal handle, and her empty stomach clenched as the door swung outwards.

There was still a vague aroma of chlorine, and a bulb glowed over the small ticket desk. A board above the entrance to the park displayed an admission price.

MAX THRILLS FAMILY PASS $18

Lana momentarily hung back. Should she wait here? They were aware she'd arrived. But when she tried the doors ahead they were unlocked too, so she stepped onto the ramp that led down into the middle of the water park. Reaching the bottom, she edged towards a paved circular area where there was another sign.

MEETING POINT

She took in what she could of her gloomy surroundings. The male and female changing rooms were to her left, as was a unisex wash area. Rivulets of rust stained the dirty tiles beneath each metal shower head. The shapes of the slides and tubular chutes towered over her, the proximity of an old childhood fear underscoring her rising terror.

Somebody was here somewhere. But she doubted that Cooper was nearby. Was she just being shown another part of Mr Whisper's history?

'Lana,' a throaty voice called urgently.

She cast her eyes about, but couldn't work out which direction it had come from.

'Lana,' it repeated.

She fumbled her phone out of her pocket. Li Jun's face was tight and strained. Lana held her finger to her lips. What the hell was he doing?

'Lana!'

There was somebody else in the car with him. She could make out their shoulder behind him and their hand around his throat as the image shook. Then she saw the blade.

'Li Jun!'

'Lana, run!'

The blade went into his larynx up to the hilt, and his mouth hinged open. The metal slid out of his neck, and Lana saw dark liquid flow over his collar before the blade was jabbed repeatedly, the force hinging his head back. The attacker was holding Li Jun's phone steady.

'Stop!'

The knife kept stabbing him, his suspended expression of panic lolling forward and bouncing as the fist kept driving the handle and the jolts squirted blood out of his lips.

# CHAPTER 78

Lana's feet shot her back up the ramp. But when she pulled on the handle of the door she found it had been locked. She tugged on the other, to no avail, and attempted to peer through the window. All she could see was her own petrified reflection. Lana took a step away and whirled around, expecting to find somebody standing behind her.

Nobody was on the ramp or in the circular meeting point. She was trapped. Now she had to go into the water park. The dizzying revulsion prompted by what she'd just witnessed made her put a hand on the metal rail to steady herself and clamp her other over her mouth. She painfully heaved once and waited for the vomit to come. But there was nothing inside. Lana retched again and groaned as it harshly tightened her abdomen.

She'd brought Li Jun to the park. He'd tried to make her see sense and call the police, but she'd refused. Lana should have sent him away. Now he'd died helping her. She recalled their conversation in the car about how everything he did was for his daughter.

Lana wiped the moisture from her eyes. She thought of Li Jun bleeding out in the car. He'd been stabbed so many times; he couldn't have survived such a vicious attack. But she still had to call an ambulance. Where was her phone?

She spotted it lying on the floor of the meeting point and trotted warily to it.

'He wasn't police!' Lana yelled for the benefit of anyone in earshot and scraped it up.

'Which service?' a female operator asked.

'I need an ambulance. A man is dying.' She told the operator where they were.

'On its way. Can I take some details?'

The police wouldn't be far behind but she had no choice. 'Just get here fast!' She hung up. 'Cooper!' she shouted at the slides. Lana whipped around again but nobody was coming down the ramp. 'Give him back to me!' She could feel control slipping and balled her fists. If they were capable of doing that to Li Jun, an innocent stranger, why would they think twice about her son?

'Help!'

Lana spun back to the park, blood and breath suspended. Had she really heard it?

'Help!'

It was definitely Cooper's voice.

'Cooper!' She ripped his name from her throat. 'Where are you?'

'Up here!'

Lana looked to the skyline of slides. 'Where!' She waited and he didn't respond. 'Cooper!'

'At the top of the serpent slide! He says you've got to come get me!'

'I'm coming!' Lana had already left the meeting point and was crossing the overgrown grass to the conglomeration of rides. She knew she was being drawn deeper into the park but figured they could have already killed her by now. Whatever they wanted her to do, she'd do it. She turned on the torch of her phone.

She was at the metal stilts of the first ride.

POSEIDON'S SPIRAL

She shone the beam to the left and saw another slide. Ducking under one of the struts, she made her way swiftly to it.

'Cooper, keep talking!'

Lana waded through the thick, pungent grass. Something scuttled away to her left. 'Cooper!'

'He says hurry!'

She reached the next and could just make out the shape of its snake head against the wisps of cloud in the inky sky. 'Are you up there?' She followed one of its tubular coils until she came to the foot of some metal steps. 'Cooper?'

Pocketing the phone, Lana climbed.

# CHAPTER 79

'Keep talking to me, sweetheart!'

But Cooper didn't reply.

Lana tripped on a metal step. They were designed for the small stride of a child and, as Lana attempted to take them two at a time, she stumbled again, smashing her shin against a sharp iron edge. She winced but tuned out the pain and dragged herself up by the handrail.

The top of the slide came into view. It was the solid black mouth of a tunnel, and she couldn't see anyone standing there. 'Cooper?' She hesitated at the last step and could hear a sob echo from within. 'Say something.'

He didn't speak, but there was a low hissing sound below her. They'd gone down the slide, and she could hear them lightly buffeting the sides of the tube. She recalled standing at the bottom of the one at Blue Crest. She wouldn't allow Cooper to be snatched away from her again. Should she follow? It was the quickest route down.

Lana covered the platform and gripped the metal bar across the top of the opening. She swung back and forth on it twice then used the momentum to catapult herself into the slide.

She shot into pitch-darkness, the twisting coils and speed immediately disorienting her. It was stifling inside and reeked of mould. It was the aroma of her worst childhood moment, the cloying scent of the bootless circuits she'd made as she'd tried to escape the construction pipe.

Lana cried out as she was tossed about and her elbow smacked against one of the turns. Under her own exclamation she thought she made out Cooper's. 'Cooper!' she called to reassure him. What was waiting for her at the bottom? She couldn't be too far behind them. Lana lifted her head but couldn't see beyond her.

She started to slow, but then felt the angle getting steeper and accelerated again. Lana discerned the silhouette of her feet as she hurtled towards weak light. But the circular end to her journey looked like it was obscured.

In a split second Lana saw the adult figure standing in readiness for her arrival, and the white plastic netting. Her body slipped inside it, and she landed hard on the tiled area in front of the slide.

Lana turned onto her front and tried to crawl out of the bag, but the opening before her closed up. A drawstring had quickly been pulled tight. Lana spotted Cooper. He was kneeling nearby with his hands tied behind his back and a grubby rag stuffed into his mouth. Dirty tears streaked both cheeks. He howled something at her that was muffled by the gag, and Lana attempted to undo the tightened circle in front of her to reach him.

'OK, let's calm ourselves down.'

She immediately recognised Clarence Belle's voice from the interview room.

'Let me go!'

Lana was about to roll away from him inside the bag, but his weight was against her waist. He'd straddled her and was pinning her on her front.

'Ssshhh. No one to hear you.'

As if in response to his statement, the sound of a siren broke into the moment and their fitful breathing was briefly suspended.

Lana felt his legs tense either side of her. 'You'd better run.'

'No need for that. They'll be busy tending to your friend.'

'He was just my driver. He wasn't the police.' Lana met Cooper's petrified features through the netting. 'Run!'

He shook his head in terror.

'I'll deal with this man! Run and don't look back!'

He still didn't budge.

'He's a bright boy, Mrs Cross. But she's right, Cooper. You can split if you like. I'm going to be very busy with your mother.'

His eyes darted right but he shook his head again.

Belle sat further forward so his weight was on Lana's behind.

She felt the air being squeezed out of her but her fingers still grappled with the drawstring.

'Leave that.'

Something solid struck her knuckles and the agony shot up her arm. She saw Cooper react as if it had been transferred to him.

'Take me, just let him go!'

The siren stopped.

Belle shifted forward and pushed her face into the tiles so she couldn't make any more noise. 'I told you not to call them.'

'He needed an ambulance,' she spat through her crushed lips.

Lana tried to protest further but tasted dirt as he applied more pressure and her teeth scraped against porcelain.

'Ssshhh.'

They could hear a vehicle door slam nearby.

Lana calculated the ambulance couldn't be too far away. She'd passed the fenced-off rides shortly after she'd left Li Jun's car. She yelled into the floor.

'Don't.'

She did it again, as hard as her flattened lungs would allow.

'We're gonna have to agree to disagree then.'

A leaden object slammed into her scalp, unconsciousness blotting out Cooper's stifled scream.

# CHAPTER 80

It felt as though it had taken Todd the whole night to get back to Sequonda, and as he dodged around an abandoned shopping cart in the dark, he nearly stepped off into nothing. He scrambled backwards. It was the end of the bank, and a riverbed lay below. He picked up a rock and threw it in to see if the blackness at the bottom was actually water. It wasn't. And the rock had taken way too long to land. It would be suicide to clamber down the sheer face. An illuminated bridge went over the dry gully into town; he wondered if Dee was waiting the other side in exactly the same position.

Maybe Todd had beaten him. If he had, lingering here would give Dee the chance to catch up. His face was so cold he hardly felt the injury to his cheek but his ankle pounded from hiking along the bank at an angle. It had been much easier than trying to traverse the debris, though.

He peered over the low wall that ran from where he was crouching along the bridge but couldn't see any movement the other side of the freeway. Should he climb over it now and make his way down the two-foot wide platform beside the traffic? It would take him at least five minutes to cover the straight road, which meant he would be a very easy target. He couldn't allow himself to get picked off when he was so close.

Fuck it. He would go. Todd couldn't afford to be out of touch with Lana any longer. He had to find out what was happening with Cooper. He stood but saw something shift in the shadows the other side.

He ducked back. Reversing along the perimeter, Todd glimpsed over the edge from a different part of the wall. No sign of anyone. Had he imagined it? He fixed his gaze on the deep shadows. Still nothing. Could he afford to risk it?

He had an idea and started to snatch up some tattered sheets of black polythene lying along the bank. Then he rapidly gathered any plastic bottles within his reach. He righted the shopping cart and put the bottles inside. Todd wrapped the sheeting around him like a hooded shawl, concealing his face. Could he pass himself off as a hobo?

Keeping low and watching for any signs of motion the other side, he negotiated the cart beside the wall. Still no trace of Dee. He took a deep breath and lugged the cart over it but the platform was too narrow for the wheels. He swung himself over and started to push it along the busy road.

The keen breeze threatened to tug the sheeting away, and he clutched it to himself while he directed the cart along the gutter.

A car beeped at him and gave him a wide berth as it passed.

He counted twenty paces and could see the smoked glass façade of a hotel up ahead. As soon as he'd crossed the bridge, he could lose himself in the city.

He shot a look over his shoulder. Dee was striding down the narrow platform the other side. Their eyes locked. Another thirty feet and Dee would draw in line with Todd. He must have been watching and broken cover shortly after he did. He turned to face forward again.

There seemed little point wheeling the cart if Dee had seen through his disguise. But Todd kept driving it on and glanced back again; this time to see what traffic was coming. An SUV was approaching and behind that was a construction truck. Todd kept going until the engine noise was loud but still far enough away to brake. He shoved the cart sideways into the SUV's path and heard the vehicle's tyres screech followed quickly by the truck's.

He checked to see they were OK. The halted traffic now blocked Dee's view of him. Todd sprinted. He pumped his arms and the polythene sheeting flew off him.

Horns angrily beeped at Todd but he didn't look back. There was a profusion of neon up ahead. He was almost inside the city. Soon he would be amongst people and have plenty of places to hide.

He gritted his teeth as each step pounded in his chest. Had Dee drawn his gun and was just steadying him in his sights? Todd wasn't even a quarter of the way across the bridge. And he had nowhere else to go but in a straight line.

# CHAPTER 81

Todd checked on Dee's position. His pursuer had trotted ahead of the truck and SUV and was now standing still, waiting for a gap in the traffic, to cross over. The SUV swerved around the cart as it continued to roll to the middle. Todd bolted ahead. If he could use the time Dee was going to take to cut over to his side, he might open up a decent enough gap. But did Dee care about discharging his weapon in front of witnesses?

'Fucking asshole.' The SUV driver had rolled his window down as he reached Todd.

He didn't acknowledge him as the vehicle kept up with his pace.

'You could have killed us.'

Todd held up his hand in apology and then fixed the driver in desperation. 'Will you give me a ride?'

'What?' The balding thirty-something man was incredulous then recoiled from Todd's facial wound.

'I'm being chased.' He tried to gauge the expression of the driver's wife, but she was hidden in shadow. 'By that guy.' He jerked his thumb back at Dee.

He'd just hit Todd's side of the freeway and was stalking down the platform, one foot on and one off.

The driver glanced in his mirror as he approached.

'Roll up the window,' his wife ordered.

The driver regarded Todd uncertainly.

'He's probably a criminal,' she hissed.

'Please, just take me over the bridge. I swear I'll jump out there.'

The construction truck was attempting to get around the SUV, and honked.

The driver squinted at Todd then in his mirror again.

'Don't get involved,' she snapped.

The driver opened his mouth to say something.

'Craig, roll up the window and drive on!'

His features were apologetic as he complied and pulled away.

The truck surged by soon after.

Todd raced for the end of the bridge, praying that a cop car would pick him up. Dee had a clear shot now. He attempted to zigzag as much as he could but there was only a tight space between him and the traffic zipping by. A painful stitch jabbed at his rib, and he wheezed in fumes as intermittent motorists blared at him. He thought of Cooper and drove himself on.

As he entered Sequonda, the gunshot he was expecting still hadn't come. Todd stepped up onto the wider sidewalk in front of the hotel and turned. Dee was standing still, about a hundred yards away. He was on his phone. Cars beeped at him but he seemed oblivious to them.

Todd charged towards the reception of the plush hotel set back in its own courtyard. A hefty doorman was there to greet him, and he suspected his luck wasn't about to change. The suited, crew cut beefcake had obviously seen where he'd emerged from and eyed him suspiciously.

'Excuse me, sir?' he said tersely as Todd slowed and tried to walk casually past.

'I just need to use the phone.'

'You're not a resident.'

'Please, this is an emergency.'

'Sorry, I can't allow you to go in there.' There was actually some sympathy in his voice as he examined Todd's bloody cheek and dishevelled appearance.

'I'll be one minute. You can walk me in there if you have to.'

'Can't leave my post.'

Todd swivelled briefly back to the sidewalk. No sign of Dee. 'Please, my child's life is at stake.'

His words had the opposite effect on the doorman. The civility drained from his expression and it was clear he thought Todd was a con artist. 'Just move on now.'

'I'm telling the truth.'

'You're not going in. Try somewhere else with your story.'

Todd knew that, short of assaulting the doorman, there was no way past. 'Can you at least tell me where I can find a phone?'

The doorman pursed his lips and narrowed his eyes.

Todd's darted behind him. Still no Dee.

'There's an amusement arcade two blocks down. You should find one in there.'


Stopping for a few seconds made running again seem twice as arduous. Todd could see a few people on the crossing ahead. He had to mingle, make it harder for Dee to make a move. But he was sure he'd called for backup. He only needed to keep Todd in sight in the meantime. If he didn't give Dee the slip soon, they'd quickly have him cornered.

# CHAPTER 82

'Mom, wake up!'

Lana could feel Cooper's hands gently shoving her back.

'Open your eyes!'

But momentarily, she only wanted to savour the warmth of her son's body as he burrowed himself up against her as he did on the rare mornings when she didn't have to leave early and the three of them could lie in.

'Mom!'

Lana jerked awake. She was lying alone on a leather couch. She sat bolt upright and dizziness prevented her from immediately standing. 'Cooper?' Her lips cracked. The dream's sensation drained away. She flinched as she touched the open wound on her scalp. Whatever Belle had used to strike her, had taken off a layer of skin.

She took in the room. Where the hell had he brought her? Lana was in a small, old-fashioned lounge – TV, two armchairs, a cocktail cabinet, and another housing china figurines. The air smelt of furniture polish, and heavy cobalt curtains were drawn. She got shakily to her feet and tugged one.

Outside was a short front yard and a meadow beyond, bordered by a pine forest. Nobody was in evidence. The sun was just rising. In the muted light, she could see the trees gently swaying in the wind.

Lana lifted the window halfway and the cool breeze blew in against her legs. She could easily escape. Was this a trick? Quickly crossing the room to the door, she tried the knob. It swung out.

She was looking into a tight hallway and when she glanced left she could see the stairs and kitchen. 'Cooper?' She called louder than she intended, and his name triggered a throbbing in her temple.

Lana stepped into the hallway and listened, dread escalating. There had to be a reason she was free to move around. She padded up the Indian runner carpet to the front door and opened it.

She breathed the cool, grass-scented air. There were three steps down and a path to a slatted white gate that led to a narrow road in front of the meadow. The house didn't have any neighbours and there were no other homes nearby. Leaving the door ajar she made her way to the kitchen. It was a compact room with an old stove, microwave, refrigerator, and wooden table surrounded by four chairs. No sign of a phone. She squinted through the panes of the back door to the long yard hemmed by firs.

A soft thump from above her.

Lana rolled her eyes to the ceiling. 'Cooper?' This was all wrong. Why wasn't she still restrained, and what had happened to Clarence Belle? She crept back to the hallway and hesitated at the bottom of the stairs. 'Who's up there?'

No response. She heard a louder thud. She had to go up there. It could be Cooper.

'Answer me.'

Lana went to the kitchen drawers to find a weapon. They were empty. She returned to the hallway, put her foot on the bottom stair and touched the white gloss-painted handrail. This had to be a test, or a trap. But she couldn't leave the house without finding out.

As she cautiously ascended she could feel her shin pulsing from where she'd fallen on the serpent slide. Stealing herself, she took the last six stairs quickly until she was standing on the landing. A door was immediately in front of her, and three more in the passage to her right.

There was a light switch to her left, and she flicked it on. The bulb in the shade above her buzzed as she waited for further sounds. Should she just work her way through the rooms?

A creak.

That definitely came from the room immediately ahead of her.

'Who is that? Say something.' Lana's muscles tensed as she anticipated the door opening. Would Belle emerge and bludgeon her again?

A muffled voice said something incoherent then whimpered. Sounded like a child.

'Cooper?'

They were clearly in pain and unable to speak. But were they alone?

Lana cocked her ear to the panel.

The moaning continued.

Lana gripped the handle, pulled it down and pushed into the room.

# CHAPTER 83

As she peered inside, Lana remained in the doorway. The curtains were drawn, so the only illumination was the light on the landing. A slice of it was across the bed in front of her. A woman was curled into a ball amongst the pillows. She choked against the white cloth gag that was in her mouth, and Lana could hear the bedstead bump against the wall.

Was there someone else in there? Lana's eyes swept the room while she pushed the door wider, and her hand scrabbled for a switch.

She babbled at Lana and yanked on the handcuffs that attached both her wrists to the bedstead.

Lana found the switch and turned it on. 'Don't be scared.'

The woman pointed frantically to the nightstand on the other side of the bed. There was a set of keys there in front of the lamp. The woman clearly couldn't get to them because she'd been cuffed to the far bedpost.

Still surveying her surroundings, Lana went to the nightstand and snatched them up.

The woman was slim, in her thirties, and wore a peach sweatshirt, jeans, and dirty, white crocs. Her dark hair was pulled tightly from her face in a ponytail, and her eyeballs bulged in panic as she tried to communicate with Lana through the gag.

Lana knelt on the bed and released the knots at the back of her head.

'Please.' The corners of her lips were raw and she ran her tongue over them. 'Unlock me.'

'Zoe?'

The woman frowned. 'No.'

But there was something immediately familiar about her.

The woman remained in a foetal position, as if expecting attack. 'Who are you?'

'Lana Cross, I was abducted and brought here. I woke up downstairs and heard you.'

'How come you're not cuffed like me?'

'I don't know. Maybe this is a game.'

'A game?' the woman spat. 'My daughter's been taken!'

# CHAPTER 84

'My son, Cooper, was snatched on Monday.' But Lana could tell the woman was still afraid of her.

'Angie,' she said guardedly but didn't move from her position.

Lana knew why she looked familiar. 'Angela Hamlin?'

'Yes,' she answered suspiciously.

'I tried to contact you through the website you set up about Theodore Lane Hewett. I spoke to your father yesterday.' She recalled the conversation with him and how he'd been waiting for his daughter and granddaughter. 'I think Lane Hewett and Clarence Belle are working together.'

'Who's Clarence Belle?'

'He brought me here. The police arrested him but he escaped custody. He has my son. When were you taken?'

'Yesterday, I think. But I was drugged so I don't know how long I've been here. Unlock these… please,' she pleaded warily.

Lana leaned over her with the key. 'How?'

'I was lured to an old water theme park.'

Lana could see a wound crusting on the woman's scalp. 'Brennington? That's where I got mine.' She dipped her head so Angie could see where he'd struck her. 'All this time I thought it was just my ordeal.' Lana fought to suppress the beginnings of another attack.

'A woman had my Stacey at the top of the slide.' Angie inhaled unevenly.

'I know this story. She's working with Belle. Hold your hands apart.'

Angie obeyed but Lana could feel her gaze on her the whole time she fumbled the key in the lock. She freed the cuffs and got off the bed.

'Looks like Belle has orchestrated all of this for a reason.' Lana examined the deep red marks around Angie's wrists. 'You kept your trip to the water park from the police?'

She rubbed them and flinched. 'They said it was the only way I'd keep Stacey alive. You brought the cops in?'

'To begin with. Until I was told what would happen.' Lana took a few paces back to give her space.

Angie woozily stood.

She supported Angie and felt her tense. 'Please, let me help you. If you've been through what I have then I think we need to trust each other.'

Angie met her eye. 'I know my Stacey is alive,' she declared. 'I can feel her.'

Lana recognised the conviction she'd been clinging to since Cooper had disappeared.

Angie straightened. 'So where is this place?'

'I don't know.'

Angie crossed the room and opened the curtains.

'I took a look outside but I don't think anyone else lives nearby.'

'We can just walk out of here?'

'Yes. That's how it appears anyway.'

Angie squinted at the nightstand and then the carpet. 'You seen a pair of specs around?'

Lana scanned the windowsill and the floor.

'Must have lost them when he took me.' Angie sucked in air through her teeth.

'You OK?'

'Dying to pee.'

A clatter from the room next door.

Lana and Angie exchanged a look. They waited.

It came again.

Lana stole onto the landing and regarded the sealed door to her left.

Angie followed her out and put her hand to her chest when a metallic rattle came from within.

Lana gripped the cold handle.

Angie nodded at Lana that she was ready for her to open it.

There was another darkened bedroom the other side. Lying on the mattress was a second handcuffed woman.

# CHAPTER 85

The woman's name was Violet Campbell. She was brawny and in her late forties, had tattoos on both her substantial arms and a bowl cut of bleached blonde hair that closely framed her face and revealed dark roots at her scalp. After Lana unlocked the cuffs, the older mother told them that she and her eight-year-old daughter, Rosetta, had been snatched two days previously. Again, she'd been warned about involving the police and directed to the water park before ending up in the house.

'I remember somebody coming into this room and injecting me. I was too weak to fight back.' She attempted to rise, but her legs wobbled and she sat down again.

'Take it easy.' Lana put her hand on her hot back.

Violet was perspiring heavily and her cheeks were flushed. She was wearing a long burgundy knitted tank top, leggings, and sandals.

'Wait.' Lana stood and headed back out of the room.

'You want me to come with you?' Angie knew where she was going.

'Stay with her.' She carefully opened the next door along. It was the bathroom – shower over the tub, toilet, and a sink. The tap was dripping. No toothbrushes or other signs of occupation.

She investigated the last room. Another bedroom. Lana switched on the light. A third woman was lying cuffed and petrified.

'Jesus.' Angie followed Lana into the room.

Lana tried to calm the girl's undiluted terror as her pupils flitted between her and Angie. 'Let's get you free.'

The girl was petite and her curly ringlets of red hair were stuck to her pale, tear-stained face. She was barefoot, her violet tie-dyed dress had ridden up her body, and she'd soiled the bed.

Lana located the keys on the nightstand. She removed her gag and released the cuffs. They both placated her until her breathing had slowed.

'What's your name?' Angie gently wiped hair from her freckled face.

'Zoe.'

Angie turned to Lana.

'Zoe Maddock.' Lana nodded. 'I'm glad to have found you. The police are searching for you and Cayla.' The poor girl seemed emotionally exhausted. 'How old are you, Zoe?'

'Twenty-four.'

'And Cayla?'

She wiped mucous from her nose. 'Six. Are you police?'

Lana shook her head.

'I'm Angie Hamlin. We've been in touch. You sent your details to my website.'

Lana explained how they all shared the same plight.

It took a while for Zoe to absorb what she was saying. 'What are we supposed to do then?' She glanced nervously about, as if someone might be listening in.

Angie found Zoe's flats on the floor and handed them to her. 'We don't know.'

Zoe slipped them on her feet. 'I have to find Cayla.' Her words were slurred, and she almost pitched forward.

Lana and Angie supported her and sat her up straight.

Violet was standing in the doorway. 'I checked downstairs. Looks like this is us.'

Zoe asked where they were and Lana told her they didn't know and brought her up to speed.

'I need water.' Zoe stood.

'Let's go downstairs to the kitchen.' Lana gripped her arm as she walked unsteadily to the door.

'Gotta use the bathroom.' Angie trotted out.

Violet was waiting nervously outside, and Lana introduced her to Zoe before they descended to the hall.

# CHAPTER 86

'Recognise this place at all?' Lana studied Angie, Violet, and Zoe as they contemplated the view from the open front door. The only sound was the light breeze and a few birds in the pines the other side of the meadow.

Violet shrugged.

'No,' Angie answered.

'Me neither,' Zoe replied. 'One of us could go get help.'

'Help?' Angie snorted. 'He knows we can't leave. We're in exactly the same position as when he brought us here. He has our children. We just have to wait for whatever's next.'

'D'you think he's watching us now?' Zoe's eyes were on the fringe of the trees, and she crossed her arms around her bony frame.

Violet breathed in fresh air. 'Probably.'

The four of them remained silent as they took in the panorama that, under normal circumstances, would have seemed idyllic.

'Let's get the water,' Lana suggested. 'Close the door.'

They made their way into the kitchen. Pulling out the chairs the three others seated themselves while Lana found some tumblers and shakily filled them from the tap.

'Tell me what you know about Clarence Belle.' Angie accepted hers from Lana.

'Who's Clarence Belle?' Violet gulped the liquid down.

Lana told them about how she'd spotted Belle in the park and confronted him, his arrest and escape from police surveillance, and his female accomplice. 'My husband was following him; if he'd still been behind him in the water park he would have helped me.' Had Todd lost him or, even worse, been attacked by Belle?

'And that's who brought us all here?' Zoe ran her fingers nervously up and down her glass.

'I recognised his voice when he attacked me at the slide.' Lana took a sip, and the cool liquid felt like it evaporated before it reached her throat. 'And he's been using an app to point me towards a notorious child killer.'

'An app?' Angie thudded her empty glass on the table.

'*Right Where You're Standing.*'

'Isn't that full of bogus information?' Zoe's hand quivered as she lifted her water.

'I was using it to try and find the man who nearly snatched my son last year.'

'Somebody tried to abduct your child before too?' Angie's features were grave.

'Yes.' Lana dropped into her chair.

'The same with my Stacey.' Angie licked the sides of her sore mouth. 'A man attempted to pull her through the railings in the skateboard park in 2012.'

Lana's attention shifted to Zoe, though she knew her story as well.

'A stranger tried to take Cayla out of her pushchair the same year, but my neighbour saw him and he fled.'

Violet nodded. 'Someone had a shot at talking my Rosetta into getting into his car in 2011.'

Lana drained her glass as the episode they all had in common sunk in. 'Did any of you ever see the man who attempted to take your children?'

The other women shook their heads.

'Last year I fought the man who tried to lift Cooper out of my back yard. I bit him. Tasted him. And I can still taste him every time I wake up playing that moment over and over in my head. My son called him Mr Whisper. I thought it was Cooper's nickname for him, but it was what everybody used to call him when he was a caretaker at Hasbland High School. His real name's Theodore Lane Hewett.'

The other three tensed.

Angie nodded. 'I set up a website about him. Zoe knows all about it. He was convicted for murdering three girls after somebody tried to take my Stacey. I'm sure it was him, and I wanted people to know how many other local crimes he could have been responsible for.'

'I've been to your website,' Violet said. 'But I never contacted you. I didn't want my name on it, or my child's. Seemed like a red rag to a bull.'

'He was locked up in 2013, though.' Zoe took another sip of water and fixed Lana. 'He couldn't have tried to take *your* son last year.'

Lana informed them of her visit to Jeanette Lane Hewett and how she'd been to Coitsville.

'Was Lane Hewett there?' Violet asked.

'Lane Hewett was sent there because he had dementia and was low-risk. The management didn't want to discuss him, but a member of staff told me they were trying to cover up his accidental death.'

'Death?' Angie frowned.

'According to the guy I spoke to, he drowned in the boating lake. But I think he's alive.'

'So what the hell's he got to do with this Clarence Belle?' Violet sighed.

'I don't know. And I've found nothing about him online.' Lana regarded the red marks around Violet's wrists.

'So, nothing's changed.' Zoe sagged. 'And nobody here knows where we are.'

Angie got up from the table and tested the back door. It was unlocked and swung open. They all took in the tiny unremarkable yard beyond. More trees lay behind it.

It occurred to Lana that perhaps the house was another slice of Lane Hewett's life. Like Hasbland and Coitsville. Was it part of the journey Clarence Belle had sent her on?

'A police helicopter could land out there and it still wouldn't do us any good.' Angie closed it again.

Lana's new company prompted her to remember the image of the three graves she'd been sent. 'I should show you all something.'

A phone rang. They froze.

'Where is it?' Violet stood.

'Sounds like it's coming from the lounge.' Lana hurried into the hallway. She entered the room she'd woken in as the phone continued its familiar warble. She tugged the drawers of the ornament cabinet. Empty.

The others joined Lana and helped her search for it. She opened the cupboard beneath the TV cabinet. Inside was her iPhone. Trembling, she took it out.

'Hello?'

'Lana.' There was no mistaking Clarence Belle's voice.

'Where are we?'

'So you've got acquainted with the others. Why don't you put me on speaker?'

She hit the button and held out the phone to them.

He waited before continuing. 'Am I speaking loudly enough for you all?'

None of them responded.

'As you've all been so patient, I've decided I'd like to give you one last opportunity to see your children.'

Lana watched the stunned expressions of the three other women mirror her own.

# CHAPTER 87

"'One last opportunity?'" Lana repeated the three words that had silenced everyone else.

'That's right.' His tone was impatient; as if it were a detail he didn't expect to need clarification. 'And I need you to continue displaying the same degree of cooperation in the meantime.'

'What the fuck are you saying?' Angie snapped.

Lana held up a palm to her. It was pointless being aggressive towards him.

'You know better than that, Angie. Stacey's not going to thank you for it. And she's been more than obedient. In fact, she's been a joy.'

Angie closed her eyes and suddenly the only sound in the room was the women's irregular breaths.

'What d'you need us to do?' Lana attempted to swallow.

'Getting to that. Firstly, I'd just like to tell you what a stand-up job you've all done with your children. They're a real credit to you. Rosetta – she's an old head on young shoulders.'

Violet glowered at the phone.

Lana wanted to drop it. Didn't want to be connected to the voice she was sharing. She could feel it vibrating down her arm.

'She's been like the mother hen of the group. Took it on herself to look after the others.'

'Let me speak to her,' Violet demanded.

'Cayla's the one who's found it the most difficult. She's got patches of this rash down one side of her back and on her arms. Is that an allergic reaction?'

Zoe's shoulders heaved, and she clamped her fingers over her mouth.

'Maybe it's just her being overwrought though. Being in a strange place with unfamiliar faces. Rosetta became very protective of her. It's been interesting watching them interact. Makes me wonder how they would have been if they'd met in a playground. Perhaps they wouldn't have all gotten along as they did. Rosetta, she would have played with anyone. The others, I'm not so sure.'

A tear trickled over Zoe's fingers.

'Cooper's been the most difficult to read.'

The women's attention was on Lana now.

'But he reminds me a lot of myself when I was his age. Withdrawing as soon as things get difficult. Artistic though. Something I never really excelled at. Hard to believe how personalities can be fully formed so early on.'

'Enough!' Angie exclaimed.

They could hear Belle breathing.

'Tell us what we need to do.' Lana coldly formed each word.

Belle took his time answering. 'OK, you've all been indulging me so I owe you that.'

Indulging? Lana couldn't conceive of a mind that would describe what they'd all been through as that.

'And I'm sure I can trust you to follow my last instructions as carefully as you have the previous ones.'

'Are we going to find them alive?' Angie clenched her jaw.

'Lana?'

'Yes?' she answered flatly.

'I want you to help me answer that question, and I'm going to have to trust you not to use this phone for anything but the app.'

She tried to focus on what he was saying but, like the others, was still considering how he'd indirectly responded to Angie.

'You remember the app?'

'Yes.'

'I want you all to cross the field, enter the wood via the gate and then search out the nearest murder site. It'll be uploaded shortly. It's only a short distance from where you are. Got that?'

'Got it.' Lana's wrist shook. The phone felt like a dead weight in her hand.

'They'll be waiting for you.'

'The children?' Violet spoke up.

But he'd cut the call.

# CHAPTER 88

Todd caught his breath in the upstairs bathroom of the indoor produce market and washed his cheek with a paper towel. There was an ugly, swollen slit underneath the caked blood. Outside he could hear the stallholders setting up for business.

He hadn't been able to reach Lana from any of the payphones he'd located. And when he'd eventually made his way back to the house where Belle had led him, he'd found the door open but the place empty. Now he was positive a guy was following him. It wasn't Dee but maybe it was his backup. He didn't know if they'd seen him duck inside the market.

He cracked the door to the bathroom and peered out. Amongst the people erecting their pitches under the slatted wooden roof he couldn't see a sign of the man who had been behind him.

He waited, scanning the owners distracted by struts and canopies until he was satisfied he could emerge. He made a beeline for a girl in a plum beret selling chalk art on slates who had just finished having an animated conversation on her iPhone.

'Excuse me.'

She looked up at him, a warm smile on her face.

It struck Todd she assumed he was a stallholder too. It was too early for customers. Better he pretended he was and not a crazy from the street. 'Sorry. I'm new.' He extended his hand. 'Todd, I'm running the artisan bakery.' He vaguely gestured over her head. 'Big ask, I know, but the battery on my phone has just died and I need to make a really urgent call.'

'Oh.' She took in Todd's unkempt appearance, then his scar and glanced around at the other stallholders.

He held up his palms. 'I just need five minutes and I'll stand with it right here. I'll toss in a rosemary focaccia…'

'Sure.' She pressed her finger on the button and handed it to him. 'Really appreciate this.'

First of all, Todd tried Lana again. Still no response. Now there was no choice. He couldn't delay any longer.

He turned his back on the girl after dialling the operator. 'Sequonda PD, please.'

# CHAPTER 89

Lana had been sorely tempted to answer Todd's call but assured the other women she wouldn't and walked in silence after it had stopped ringing. At least it meant he was still alive. Or perhaps it was Belle's trick to test her obedience. She couldn't risk Cooper's safety now.

They'd left the house and made their way across the dewy meadow. Now they were at the wooden gate to the forest. They passed through it and entered the cool shade of the pines.

'OK.' Lana tapped the *Right Where You're Standing* app. The others gathered around her.

*'Finding nearest murder site…'*

But the white grid remained on the screen.

'Should it normally take this long?' Zoe brushed a red curl from her face.

'There's hardly any reception.' Lana was about to move back to the gate when the map appeared. 'We're in Braddock.'

'Braddock?' Violet said incredulously.

'You know it?'

'We haven't come far. That's only on the outskirts of Sequonda.' Angie squinted.

A pin appeared in the map and it zoomed in to an area surrounded by a flashing yellow outline.

A box popped up. *'(Posted today - awaiting authentication)'*

'What does that mean?' Zoe asked.

'It means the information hasn't been substantiated.' Lana shuddered as she guessed what was about to display itself.

More text appeared:

*'Chute Pines Bunker. Contains human remains believed to belong to victims of Theodore Lane Hewett (awaiting authentication).'*

'So, is this a murder site that only Clarence Belle knows about?' Nobody answered Zoe.

'Let's go.' Violet was first to head off.

'Please, tell me.'

Lana couldn't bring herself to utter what she and the others expected to find there.

# CHAPTER 90

Chute Pines Bunker was four minutes away. Lana and the three women hastily crossed a crumbling bridge over a railway track. None of them were dressed for the chill in the morning air.

The four of them slowed as a man walking a husky rounded the corner at the end of the bridge.

'Careful,' Angie cautioned as he approached.

The paunchy man was wearing a camouflage hunting jacket, and a dark beard covered the bottom half of his face. As he got nearer, Lana studied his features.

'Let him pass,' Violet said through the side of her mouth.

The group parted as he reached them.

He smirked as he breezed by. 'Morning.'

They all stopped to observe him tramp to the other side of the bridge. As they watched him go Lana knew they were all thinking the same: it didn't matter whom they came into contact with along the way, they were on their own and had to do exactly what they'd been instructed if they wanted to see their children again.

But was what Belle had posted on the app another cruel piece of torture or a fulfilment of their worst fears?

They were now travelling along a wide, straight trail through tall fragrant pines each side. They were much denser further on and their route headed straight into a patch of darkness at the end. She examined the map. The bunker lay just beyond, in the north of the forest. She googled it.

Ex USAF underground munitions storage facility used in WWII when nearby Oakley Farm was converted into an ordnance depot and headquarters. Chute Pines was chosen for this purpose due to its proximity to railroad.


'Looks like we're not just going to find a hole in the ground.' Lana showed what she'd found to the others. They stopped to read it.

'So we should be preparing ourselves to walk into a trap?' Zoe anxiously scanned the trees around them.

'How?' Angie tightened her ponytail. 'He's luring us underground.'

'If he's hurt Cayla, he won't be coming out of there alive.' Zoe's expression appeared as if she was already projecting herself to that moment.

'If he's there, whatever's about to happen, it will all be on his terms.' Angie started striding ahead again.

'Wait. We need to stick together!' Violet called after her.

'I only care about my Stacey.' Angie didn't look back. 'You do what you want.'

'Wait!' Zoe yelled.

They watched her ponytail bounce as she marched on.

Lana considered calling after her, but knew it was futile. With her daughter's life at stake, there would be no reasoning with her.

'But we have to decide exactly what we'll do if, when, we get there…' Violet tailed off and bowed her head, her bowl cut of bleached hair hanging away from her grim features.

Lana knew none of them could countenance the outcome they all dreaded was awaiting them. 'Come on. We can't let her go in alone.'

They all trotted to catch up with Angie and continued down the path into the shadows ahead in silence.

# CHAPTER 91

The female stallholder was hovering nearer to Todd. He'd been put on hold by the desk at the precinct while they tried to locate Detective Huxtable. 'Sorry, just one more minute, I promise.'

'Someone's meant to be calling me back.' She sounded peeved.

Todd's eyes wandered the market for any sign of the man he thought had been behind him on the street.

'Huxtable.'

'Detective Huxtable, it's Todd Cross.' He didn't wait for a reaction. 'Have you heard from Lana?'

'Only to tell me that you were both OK but that was yesterday. Look, there's been a development. Styx36 has just posted a new murder site on *Right Where You're Standing*. I've sent my men over there to check it out and am just on my way—'

'Where?'

'It's time you gave yourself up, Mr Cross.'

'Where?'

'Just find an officer and surrender yourself.'

Todd immediately cut the call and turned to face the stallholder. 'I just need it for one more thing. Please, I can't impress on you how important this is. I need to quickly download an app. Can you put in your password so I can?'

'No. I really need it back now.'

'I'm begging you. This is my child's life at stake!'

She nodded, stricken by his sudden outburst.

Todd searched for *Right Where You're Standing* in the app store and hit the 'get' button. It asked him for the password, and he handed it to the stallholder. She quickly entered it.

'Thank you, thank you.' Todd watched the clock face steadily fill up as it downloaded to the phone.

# CHAPTER 92

'There.' In the weak sunlight spilling in through the canopy above, Violet had spotted the door.

Nobody spoke as they made their way through brittle leaves towards it. It was set into a large corrugated panel about ten feet square. The bunker's roof slanted down into the ground, the rest of it hidden beneath the soil. The iron was stained green with lichen and there was a thick carpet of moss on the turf surrounding it. But half a semicircle of sooty earth had been exposed where the door had recently been swung open.

Angie put her fingers into the recess of the handle.

'Wait up.' Lana peered into the gaps of the trees. A few birds warbled low in the branches above. No signs of movement but it would be easy for anyone to remain concealed behind the trunks and dense shadows.

'For what?' Angie pulled on the door and it juddered out. She hesitated, though, as an even deeper darkness beckoned. 'Use the torch on your phone.'

Lana closed the app and switched on the light. It illuminated the top of a flight of concrete steps leading down.

Angie put her hand out for it.

'I'll go first.' Lana stepped past her but immediately felt the apprehension of what lay below congeal inside her.

'We stick together,' Zoe's voice echoed back.

The others followed Lana down.

The air smelt of soil and engine oil. Lana counted fourteen steps before she hesitantly placed her foot on the floor. She played the beam along the narrow corridor in front of them. About a hundred yards away was a weak yellow light. 'Up ahead,' she whispered and moved forward so the others could gather there.

'Maybe one of us should have stayed outside. Just in case he tries to lock us in here,' Violet said breathlessly.

'Go back if you think you'd be able to stop him.' Angie pushed past Lana.

'Angie,' Zoe hissed.

Lana directed the torch around the ceiling and created magnified shadows of the cobweb tendrils lining the corrugated walls. There was a panel of bulbous switches to her right. She flicked them all down but nothing happened. 'If there was power, there isn't now. We can only go one direction, though.'

They followed Angie to the end of the passage, and she gestured for them to stop as they reached the tight right turn. They craned round to find a single oil lamp burning inside a recess in the wall. Beyond it was a circular, tiled tunnel.

'Stacey!' Angie yelled.

Her voice bounced away from them.

'Jesus, how big is this place?' Violet rubbed the tops of her arms.

But it wasn't the scale of it that dismayed Lana. It was the fact it sounded so empty and dead. Was Cooper really down here?

'There's another light up there.' Zoe pointed.

It looked like a second lamp had been positioned further down the tunnel. They continued, and Lana could feel the temperature drop. She recalled the waterway she'd explored with the police officers. How many abandoned places like this had been exploited by people like Clarence Belle and held the answers so many parents were searching for?

As they rounded the curve of the tunnel the lamp came into view. It was hanging from a rusty nail, and its eerie, guttering light flickered over the dirty tiles.

'Quickly.'

The four of them froze.

'We all heard that then.' Violet glanced over her shoulder.

The word had barely been spoken. They waited but the tunnel was silent.

Lana shone the torch around. 'No one up ahead. Sound travels in places like this.'

'Where are you?' Angie said defiantly.

'Keep walking,' the sibilant voice quietly replied.

What other option did they have? They advanced past the lamp but now Angie wasn't pacing ahead. She stuck with the other three.

Lana's torchlight gradually lit up the end of the tunnel and a square concrete entrance. Beyond was solid blackness. They halted and listened. Not a single sound; the air seemed briefly anaesthetised.

Lana cast the torch down to the floor and broke the atmosphere as her feet scuffed forward. She stepped through the doorway and knew they were no longer in a tunnel. The echo of her footsteps sounded less enclosed.

'Lana, wait!' Zoe exclaimed from behind her.

A motor started up.

# CHAPTER 93

Lights overhead flickered on, and Lana quickly absorbed their surroundings. They were in an expansive, high-ceilinged room about eighty feet square. There were no other doorways bar the one they'd entered through. The height of it was obviously to accommodate munitions, but it was now vacant. A large concrete cube, about four feet high, with a heavy metal chain attached to it was in the middle of the floor.

Beyond it, in the far right corner, was the source of the engine noise. It was a large, red-painted, antiquated generator on wheels that was plugged into a power box on the wall. Clarence Belle was standing beside it. He was wearing a denim shirt and pants, thick-soled leather boots, and an ebullient expression on his tightly packed features.

The purring generator made a series of grating sounds, and the bulbs briefly dimmed.

Lana wanted to harm him. Wanted to tear lumps out of his smugness for what he'd done. But she suspected it was pointless even considering overpowering him. There was still no sign of the children. Nothing had changed, and his body language said he seemed confident they'd understand that.

The lighting dipped and brightened again, and Lana regarded the dingy area to the rear and left of the room. A two-seater couch and an armchair were positioned on a square of carpet and illuminated by a standard lamp with brass tripod legs.

'What the fuck is this? Where are the children?' Angie skirted the others and approached Belle.

He held out a palm. 'If you want to see them again, you won't come any closer.'

Angie kept walking but slowed.

'That's four steps too far. Back it up.'

Angie halted then reversed a couple of paces.

'Keep going. Now the rest of you come join her.'

Lana was the first of them to respond, and the other two followed.

Belle ambled over to the leather couch and sat down in the middle, his frame perching on the edge. He contemplated the four women with his darting gaze and ran a hand through his straggly auburn hair. His features looked jaundiced in the glow of the buzzing strip lights above, and he gripped his knees tight, as if he was on a ride. 'You didn't have far to come from my family home.'

Nobody reacted.

'From the house, I mean. Not a great distance, was it? Far enough, though. Sufficiently isolated so that nobody can hear. I was in that little front yard with my sister when Theodore Lane Hewett stopped in his car.'

Lana didn't turn to the others. Knew their silence meant his statement had momentarily blindsided them as well.

'I was four at the time. He was still a teenager.' His eyes flitted between theirs. 'Ended up here with him. Had a set-up just like this.' He opened his hands at the furniture.

'I don't care what your fucking twisted motives were for doing this. Where's Stacey?'

Belle lifted an eyebrow at Angie. 'I thought you'd be a little more interested in this story, Angela. You've collated so many for your website. Don't know how long it lasted. But we got out, me and my sister.' He leaned back, leather squeaking, as he allowed them to digest what he was telling them.

Lana remembered the woman's voice on the phone when she'd last spoken to Cooper.

'We ran home, through the forest and over the bridge. We told my parents everything that happened. Where we'd been taken and what he did to us. They comforted us and put us to bed with a glass of warm milk. The next day they told us we had to treat it like a bad dream; that we had to forget all about it. They didn't want people to know we'd been damaged. They were ashamed of us. Never called the police. Just stood by and did nothing.'

The generator rattled again.

Belle shot it a look as the lighting blinked. It settled down. 'I'm telling you this in case you think I can't empathise with what your children have been through. But, believe me, they'd be better off dead, so they don't have to carry all that guilt and shame into adulthood.'

'You son of a bitch.' Angie marched over to where he was sitting and knelt against his chest so that he was pinned against the leather. 'You tell me right now before I kick the shit out of you!'

Belle didn't attempt to extricate himself and remained calm. 'Do what you want to me. But is that going to be worth never seeing your child again?'

Angie balled her fist and punched him in the middle of his face.

'Angie!' Lana yelled and covered the distance between them. 'Stop!'

Twin streams of blood poured out of Belle's nose, down his chin and onto his shirt. 'And there's only one way you're going to be *able* to see them.'

Angie gripped his jowls in her fingers, forcing the blood out of his nostrils. 'Tell me!' His face trembled as she squeezed harder and her nails went in.

'Enough!' Lana locked her arms under Angie's and levered her back.

'Get the fuck off me!' Angie wriggled from side to side.

Lana released her and stood back with her hands raised. 'Think of Stacey. This isn't helping.'

Angie rounded on Lana, keyed up and lips drawn.

'I'm not going to allow you to risk everything we've been through.'

'Lana's right,' Violet placated.

Zoe nodded. 'Please.'

Angie's chest heaved, and she pointed at Belle. 'Tell us now.'

He got to his feet and nodded behind them. 'That's the only way you'll know.'

They all swivelled to the concrete block.

'What are you talking about now?' Angie spat.

Belle wiped blood away with his sleeve. 'Take a closer look.'

Zoe and Violet went tentatively to the cube.

Lana's attention returned to Belle as he inspected the blood on his shirt cuff. 'Tell us.' She knew she wasn't going to be able to control her rage much longer either.

'You'll work it out.' He sniffed blood and mucous back into his nose.

# CHAPTER 94

As Lana reached the block she could see the cuffs attached to the heavy metal chain dangling from its side. There were four sets, one loop of each already secured to the thick links.

'No way.' Zoe took a pace back and spun with fearful eyes to Belle.

'What is it?' Angie was behind Lana. 'Fuck you.'

His gaze slid to each of them as they all faced him, an implacable expression primed and ready. 'Let me save you time and discussion and tell you this is your only option.'

Angie's fists were solid again. 'Maybe I'll keep beating it out of you.'

Belle stood his ground. 'I just told you what I've already endured down here. D'you really think that's going to work? You can beat me to a pulp and I'm not going to tell. But every time you strike me you can cross off the name of one of your children.'

Angie's body remained rigid.

'Angie, let's take a breath,' Lana cautioned. 'He has an accomplice, remember?' She raised an eyebrow at Belle. 'Your sister?'

Belle didn't react.

Angie whipped her head to her. 'I'm not handcuffing myself to that.'

'What other choice do we have?' Violet said quietly.

'And what do you think's gonna happen when we do, huh?' Angie jabbed her finger at Belle. 'He's trapped us down here, and once we're chained up he can do whatever he wants. He still hasn't told us if our children are even alive.'

'I haven't said they're dead, have I?' He licked the blood off his mouth.

'Are they?' Lana fixed him.

'I'll only answer that question once you're wearing the cuffs. Not a moment before.'

Only the puttering generator filled the silence.

'And if we refuse?' Zoe asked, ashen.

'You walk out of here. Go home. Call the police. Do what you want. The cops are probably already on their way. I intend to take my life today, and then you'll never know where your children are. This is going to be your one and only opportunity. Think very carefully.'

Lana doubted he was bluffing. Prison was the only place Belle could go now. He had nothing to lose. 'We've all cooperated this far. We give you our word we won't touch you again.' Lana knew she had to delay their moment of submission. If he couldn't be reasoned with, she needed to buy time while she tried to think. 'Angie?'

Angie appeared poised to assault him again.

'Angie,' Lana repeated sharply.

'Please,' Violet pleaded.

Angie eventually nodded.

'I believe you're as good as your word, Angela. And I understand everyone's feeling tired and emotional. But the fact is, this is strictly non-negotiable. You will *all* cuff yourselves to the chain before we go any further.' Belle folded his arms.

The four women remained motionless.

'And I wouldn't be exaggerating to say there's a time factor that should really accelerate your decision-making process. Be a shame if your hesitancy now soured everything at the last minute.' He sucked his bottom lip.

Violet stepped forward and picked up the end of the heavy metal chain. It scraped against the concrete floor as she put the first cuff around her wrist and clicked it in place. 'You heard him,' she said and blew the fringe of her bleached hair off her sticky forehead. 'All of us.'

Zoe was next. Her thin arms hefted the heavy length of chain next to Violet and snapped on her cuff. It weighed her down, and she struggled to stay upright.

'Angie?' Lana examined her profile, which was still set defiantly towards Belle.

She blinked a few times and then turned slowly to the other two, shaking her head as she joined them.

Lana immediately followed, seizing her cuff the same time as Angie and sliding it around her wrist.

The metal locking shut seemed to satisfy Belle, and the motor of the generator thrummed as he regarded them. 'Thank you.' There was a vague trace of relief in his voice.

Lana didn't look down at her cuff but kept her other hand covering her wrist. She'd complied the same time as Angie but hadn't locked it. She hoped the click of Angie's loop had sold it, though.

Belle grinned, his split lip an angry red.

# CHAPTER 95

'Where the hell are you taking me?' Todd leaned forward to the cab driver in exasperation.

'Don't sweat it,' he replied as the taxi shuddered out of a hole in the dirt track. 'Freeway is murder this time of the morning.'

Tall hedges pressed in at the Honda Civic from both sides, and Todd met the middle-aged driver's eyes in the mirror.

'I promise this is the quickest route. Came up to Chute Pines when I was a kid. Used to be a service road went all the way to it, but it's overgrown now. I still know where the entrance is, though.'

The hedges dropped to a lower level, and Todd glanced right to the freeway. The traffic was almost at a standstill.

'What'd I tell you?'

Todd could hear sirens and made out three patrol cars crawling through the middle of the jam. They looked like a slow-moving zip. It was going to take them some time to get clear.

A few moments later the cab pulled up at the left side of the road.

'Climb that gate and keep straight.'

Todd was already out.

'Hey, you gonna pay me!'

He vaulted the gate and dropped down onto the forest floor. Todd took out the iPhone the stallholder had let him borrow and checked his position on *RWYS*. He was close.

The quiet of the forest was suddenly hacked up by a deafening sound above. Todd looked skyward and saw a police helicopter sweeping overhead. But the tall trees were so tightly packed it didn't look like it was going to be able to land.

Until the patrol cars made it through the traffic, Todd was alone. He pumped his arms and wondered what he needed to prepare himself for when he reached the bunker.

# CHAPTER 96

'Theodore Lane Hewett used cuffs. I can still feel them cutting into my wrists.'

'Where's Cayla?' Zoe blurted, hysterically. 'We've done what you asked.'

'I'm coming to that.' He sauntered towards them.

'You said there was a time issue,' Angie snarled. 'Start talking.'

But Lana knew they were now the captive audience he wanted. What was he about to do to them? They couldn't fight back. At least, that's what she wanted him to think.

'Do you understand why bringing you here was necessary?' His gaze dropped to examine the chain.

Lana had to keep him distracted from her loose cuff. 'If Lane Hewett did those things to you here, why would you ever subject another child to the same experience?'

Belle was happy to evangelise. 'I spent a lot of years watching the lives of others as an outsider. You can't participate when something like that happens to you. And as I grew up I came to the same conclusion that others who hide a moment so loathsome in their past do. The only way to get that innocence back is to take it.' He paused, inhaled, and his shoulders straightened, as if the truth of the statement had given him strength. His eyes went to the floor. 'Toby Morrow was my first. At the water park. I took him from the serpent slide. Thought what I needed was sexual. Like it was for Theo. But when I was done I found it wasn't.'

Lana registered Zoe sagging. Was she about to pass out?

'When he was incarcerated I went to see Theo in prison. Wanted to figure out why I couldn't feel the release I needed. I never told him who I was. Couldn't tell him I wasn't the same frightened person he'd taken. That I'd transformed beyond all recognition. Said I was a journalist writing a book about him. He enjoyed me peeling away his brain. Liked the prestige. It was the one way I could ask him the most intimate questions. How I could look at what had happened to me square in the face. By the end of six months, I understood him. And I understood what I'd done even more. Theo had been abused by his mother and father. He taught me about the inevitability of what I did. What I wanted to keep doing.'

Lana recalled what Jeanette Lane Hewett had told her about her husband's prison visitor.

'He told me about the ones who had escaped him. Even after all his planning. He used to tell his wife he was going on weekend fishing trips. But he was casting his net wide. Theo was meticulous about which ones he would take. That's what I learnt from him. He watched them for weeks. But some still got away. He told me he was going to find a way to get back to them. When I heard about his escape from Coitsville, I knew he had. He didn't have dementia. That was an act. He did have colon cancer, though. Called me after he'd broken out and said he was starting again. Casting his net. Last time we spoke he sounded so sick. He told me about Cooper. He was his last child.' Belle slid his gaze to Lana. 'Said he'd failed, that he wouldn't ever finish and give me the ending to the book he wanted. That was the last I heard from him. But I knew all of the children who had escaped Theo. Exactly who they were.' He studied each woman in turn. 'And it struck me, after what he'd taken from me, they were the one thing left I could take from him. He was weak, as I had been down here. But I was strong. I could finish. Be his final chapter. And my own. They'll always be his victims, though. I'll always be as well.'

'You *are* a victim.' Angie's voice was tractable now. 'And I understand everything you've told us but you have to stop this now. It's not too late. Release us and tell us where they are.'

Lana knew what Angie was doing. 'She's right, Clarence.'

He regarded her sharply.

'If you harm them then Lane Hewett will have succeeded at what he did to so many other innocent lives. But you can still save them, and you can still save yourself.' But Lana couldn't detect a glimmer of indecision in his expression.

'No,' he said resolutely. 'It's too late for that.'

'Let them go. We'll all walk out of here. We'll never tell anyone about this, will we?' Angie looked at the others for agreement.

Belle leaned forward and swiftly snapped the loop tight around Lana's wrist.

Lana waggled her hand in the cuff. It was now securely attached to the chain.

'Maybe Cooper should be first.' Belle slid the cuff keys out of his pocket, showed them to Lana and then hurled them to the back of the room.

# CHAPTER 97

Belle headed towards the couch. 'Sorry you didn't get to enjoy the free vacation I set up for you, Lana, but I had to entice you to Sequonda somehow. And it's been fun using your morbid fascination with *Right Where You're Standing* to introduce you to my mentor. I'm sure the fact Cooper was Theo's last child made you special to me as well.'

Lana felt her circulation pumping hard against her restraint. Belle had planned as meticulously as Lane Hewett and lured her hundreds of miles to a place she never conceived would be the home of the man she'd been searching for.

'This has been a logistical *and* emotional challenge.' He reached the couch but didn't sit. Instead, he put his foot against the edge of the seat and shoved. It trundled away on its wheels, and he did the same with the armchair. 'Not Theo's furniture but I've tried to replicate as closely as I can.' He bent to the edge of the faded carpet and whipped it back. It revealed a square hole in the floor that had been crudely plugged with a piece of wood about four feet square.

Lana gripped the chain tighter as he tugged it out.

'But this is definitely his pit.' He dumped the wood beside it. 'Can't remember how long he kept me cuffed down here while he dealt with my sister. But when he yanked me back out I was just glad to be in the light, whatever he did to me.'

Lana could see the top of a ladder against the rim of the pit.

Belle turned his back to the hole and stepped down onto the first rung. 'Bear with me.' He steadily dropped inside and the top of his head vanished.

Lana focussed on where the keys had landed and pulled on the links. There was no way the solid block could be shifted even an inch.

Angie tugged hard on the cuffs. 'Can you get free, Zoe?'

She had a slender wrist, but her loop was locked tightly around it. She struggled uselessly.

'We've got to get loose. Even if we have to break a bone.' Angie forcefully jerked hers, the metal cutting into her skin.

'Angie!' Violet was horrified.

Angie didn't stop and hissed in pain as she continued to wrench against the chain.

Their activity ceased as something appeared at the top of the ladder. It was a tied canvas sack, thick yellow rope in several knots about the neck.

Belle grunted as he heaved the weight over the edge of the hole and climbed out after it.

Lana could tell the sack contained a small body, and her breath halted as he pushed its motionless bulk clear.

'Either I'm out of shape or your son is.' Panting, he reached into his back pocket and slid out a slender-bladed knife.

The graves she'd been sent an image of had to be down there. 'No!' Lana yelled.

But Belle knelt, hitched the sack upright and sawed at the rope.

Lana heard the chain rattle frantically as the other women fought against it. They knew they couldn't escape but none of them could stand by and watch. As Belle's parents had.

The rope fell away, and Belle seated himself with his legs around the sack and tugged the top of the canvas past the face it concealed. It was Cooper; he was gagged with a chain, his eyes closed, and his pale expression blank.

He looked like… Lana wouldn't accept it.

The generator made a grinding sound. The lights went out and came up again, illuminating his empty features.

Belle slid the sack down as far as his shoulders. 'Theo had been talking to this one for days before he made his move. Had taken a real shine. Said you put up one hell of a fight, Lana and gave him a bite on the leg to remember you by. But Theo was weakening then. I guess that's when he realised he couldn't do it any more. Said his cancer was eating him up but I think he'd spent too much time in prison.' Belle gently wiped away Cooper's fair hair where it was plastered to his forehead and placed the tip of his knife to his ear.

# CHAPTER 98

Stanley de Souza's voice played back in Lana's head: *'Police were unnerved by the casual nature of Lane Hewett's testimony and how he recounted pushing the tip of his blade into the ear canals of victims as the hardest thing he's ever had to do.'*

'Don't disappoint me now.' Belle shook Cooper.

His head waggled but he didn't stir.

'Cooper!' Lana was only vaguely aware of the agony as her body leaned back, her locked arm stretching as she tried to twist her wrist clear of the cuff.

'Cooper, your mother's here. Don't you want to see her again?' Belle slapped his cheek gently. 'Open them.'

Cooper's eyelids fluttered, and he was staring directly at Lana.

'Cooper, I'm here. Look at me!' She could see Belle's legs tense around her son to hold him place. He was still drowsy. Did he even know she was there? 'Cooper, wake up! Try to get free!'

But Cooper's numb expression didn't alter.

'Ketamine. Theo's drug of choice. He used it on me here. If he hadn't, I'd have remembered everything he did to me.'

The generator clattered again, and the strip lights shimmered.

'Please, I'll do anything you want!' Lana screamed.

A muffled cry for help came from the pit. A girl's voice.

'Cayla!' Zoe wailed.

'They're all rising and shining now.' But he was still considering Lana's plea. 'You'll do anything I want?'

She nodded vehemently.

'But you already are.'

Lana watched Cooper's eyeballs roll back in his head. 'Cooper!'

'Fucking son of a bitch!' Angie yelled.

The others knew they were about to be subjected to the same.

Lana caught a movement to her left. Violet had a paring knife in her hand. Had she brought it from the house? Her attention darted back to Cooper.

Belle nudged him harder. 'Come on, I want you bright and bushy for this.'

While he roused Cooper, Violet slipped free of the chain.

Lana bit her lip hard as Belle remained distracted and Violet slunk stealthily forward, blade gripped firmly in readiness.

# CHAPTER 99

Violet changed course. There was scarcely time for Lana to question how she'd released herself but, as she watched her dart towards the crumbling side wall, she assumed she was attempting to steal her way around to Belle.

But when the generator stopped stuttering, and the lights intensified again, she saw the other figure that Violet was stalking.

It was Todd. He was using the intermittent darkness to sidle along the wall to where Belle was holding Cooper.

Lana swivelled to Angie and Zoe who were frozen and had their gaze locked on Violet. She regarded the cuffs Violet had slipped from. The free loop was hinged open. 'Todd!'

But Violet had already reached him. He turned to silence Lana, and she lunged. He tried to block her but, as his body angled away, the knife went into the side of his neck. He staggered.

Lana sank to her knees, cold realisation choking her exclamation. Violet hadn't escaped. She knew how to release the cuffs.

Todd toppled onto his side.

'I thought Daddy was still in the hospital.' Belle watched him writhe on the floor.

'Todd!' Her weight dragged at her arm connected to the chain above.

'Nice interception, Mya,' Belle addressed Violet. 'You OK?'

She nodded and glanced back to where Lana, Angie, and Zoe were still tethered.

'Did you know he was coming?' Belle narrowed his eyes at Lana.

Hers darted between Cooper's lolling face and Todd. Dazed, she shook her head.

'This is Mya. Styx36 and Ambuscade1 to you, Lana. She knows what it's like to suffer down here too. We both brought this place out with us. Today, neither of us will leave. It's a shame that we've shared for too long; when I strangled Toby Morrow she was the only one who understood.'

Lana recalled the image that had been sent to her. There were three children's graves in the pit. Not four. Mya was Clarence Belle's sister. She'd been planted amongst them, had been monitoring them every step of the way. And she'd been the first to put on the cuffs. She could hear Angie cursing her, but as she hauled hopelessly at the cuff again, Belle still held his blade to Cooper's ear.

'Let's end this quickly, Clarence. The cops will be here any moment.' Mya ran a hand through her bowl cut of bleached hair. 'Work faster. I'll finish him.'

'Careful.' Belle was studying Todd.

But he'd stopped moving and Lana could see blood pooling around his shoulder.

# CHAPTER 100

A red puddle flowed away from Todd. He could feel his blood pumping against the knife blade in his neck and was looking along the concrete floor to Mya's sandaled feet. Beyond her he could see Lana kneeling beside the other two women. He struggled to discern what the voices around him were saying.

Lights fluttered above. Or was his grip on consciousness weakening? He wouldn't allow himself to black out, let alone die, after he'd got so close to saving Cooper. Lana was helpless. Had to get to his feet.

'Listen,' Mya hissed.

Todd strained to hear above the thudding of his heart.

Under the rumble of the generator was another steady beat. Faraway footsteps.

They slowed and stopped.

'The sound carries down here,' Belle whispered. 'They're still in the first passage.'

'They'll be able to hear the generator.' Mya's sandals moved out of Todd's field of vision.

His dark pool expanded again.

'Help us!' A female voice.

Lana's? But sound was getting smudgy.

Todd cracked his eyes again and saw the figure standing in the doorway behind Lana. It was Dee, and he was holding a handgun.

*Stay awake.*

Black silence snapped shut.

# CHAPTER 101

'Jesus, what the fuck is this?'

Lana had never seen the man with the gun before.

He quickly took in the room. 'Looks like I'm the only person with one of these.' He indicated the weapon as he approached the block.

Lana turned back to Belle. He was still holding the knife to Cooper's ear. They'd already been told what would happen if they opened their mouths.

'Please help us,' Mya whimpered.

The generator stumbled and the light faded.

Should she warn him about Mya? Belle only had to exert the slightest pressure with the knife. She had to stay silent. But would Angie and Zoe? Their children were still in the pit. If he was shot, Belle couldn't harm them. Would they jeopardise Cooper to save them?

'I suggest you leave, friend.' Belle's eyes darted.

'Please…' Mya took a step towards him. 'Help us.'

The gunman pointed the firearm directly at her. 'Just hold your horses.

'Turn around and walk out of here.' Belle struggled to his feet and propped Cooper against his legs, the blade still against his eardrum.

The gunman swept his weapon back to Belle. 'Sit yourself back down.'

Belle didn't comply. 'Your gun doesn't have any currency here.'

'How d'you figure that?'

The generator triggered the strobe of the overhead lights again.

'She's with him!' Zoe howled.

Mya chopped at the gunman's wrist. The pistol bounced across the floor and they both chased after it.

But as the gunman reached her, she spun with the weapon raised.

The gunman hoisted his arms. 'OK. OK. Who the fuck are you people?'

Belle nodded, relief registering. 'Shoot him, Mya.'

Mya cocked the hammer.

Todd was on his feet, pulling the knife from his shoulder.

'Behind you!' Belle warned.

Mya swung the gun to Todd but he'd already plunged the blade deep into her back.

# CHAPTER 102

Lana watched Mya crumple and the gun slip from her hand. It skated along the floor and came to a standstill by the cube.

'Mya!' Belle sounded like a wounded animal.

The gunman squinted behind him to the weapon.

Todd stumbled forward and collapsed against him.

'OK, good work, Todd, but you're getting blood on the suit. Get the fuck off me.'

But Todd clung on as he nodded at the weapon in front of Lana.

Lana crawled under the chain as far as she could go and reached out to it. The gun was about a foot away.

'Quickly!' Angie dropped to her knees as well.

The gunman clocked Lana grappling for it. 'OK, don't go playing with that.'

Lana saw Todd's elbows lock around the gunman as he tried to hold him fast. She stretched as far as her arm would allow, but the barrel was still two inches from her fingertips.

'Leave it alone! Get the fuck off me, Todd.' The gunman grabbed a handful of Todd's hair and tried to snap his head back.

Angie shifted towards Lana so she wasn't restraining her but it made no difference. Lana's body trembled as her cuffed arm started to come out of its socket. She glanced over her shoulder to see Zoe contemplating them, her expression vacant.

'Move forward!' Angie shrieked. She seized Zoe by the leg and toppled her.

The chain slackened and Lana reached again. She touched the gun. But as her fingers encircled the end of the barrel, Mya slithered over to it, the handle of the knife still protruding from her back. She tried to wrench it clear, but Lana kept it pressed to the floor.

Then Mya was on her feet, and she stamped on Lana's hand. 'Let it go!'

Lana screamed and had to.

'Fucking bitch!' Angie clutched Mya's leg.

Mya keeled on top of Angie, and they both fell backwards, dragging Lana away from the gun with them. Mya disentangled herself and shunted forward on her buttocks. Lana followed but heard the noise of metal scraping on concrete as Mya snatched up the gun. Lana lifted the chain and slung it around Mya's throat.

As she gripped the links and tugged on them, Todd held her gaze as he slid down the gunman's body and was repeatedly slugged in the head. His attacker kicked his face and twisted to where the four women were lying in a heap.

Lana felt the handle of the knife in Mya's back against her chest. She jerked the chain and thrust herself forward, and Mya gasped as the blade went in deeper.

But Mya raised the weapon at the gunman as he approached. He halted, his hands raised.

'Mya!' Belle's voice was nearby.

Lana couldn't see Cooper. All that was visible beyond Mya was her extended arm and the gunman frozen and waiting for the outcome of their fight. Mya had to be dealt with first.

Mya tried to keep the gun trained on him, but Lana could feel her body slackening. She yanked on the chain and the handle dug painfully into her sternum. With one last tug and thrust she screamed.

Mya's arm remained straight.

Panic swept the gunman's expression.

Tears blurred Lana's eyes. The handle was stabbing her. She rammed herself against it again.

The gun tumbled from Mya's hand.

Lana felt her go limp. But she wasn't about to release her. Where was Belle?

The gunman picked up the weapon. He turned and behind him she could see Belle had attempted to surprise him and was only paces away. His knife was gripped tightly in his fist.

'No currency here?' The gunman aimed and fired.

A chunk of Belle's head launched from him as his body dropped.

But Lana's attention was fastened on Cooper.

'Cooper!' She shoved Mya aside, ignoring the agony of the handle unsticking from the indentation in her chest. 'Cooper!'

The gunman was speaking, but she wasn't processing what he was saying. All her brain was telling her was that Cooper was lying half out of the sack, his eyes closed. But his mouth muttered against the chain. His lips were moving.

# CHAPTER 103

When Todd regained consciousness, he was being carried up the steps of the bunker. He could feel a strap tight across his chest, and his first instinct was to try to remove it. His heart surged. He remembered Dee battering his head, but had no recollection about what had happened afterwards.

'It's OK. Don't try to move.' A youthful girl was above him, and he could smell cinnamon on her breath.

'Cooper.' He unstuck his lips and felt them throb.

'Don't struggle. We're just getting you out.'

A thud behind him. The gurney jolted and cold daylight and air was in his face. He could hear voices around him. A uniformed police officer brushed by.

'You've lost a lot of blood. We're going to put you in the ambulance now.'

'Let me see my family.' But he glimpsed Lana. She was by the entrance to the bunker with a tanned man with white hair in a leather coat and the two other women who had been chained up. They were standing around three children.

One of them was Cooper. Something burst inside him.

'Dad!' Cooper left the group and ran to him.

Todd touched his son's warm head. Instantaneous tears streaked hot down the sides of his face. 'How you doing, Squidge?'

''K.' His eyes roamed Todd's swollen features with alarm.

Todd nodded. 'So am I now.' He brushed Cooper's dirty cheek. 'Really. No problemo.'

Lana's hand was suddenly gripping Todd's, and it felt boiling.

'Todd.' Her expression was tightening but it already looked like she'd been crying.

'You both OK?' He tried to sit up but couldn't.

'They've checked Cooper over. He's fine, though. So are the other children.'

He dizzily regarded them. 'Others?'

'Mrs Cross, we have to get him to the hospital now.'

Lana stepped back. 'Stop talking. I'll explain later. Don't worry about us.'

'Listen.'

Lana bent forward to hear him.

'What happened to the guy with the gun?' He didn't want to use his name with officers around.

Lana glanced back to the man in the leather coat to check he wasn't in earshot. 'Said he never wants to see you again. Then he disappeared before the police arrived.'

'You don't know who he was,' Todd instructed her.

'That's right, I don't,' she said significantly.

'Mrs Cross…'

Todd was being lifted. 'He just walked in with a gun.'

Lana leaned closer. 'That's what I just told Detective Huxtable.'

Todd released her as he was slid into the ambulance.

# CHAPTER 104

Lana stood stiffly up from her uncomfortable plastic chair in the private intensive care room and stretched. It had only been two days since she'd last attended Todd's bedside after he'd been pushed from the bridge. She looked down at the plasters over his inert features. He'd spoken to her for five minutes after they'd admitted him but now the painkillers had knocked him out. That was for the best. The doctors had said he'd lost a lot of blood and that the transfusion hadn't been a second too early.

She'd held Cooper until exhaustion had claimed him, and he was now fast asleep in the TV lounge. The doctor wanted to thoroughly examine him when he woke but her parents were watching over him in the meantime. They'd jumped on a flight as soon as she'd called them.

Everything sounded small, as if her brain could barely process everyday sounds while it dealt with what she'd experienced in the bunker. But she knew its repercussions wouldn't truly impact her until she was safely home with Cooper and Todd. She rubbed the bandages around her wounded wrists.

But it was Li Jun's death that was still playing on a loop in her head. When the time was right, she would speak to his family. Where would she even begin with that conversation? Even though she'd come so close to losing her own child, Lana couldn't imagine what they were going through right now. He'd said Mei Lin was only two and a half. She hoped that would make her resilient to the trauma.

Huxtable was biding his time and said they couldn't return to Jaxton until they'd submitted to further interviews. Lana had already assured him she didn't know who the gunman was, and she hadn't been lying.

Todd had deliberately said nothing about him when they'd spoken earlier. He knew if he told Lana any more it would implicate her. His need to find funds for the private detective he'd engaged had forced him to make some misguided choices but she had to put her anger on hold. As she and Todd had saved the gunman's life, she sincerely hoped his parting words and sharp exit from the bunker had been the end of his association with them. If he hadn't walked in there when he had, however, things could have ended very differently.

Todd had given Huxtable the location he'd followed Clarence Belle to, and the detective had already raided it. The empty property belonged to Mya. The hidden cellar of the derelict house had contained three children's airbeds. Belle's sister was an IT support analyst, which explained how she'd effortlessly hoodwinked Lana with the online shopping vacation and through the *RWYS* forum.

Lana strode out of the room and down the busy corridor to the tiny TV lounge. The window there told her it was night outside. Cooper was asleep on Grandpa's lap. Both her parents were flaked out. Lana smiled at the only other occupant, a young mother standing by the coffee machine gently bouncing her baby.

Lana entered the room and tenderly touched the back of her son's hand. He didn't stir. She watched him for several minutes, his serene face riding the swells of her father's chest, and then headed out of the building to the car park.

# CHAPTER 105

Lana switched off the engine, the grim street even more foreboding as soon as she killed the headlights. Nobody around. She hadn't had time to be scared the last time she'd been here.

She considered how she'd sought out dark places after Cooper had nearly been abducted by Mr Whisper, combating her debilitating terror by facing it full on, as Clarence Belle had when he'd gone to visit Lane Hewett in prison. She'd submerged herself in the evil crimes of the people on *Right Where You're Standing* in an attempt to glimpse the face of the man who had paralysed her. Clarence Belle had looked straight into it and seen himself there.

Lana got out of the car and crossed the street to where Li Jun had recently dropped her. Something Jeanette Lane Hewett had said to her during their encounter had given her cause to call on her one last time.

Lana pushed the door to the second-hand book exchange.

Jeanette stood up from adjusting the dehumidifier and immediately recognised her. 'I thought you'd come back here.'

'Sickness and health, Jeanette?'

She wrinkled her features, but Lana could see she knew exactly what she was referring to.

'He had colon cancer when he escaped from Coitsville. Where else would he go?'

'I've said all I need to you. I'm closed.'

'This is where he came, isn't it? Pointless denying it now.' Lana recalled Jeanette's exact words: *I'm still his wife, though. I made the vows. Sickness and health.*

'And I suppose you've told the police,' Jeanette sighed with resignation. The old woman appeared as if she would shrivel and blow away.

'I want peace of mind.'

'How?' Jeanette jammed both her hands into her apron as if staking herself to the floor for support.

'Tell me when he died. And exactly where he's buried.'

'He's dead and gone. Isn't that peace of mind enough?'

But she'd paused before responding, and Lana had seen the brief flash of relief in her expression before her answer. That was when she was positive that what she suspected was true. 'He's still alive, isn't he?'

Jeanette's frown was too deep. She couldn't have misunderstood what she was being asked.

'Jeanette, is he still here?'

Jeanette's shoulders sagged, as if the pretence had finally exhausted her.

Lana headed for the doorway she'd seen Jeanette emerge from on her previous visit. She was in a tiny kitchen area but there was a door to her right. She yanked the handle and found a flight of stairs behind it. Jeanette protested, but she'd already started to climb.

She reached a door at the top and opened it. Jeanette was unsteadily following her. Lana closed it and noticed the key in the lock. She turned it and peered down the musty passageway she was in. Stacks of mildewed books lined both sides but there was an open room to her right.

'Come out of there.' Jeanette knocked weakly on the panel.

Lana reached the doorway and looked inside. It was a bathroom, yellowing green shower curtain hanging over the old tub. Three paces took her to another sealed room.

'Open it!'

Lana depressed the handle and pushed in. She was in a poky bedroom and a king-size took up the whole space. Mothballs and lavender pervaded the air. The blankets were twisted up in the middle of the mattress. Empty.

There were two more doors at the end of the passageway, and she opened the one immediately in front of her. It was in darkness, the thick brown curtains drawn over the small window.

Even though she couldn't see the man there she could smell him, the sour sweat aroma vividly reminding her of her struggle in the yard.

'Unlock this… please!'

Lana found the light switch inside the door and flicked it down.

The figure lying in the single bed reacted to the sudden illumination from the shade above. His brows knitted and he lifted a palm to shield him from the glow.

His features were emaciated, paper-thin yellow skin stretched tight over angular bone, showing the dark blue of his busted veins, but Lana could still perceive the face of Theodore Lane Hewett.

'Mr Whisper.'

His watery blue eyes darted.

Lana could hear his breath bubble in his chest. It was obvious he could barely move. 'You tried to steal my son.' She searched him for a reaction. There was none. 'My boy, Cooper, remember?'

He cowered as she approached the bed. But his appearance didn't temper the rage that had remained as raw and vital as when he'd first triggered it. She grabbed the blanket and sharply tugged it back.

She heard him whimper; saw how pathetic his skeleton was, his powder blue pyjamas flapping off his frame. She seized his silvery white leg and registered the scar from her teeth there. 'I gave you this. Remember me?' Lana glared down at him unblinkingly, looking for a sign that he did.

He shook his head, panic in his weak regard. He looked like a frightened, flinching animal.

'Tomorrow, you said.'

He shook his head again.

'Tomorrow is today, Theo.'

Then his eyes sharpened insolently; the calculating intelligence and malignancy still within him fixing her with amusement from behind his ravaged face.

'There you are.'

But she could understand why a feeble smirk played about his thin lips. What could she do to him now? He would be dead soon and had hardly any time left to pay for the myriad crimes he'd committed against so many other children and parents.

Jeanette kept rapping her knuckles on the door.

Lana took out her phone. 'I hope you're not too comfortable where you are, not thinking you're going to pass away peacefully under the care of your wife. One call and you're arrested. You'll be dragged out of your bed and, however long you've got left, you'll spend it locked up where you should be. Not in Coitsville. We both know that was a sham.'

The old man's gaze dimmed, and she was looking at a petrified patient again.

'I'm going outside to call the cops now.' Lana watched his nose wrinkle into a sneer before she turned her back on him. She hesitated in the doorway. 'Or maybe I'll do it tomorrow.'

'Whore!'

Lana heard a thump and when she glanced back the old man had made a lunge for her and fallen. He was lying on the grubby carpet, his mouth against it but one eye rolled up to her. He looked like a cloth bag of bones.

She retraced her steps and unlocked the door. Jeanette scuttled past her to attend to her husband, and Lana made her way down the stairs.

She strode out of the store and got into her car. After she closed the door she turned her phone over in her sweating hands. They were shaking uncontrollably.

But she'd looked him in the eye and knew she didn't need his death to release her.

Lana could stop looking now. Walk away from the shadows and be present again. They'd lost too much precious time already, so when they were all fully healed, she was determined her family would move out of the fortress of their apartment and go back home.

Lana waited until her breathing slowed then dialled.

'Detective Huxtable, please.'

# A LETTER FROM RICHARD

Thanks for choosing *Hide and Seek*. I hope the story really hit the spot for you. My criteria are only ever to write the sort of stories that I would enjoy reading so I sincerely hope we share the same taste in dark suspense. I have another thriller being published by Bookouture very soon so, if you're interested, please sign up to the mailing list via the link below for updates on this and other projects:

www.bookouture.com/richard-parker

If you'll forgive me, I'd just like to make a brief plea on behalf of all authors you might have enjoyed. None of us relish badgering readers for reviews. We'd all rather be writing. Thankfully, because of some passionate bloggers out there who supply their critiques and promotion skills free of charge it's possible for up-and-coming authors to break through. But readers posting a very brief review on Amazon can also work wonders. It's nothing to do with massaging a writer's ego. Ratings ensure that new books can rub shoulders with the more familiar names and keep things really interesting. Thanks for any time you can spare to do this and hope your next read keeps you turning the pages into the small hours.

Please also feel free to get in touch with me on Twitter, Facebook, or Instagram. Writing is a lonely business so it's always great when readers say hi.

# ACKNOWLEDGEMENTS

To every reader who has energised my characters and stories with their imagination, thank you for giving me the time of day. I wish I could sit with you and watch your every reaction. Behind every book is an understanding partner and I'm lucky enough to have Anne-Marie waiting for me when I emerge from the office. Love you for the patience, smiles and support you've always given me. This wouldn't be written without you. A permanent hug to my mum and dad for reading everything I write and for always taking their son's inner psychopath with a pinch of salt. Huge appreciation to ace editor Natalie Butlin (who has a great taste in hot dogs) for intelligent input that makes hard work seem fun and for the hugely creative notes that significantly elevate my work.

There aren't enough personalities in publishing but Kim Nash makes up for that by being a one-woman army of positive publicity energy. Feel blessed that Oliver Rhodes and the awesome Bookouture team have my back. Special mention to Lisa Brewster at Blacksheep for the popsicle wasp cover design, Alex Crow for his ad campaigns and Kate Barker for overseeing the audiobook.

Many authors' work wouldn't see the light of day without the generosity and enthusiasm of committed bloggers who will happily promote them for no other reason than their love of books. Heartfelt thanks to anyone who has given up their time to post a review. These include the boundless energy of people such as the award-winning Noelle Holten, Jen Lucas, Sean Talbot, Joyce Juzwik, Lorraine Rugman, Nicki Richards, Sarah Hardy, Ellie Smith, Joanne Robertson, Susan Hampson, Kate Moloney, Amy

Sullivan, Magdalena Johansson, Kaisha Jayneh, Tom Bromley, David McNeil, Shell Baker, Rebecca Pugh, David Carr, Mandie Griffiths, Gemma Burrows, Kelvin Jones, Sophie Burrow, Jo Ford, Kaz Lewis, Fran Hagen, Lisa Drewett, Carole Whiteley, Tracy Unsworth, and Scott Griffin. Apologies to anyone I've missed. Get in touch and I promise to slip you in the next one!

Lightning Source UK Ltd.
Milton Keynes UK
UKOW01f2136150917
309277UK00004B/335/P